Reckless Brilliance

Powerful Minds, Volume 1

Lloyd G Miller

Published by Lloyd G Miller, 2018.

This is a work of fiction. Similarities to real people, places, or events are entirely coincidental.

RECKLESS BRILLIANCE

First edition. February 22, 2018.

Copyright © 2018 Lloyd G Miller.

ISBN: 979-8224079285

Written by Lloyd G Miller.

Table of Contents

RECKLESS BRILLIANCE
Lloyd G. Miller

Flash Forward

When George awoke, he found himself chained to a cinder block wall in a windowless room. His arms ached from supporting his body weight. His body was stretched into an "X" shape with his feet being pulled down and spread by chains. George was not blindfolded, and the two men in the room wore no masks. That meant one thing, they were planning to kill George after extracting from him all of the information that they wanted. The jig was up. George's brief life would soon be over, probably after excruciating torture. How had he let his studies in ways to accelerate the learning process lead him to captivity and probable torture and death?

Chapter 1 - Planarians

Dressed in a tuxedo, George Horton walked forward to accept the Nobel Prize in Physics for his brilliant discoveries that held the promise of clean, safe and inexpensive fusion energy. There were gasps from the audience as they realized how young he was for someone receiving such a prestigious honor. He turned and smiled at the crowd. An elegantly dressed woman on the front row with long, raven black hair and big brown eyes caught his attention. As they made eye contact, she blew him a kiss. She opened her mouth as if to call to him. "George, dinner's ready," shouted his mother, awakening him from the slumber he had drifted into while studying his geography book. As he bolted upright, the page that was stuck to his face ripped, leaving a section still clinging to his right cheek. Under the textbook lay his completed algebra assignment that he had whipped through in a few minutes.

As George walked into the kitchen, he could see through the archway that his dad was watching a football game on their old black and white television set. "Mom, when are we going to get a color TV like the Medefins have?" The Medefins were close friends with whom they often got together for dinner and board games. George liked going to their house, but lately, Margaret, their only child, had been giving him the eye. Why did she have to ruin a perfectly good friendship by trying to turn it into something that it would never be? Margaret was nice enough and smart enough, in fact, she was always top in the class, but George was not and never would be attracted to that red hair, freckles and gangly body. She was nothing like the woman of his dreams.

"When the price comes down a little more, we will buy a color television set," responded his mother. She had been saying that for years. George's father turned off the TV and the three of them sat down to a dinner that included hot, freshly baked whole wheat bread and an abundance of vegetables from the family garden. Partway into dinner, George's mom started with the questions. "So, George, how are your geography studies coming? You didn't do so well on that last quiz."

"I was just studying the book before dinner. My algebra homework is all done."

"So you have worked out how to study with your eyes closed and while you sleep. That's amazing!"

"I try to stay awake, Mom, but reading about geography is so slow and boring. Why can't someone develop a machine to speed things up, or why couldn't it be like that episode of the Outer Limits that we saw where the guy just seemed to know everything overnight."

"Well, we don't live in the Outer Limits, we live in Bountiful, Utah and here and now you have to keep your eyes open and read the book to learn. Study hard and maybe someday you can be the one to invent the machine."

After dinner, George returned to his room to study. He looked longingly at his bookshelf full of mathematical, science and science fiction books. He hardly ever fell asleep reading them. Many of the books on his shelf belonged to his older sister, Stephanie. She was away to school at Stanford University in California. Ironically, it was not her straight "A" grades or her high test scores that earned her a full scholarship. It had been her legs. She was the fastest sprinter on the Stanford women's track team. Her demanding coach only allowed her time for brief visits home. When she came, she dropped off her textbooks from the previous semester. Fortunately for George, she majored in statistics. He had spent hundreds of hours studying the books and working the problems. He had learned advanced calculus and statistics all on his own. He finally dropped into the chair next to his desk and picked up the geography book. George was constantly frustrated by his difficulty remembering detailed facts and dates. He remembered principles easily, which enabled him to master complex math, but he stumbled in classes like spelling and history that required rote memorization.

He tried to remedy the situation. He spent his own hard-earned money, earned from mowing lawns for neighbors and doing other odd jobs, on memory training books. He learned tricks like the loci method and association that allowed him to memorize flawlessly long lists of items, but he found these techniques of little use for most practical matters.

The next evening George was surprised when his parents postponed dinner to watch all of the news. There was word about an American navy ship, the USS Pueblo, that had been captured by North Korea. George had never paid much attention to the news and did not understand much of the background to the story. His parents were very upset. They expressed to each other feelings of helplessness. The United States government hesitated to take any direct action to get the men and ship back, for fear of starting another world war. The country was already deeply embroiled in Vietnam and many Americas had lost their lives in the conflict. His parents worried that communism would take over the world, robbing everyone of their freedoms.

As George lay in bed later that evening, sleep that normally overtook him quickly was slow in coming. He thought back to the "duck and cover" drills that he and his classmates had been taught years earlier in school. Students were asked to kneel under their desks and put their hands over their necks to protect them from the flying glass that would result from a nuclear attack. All of his old fears of the Soviet Union and nuclear war returned to him.

Two weeks later, when George walked through the front door, he noticed a new television set in the living room where the old one had been. He raced to it and turned it on. Beautiful, living color appeared in a commercial for Tide detergent. However, when the commercial ended and regular programming returned, it was in black and white. He changed the channel and the Gilligan's Island rerun was in color. His mother entered the room. "So, you just start watching TV. You don't even come say hi to your mother."

"I'm sorry, Mom. It's just so exciting having a new color TV."

"Even so, the one hour limit on school nights still applies. Choose wisely what you want to watch." George's favorite TV show, a series about science, was on at five so he turned off the TV. Suddenly a book came flying at George's head. He snatched it out of the air before it hit his face.

"Mom, I wish you wouldn't throw things at me like that."

"You left the book in the kitchen. Since you don't do any sports, I have to do something to develop your hand-eye coordination. When I was your age, I was out most nights playing some kind of ball game with the neighbor kids. I wasn't sitting around watching TV."

"Television wasn't even available when you were my age." His mother just smiled and returned to the kitchen. He went right to work on his homework so that his mother would not have any reason to block him from watching his show. The time passed slowly, but finally, it was time for his favorite series.

This episode told of an experiment with planarians, a kind of primitive flatworm. Scientists placed planarians in a flat, water-filled pan painted with white and black regions. The planarians were taught to stay in the white areas of the container by shocking them whenever they entered a black region. After being well trained, the planarians were cut up and fed to untaught individuals. This second group of planarians knew to avoid the black areas without having to be taught. They had gained knowledge simply by eating. The possibilities that this discovery held for the human race excited George. He daydreamed about being able to learn huge amounts of information effortlessly.

George set out to duplicate the experiment. During a family outing, he collected some planarians at a mountain stream up in Lambs Canyon, located near Salt Lake City, Utah. He brought them and gallons of stream water home. He created a workable number of planarians by cutting them into pieces and letting each piece grow into a full-grown planarian. He painted the bottom of a rectangular cake pan with black and white areas. He filled the pan with a half-inch of water and a planarian. He wired up the apparatus with the pan grounded and a conductive grid floating on the water. He could electrify the grid using a push button. He used a variable electrical transformer to adjust the voltage to a level that was very uncomfortable but not lethal to the planarian.

Now that things were set up, George began teaching the planarian that he identified as P1. It took about forty minutes for the initial instruction, but the lesson had to be repeated every day for a week in order for the learning to become semi-permanent. When he was not teaching the planarian, he put it into an unpainted pan so as not to undo the lesson. He cut P1 in half to see which half retained the knowledge. Not surprisingly, the head end did but not the tail end. He repeated, cutting the head end smaller and smaller to determine just where the knowledge was stored. Finally, he fed this small portion of the head to P2. Within eight hours, P2 knew to avoid the black areas without ever having to be trained. Furthermore, it did not forget. It never needed a refresher course. That part really thrilled George. He repeated the experiment many times with variations to the procedure.

After three months of experimenting with planarians, George was ready to try a similar experiment with a higher life form. He moved on to a much higher life form, mice. At first, he had absolutely no success. Feeding the brains of mice that had learned to navigate a maze did not enlighten those that feasted on their brains. They did not learn a thing from their meal. George had always prided himself on being able to solve a mystery with a minimum of clues. He stopped testing for several weeks and just thought about why the transfer worked for one species and not another. He came up with two possible explanations. Either the nervous system of the planarian was unique and something special about it allowed memory transfer to work, or something about the two digestive systems was responsible for the differences in results. After extensive study at the nearby University of Utah library, George discovered that the digestive system of the planarian did not completely breakdown moderately sized organic compounds as did those of mammals. Probably the information was transferred in the form of proteins that the mouse digestive system broke down into its amino acid building blocks.

George was ready to experiment again to verify and refine his hypothesis. He ground up and filtered the entire contents of the skull of a trained mouse, M13, and injected it into the bloodstream of M20. He kept the syringe refrigerated and injected the solution over a period of several days. M20 did not gain all of the training of M13, but it did seem to have gained something. As expected, M20 died within two weeks of the commencement of injections. In his systematic way, George repeated the experiment over and over, isolating what part of the contents of the mouse cranial cavity had to be transferred. To his surprise, it was not the brain at all, but it was the fluid that constantly bathed the brain that allowed memory transfer. Eventually, George found that the best results were obtained if 0.1 milliliter of fluid was removed from one mouse and transferred directly into the same part of the cranial cavity of the recipient. The procedure had no negative health effects on either mouse. The recipient did not show any memory transfer for several hours. About 90 percent transfer occurred after one week. Around 96 percent transfer eventually occurred. To George's delight, the recipient showed indefinite retention, whereas the donor had to be periodically refreshed in its training.

After continued experiments with various small mammals, George formed a hypothesis of why all of this worked. He decided that the brain has a copy of all of the individual's permanent memories. It also creates a backup copy in chemical form in the cranial fluid. That way, when an injury to the brain such as a concussion creates memory loss, the loss can eventually be restored from the chemical backup. When the transfer is made from one individual to another, initially there is only one copy of the new memories. As the new memories are copied into the nervous system, the brain is able to organize the information in a much more systematic manner than it would be organized when it is obtained over the course of hours, days or years of learning. Consequently, the information is much more readily recalled. George's memory transfer system did not work between different species and attempts at cross-species transfer sometimes resulted in apparent insanity.

Chapter 2 - Smart Poodle

After more than a year of experimentation, George was ready for some serious memory transfer. He had not spent much time training his dog. It was an intelligent mixture, collie and poodle, but George had been given the dog as a pup shortly before he began the memory experiments and had, to the dismay of his parents, almost totally ignored the dog. "George, it is disgraceful the way that you have neglected Einstein. I am going to lock you out of that workroom of yours if you don't teach him something. I'll give you two weeks to show improvement," commanded his mother. Being one never to do things the normal way, George devised a plan. The next-door neighbor, Mrs. Austin, had a well-trained poodle. George would have to find a way to get access to Fluffy's cranial fluid. Fluffy usually stayed in the house, but sometimes when the Austins had company, she was shut up in her portable kennel on the back porch, which was not enclosed.

George learned that the Austins were entertaining that Friday night. He had chloroform on hand for use in his experiments and he purchased some gauss bandages. About eight o'clock, when the party was in full swing, George climbed the fence to the Austins' backyard. Fluffy began barking immediately as expected. George ran up to the kennel and tossed a wad of chloroform soaked gauss through the door grating. Then he ran to the back corner of the yard and hid behind a bush. George could see Mrs. Austin looking out of the window, but upon seeing nothing unusual and Fluffy quieting down, she went back to partying. Fluffy had really quieted down, all the way to unconsciousness. George quickly crept back to the porch and removed Fluffy from the kennel. He carried her back to his hiding spot behind the bushes and performed the extraction. He figured that about two milliliters would be appropriate for an animal her size.

George began to carry Fluffy back when the backdoor of the house started to open. He quickly ran back behind the bushes. It was Mrs. Austin. She came to get more soda from the back porch where it was staying cool. She noticed that Fluffy was not in the kennel and looked very alarmed. She started calling her and walking around in the backyard. George's heart began to pound so loudly in his ears that he wondered if Mrs. Austin could hear it. He decided to shove Fluffy out where she could easily be seen. George crawled further back into the bushes. The ploy worked. Mrs. Austin eventually saw Fluffy and with a scream, ran to her. She scooped up Fluffy and ran back to the house yelling, "Someone has poisoned Fluffy," over and over. As soon as she ran in through the back door, George bolted over the fence and ran into his own house. Fortunately, Fluffy had begun to regain consciousness before Mrs. Austin had even reached the door. To Mrs. Austin's relief, Fluffy was unharmed.

George took Einstein into his "laboratory" and put him out by holding a chloroformed pad to his muzzle. In the privacy of the laboratory, he injected Fluffy's cranial fluid into Einstein's skull.

The next morning George was up early, going through the motions of teaching tricks to Einstein. Einstein was a very fast learner, or so it appeared to George's mother. She was very pleased and impressed. "George, did you hear or see any strangers in or near the Austins' backyard last night?" she asked. George had always been extraordinarily honest, not only in telling the truth but in observing all laws. He even went out of his way to use the crosswalks when crossing a street. George was glad that his mother had phrased the question in such a way that he could give an honest answer without revealing what had happened.

"I heard Fluffy bark and later heard Mrs. Austin screaming and yelling, but I didn't see any strangers."

"Mrs. Austin is really shaken, so keep your eyes open for strangers hanging around the neighborhood." As his mother began to walk away, she spun and threw something at him. He tried to catch it, but it went through his hands and bounced off the wall. "Well, that performance is totally unacceptable. Give me 30."

"Thirty, what happened to 20?" His mother usually made him do 20 pushups when he missed a throw.

"You're nearly a man now. It is time to up the ante. Here, I will do two for every one of your pushups and with better form." She got down on the floor and did the pushups twice as fast as he did his, doing 60 for his 30. When she finished, she leaped to her feet, not even breathing hard. His mother was determined to make an athlete out of him even if she had to embarrass and shame him into it.

Einstein continued to amaze the family and the neighborhood. George had never cared much for animals but was actually becoming quite fond of Einstein. This also pleased his mother.

One evening, after finishing his homework, George slipped into his laboratory to do some experiments on the mice. He finished and quietly worked his way towards his bedroom. He overheard his parents softly talking at the kitchen table. "Vernon, can't you see that you need to give more direct guidance to George. He has no social life. His grades are disappointing for someone so smart. He has few positive experiences with girls his age. He is even picked on and bullied at school. Imagine that, our son, who is taller than average for his age and in good physical shape, is the frequent target of bullies. If that were not bad enough, he lacks social skills and either talks excessively, babbling about some scientific principle or he says nothing at all. There is no balance in his life."

"I just have a different style than you have, Grace. I do have talks with George, but I like to wait for teaching moments when he will be more receptive to my counsel. I prefer to leave him some room to figure things out for himself. That's what I did with Stephanie, and look how great she turned out. The fact that we have different styles of parenting is a good thing. Sometimes one approach or the other may be more effective. Right now, it appears that your frequent course corrections are working. George has not rebelled against them." His parents moved into the master bedroom and George could no longer follow the conversation.

George really liked his father's approach to parenting, but he also realized that being a little lazy and easily sidetracked, he needed his mother's nudging and needling to keep him on task when doing the less pleasant things. Even though it hurt to hear what his mother said about him, he wasn't angry. He knew that everything that she said was mostly true, but he didn't really care, because his discoveries would solve everything. He just knew it.

Chapter 3 – Friendly Help

George was anxious to try the memory transfer on himself but had one major technical challenge. How did he inject the fluid into his own cranial cavity? It was not difficult to do to someone else, but he could not safely inject fluid into the back of his own head just behind the bottom edge of the skull. It was just too risky. An awkward rotation of the needle might cause brain damage. He had to get someone to help. Involving another person would require George to trust that person and bring him into his confidence. His assistant would probably want the same benefits, the benefits of instant learning. George decided to press forward with his research and hoped that a solution to the self-injection problem presented itself.

George did tests to determine the out-of-body lifetime of the cranial fluid. He did many experiments on mice. He discovered that the extracted cranial fluid stayed fresh about as long as milk. Like milk, its lifetime was dependant on temperature. Frozen fluid seemed to last indefinitely, although there was a small loss of memories with freezing. He also found that similar to milk, the fluid had a soured smell when it went bad. If the fluid was just a little spoiled (just a hint of odor) the memory transfer was less complete but worked. If the fluid had a strong odor, no memory transfer took place and the recipient usually got very sick for a couple of days, but none had died as a result. George also tested to see the effects of the death of the donor on the fluid. It appeared that as soon as the donor died the deterioration process began. If the body was kept cold, the fluid stayed fresh for days.

Next, George began to think about whom to use as a donor. He thought that maybe an alcoholic bum would be a safe bet. George could just make the extraction while the donor lie in the gutter, so to speak. During this time, events occurred that helped George make up his mind on two issues, how and whom. George's mother was so pleased with her apparent positive influence on him that she decided to press him in a couple of other areas. George was doing poorly in his Spanish class. It was just too much memorization. His mother told him that if he did not raise his grade to at least a B- that she would lock him out of his workroom.

Mrs. Horton also had plans concerning George and Margaret Medefin. Margaret's mom was Mrs. Horton's best friend. They had always hoped that someday romance would blossom between George and Margaret. Both mothers had observed that Margaret had liked George for years and was not shy about expressing her affection. She seemed like the ideal girl for George. Why was he being so contrary?

It was the middle of her son's sophomore year of high school. Soon they would each turn 16 and be allowed to date. Mrs. Horton feared that George would just stay home and spend time in his "laboratory". When George had turned 14, Mrs. Horton started encouraging him to attend school and church dances, but so far, he had not attended a single dance. There was a school dance Friday night after the basketball game.

When George got home from school, his mom began to encourage him to go to the after-game dance and dance with Margaret. He knew that his mother would be relentless in her pressure, so he gave in without much of a fight. Friday night George showed up at the dance just twenty minutes before it ended. That way he would only have to dance with Margaret once or twice. When Margaret saw him approaching, she lit up like a supernova. She jumped up with enthusiasm when George asked her to dance. The last dance for the evening was a slow dance. Margaret kept snuggling up to George while he kept trying to put distance between them. Somehow, after the dance, Margaret talked George into walking her home. She clung to his arm all the way home. The damage was done! Everyone who saw them together would now think of them as a couple.

Margaret's mom called George's mom early Saturday morning to rejoice in their matchmaking success. At first, George was mildly disgusted, but then an idea came to him. There was no one more willing to do him a favor than Margaret Medefin was. She was also the kind of girl that could keep a secret. She was not the gossipy type.

Monday, before history class started, Margaret plopped down right on George's desk and stayed there until the bell rang. Everyone was looking and commenting. Just before the bell rang, Margaret slipped into the chair next to George. George decided to make his move. He slipped Margaret a note asking her to meet him behind the gym after last period. Margaret fidgeted in her seat throughout the class, filled with excitement. After school when George approached the back of the gym, she was waiting for him.

"Margaret, I have something very important to tell you, but you must keep it a complete secret. Can you keep a secret?"

"You can count on me to not reveal a secret." One thing that George did like about Margaret was that she didn't talk like a "valley girl". She did not use the word "like" in every sentence and she did not say, "You know," very often. She was actually quite articulate for her age.

"You have to promise to not reveal to anyone what I'm going to tell you, even if your life depends on it."

"That depends. Have you done something illegal or terribly wrong?"

"No. I have broken no laws, at least none that I know of. You've known me your whole life. You know how honest I am. And I have never done anything very wrong in my life."

"I know. That's why I have always liked you. I'm sure there must be a good reason why you want this to be kept secret and I promise to keep your secret, even if I get in trouble by keeping it a secret."

Although George had never been attracted to Margaret romantically, he did like her as a person. It was hard not to like someone who liked you for the same reasons that you liked yourself. He told Margaret all about his research as he walked her home. After dropping off her books at her house, they walked to George's home. He noticed Mrs. Medefin at a window smiling as she watched them walk away. George told his mother that he wanted to show Margaret his laboratory. It made his mother a little nervous when he shut the door behind them, but Mrs. Horton decided that sometimes a mother has to take small risks to get what she wants.

George spent hours that day teaching Margaret the techniques for extraction and injection. He even let her practice by injecting a sterile saline solution into Einstein's cranial cavity. The trick was to find the bottom edge of the skull and insert the needle just below the skull, angling the needle upwards. They took a break about every thirty minutes so that his mom would not get too concerned about the closed door. Margaret had an interest in photography and even had a small darkroom at her house. They decided that they could use the darkroom for doing the injections since it would not seem unnatural to lock the door of a darkroom while inside.

The rest of that week, George spent watching the transients that slept under a highway overpass not far from his home. He identified a man who appeared to be about 55 years old who spoke only Spanish. He often drank himself into a drunken stupor. George started carrying his extraction kit with him. Since it was late autumn, it grew dark by six. On a Thursday evening, he found the man face down in the weeds. It was a simple matter to make the extraction, much easier than with Fluffy. When George got home, he called Margaret and asked if he could come over. They never discussed anything confidential over the phone. George's mother had a habit of listening in on phone conversations.

Margaret told her mom that she and George would be developing some film in the darkroom and would lock the door so that no one would open it. It was actually the truth. Like George, Margaret never lied. They quickly developed the film. George knelt with his elbows on a padded chair. After Margaret prepped the back of George's neck using an alcohol wipe, she held a chloroform soaked cloth to his nose and mouth until he passed out. Margaret did very well at performing the injection, completing her task in a matter of seconds. However, it took a long time for George to regain consciousness. Every few minutes Mrs. Medefin would come to the door and ask if everything was all right. It was her way of making sure that no necking was going on in the darkroom. Finally, George regained consciousness. At first, he did not know where he was or what he was doing in a darkened room with Margaret. Once he was reoriented, he and Margaret quickly made their exit.

The next morning George awoke with a mild headache but other than that felt fine. He showered and shaved, but as he unscrewed the lid from a bottle of after-shave lotion, the smell of alcohol aroused a craving in him. He quickly resealed the bottle. Shaken, George quickly dressed and entered the dining room. He looked at the sugar bowl on the table and said to himself, "Azucar." He noticed that it was sitting on a tablecloth and said, "Mantel." The system was working for George.

As George walked to school that morning, he began to feel anxious. Why was he feeling this way? Memories from the life of the man from whom he stole memories, Jose Mario Martinez, came into his mind. Jose had always been short and from his first day of school, the bigger boys bullied him. As George arrived on campus, he began to see things as though through the eyes of Jose. Jose had only an elementary school education and had attended a very small, humble establishment of learning. Viewmont High seemed enormous to him and the students that he saw were so tall. The feelings of dread almost made George turn around and go back home. George suppressed the memories and feelings and asserted control over his emotions.

Later that day in Spanish class, George was quick to answer questions and even carried on an extended conversation in Spanish with the teacher. When George got home from school, he stood in front of the mirror in his room looking at himself as if through the eyes of Jose. George had always compared his physique to his father's and thus always came up short. To Jose, his six-foot frame was enviable. George had never been one to admire himself in the mirror like so many teenage boys do. However, seeing himself through Jose's perspective, he realized how lucky he was to be tall with narrow hips and broad shoulders. It was too bad that he didn't do much with this excellent body.

That evening Mrs. Lemon called Mrs. Horton to report on George's extraordinary improvement in her class. Mrs. Horton was thrilled. She could hardly believe what an influential parent she had become. Meanwhile, George was becoming aware of useful information other than just the Spanish language that he had gained. He found that he now knew much about the history, geography and traditions of the Mexican people. Jose was from the state of Chihuahua. George had not even known that Mexico had states. George also learned that Jose was only 47 and had a wife and children from whom he had become alienated due to his alcohol addiction. Jose actually had many skills in farming and construction. He was even a fair auto mechanic. George felt a great concern for Jose. He understood the anguish of Jose's broken heart. He missed his family terribly, including his parents and siblings but did not know how to get out of the rut of alcohol addiction that entrapped him.

Since George now knew Jose's habits, it would be easy to find him. The next day after school, George filled a grocery bag with food and headed out to find Jose. Fortunately, he found Jose mostly sober. He addressed Jose in his native tongue and explained that he had been observing him and had brought him some food. With his knowledge of Jose and increased understanding of people, gained from Jose's memories, it was easy to engage Jose in conversation and eventually get him to open his heart to George. Jose felt that if he could stay busy working he could stay sober, but when he could not find work he became discouraged and drank. As they conversed, George was surprised that even though he was familiar with the meaning of every word that Jose was using it was difficult for him to understand Jose when he spoke at his normal fast pace. It occurred to George that just having someone's memories was not enough. There must be changes that take place in the brain associated with a skill that made certain activities automatic. If he wanted to speak and understand the Spanish language as well as Jose did, he would have to speak it and listen to it with some frequency, at least in the beginning.

An idea came to George. He had several hundred dollars in a savings account. With his savings, they could buy an old car with mechanical problems, fix it up and then sell it for a profit. That Saturday the two of them went looking for just the right car. They found a 1961 Ford Falcon with a blown head gasket. Gaskets are relatively cheap, but normally the labor to replace one is expensive. George asked his parents if he could buy the car with his own money and fix it up. He explained that a friend who knew a lot about cars was going to help him. His mother thought that it was a wonderful idea, something a normal 15-year-old boy would want to do. His dad even offered to buy any tools that he might need and to let him park the car in the garage. The car ran in its current condition, although with much smoke. His father made the purchase in his name and drove the car home that same day.

George's parents were surprised to find that his friend was an older man and an illegal immigrant. George explained that Jose had helped him with learning Spanish and that he was trying to help him in return. On finding that Jose was homeless, George's mother insisted that he sleep in the spare bedroom and eat at their table. Fortunately, Jose had remained sober and the added attention gave him greater reason to stay sober.

Most women would have been afraid to have a stranger sleeping in their home. Mrs. Horton was not the least bit afraid of Jose. She grew up in Idaho on her parents' farm. She had three older brothers, one younger brother and a younger sister. Mrs. Horton stood six feet tall and although of slender build, she was well known for her incredible physical strength, superior to many men who greatly outweighed her. She grew up bucking hay and doing other hard physical labor right along with her brothers, whom she adored. From early on, she demonstrated incredible athletic ability, being not only strong but also fast and agile. When she was not working with her brothers, she was playing sports with them. When teams were chosen, she was picked before most neighborhood boys. To Mrs. Horton, Jose, who was over a head shorter, was no threat at all.

Not only could Mrs. Horton defend herself, but she had excellent backup in her husband. Mr. Horton was a tall, powerfully built man. He likewise had worked hard on a family farm. Although not as talented in sports as his wife, Mr. Horton possessed considerable physical prowess. Naturally, with his parents' backgrounds, George was a great disappointment, having no interest in hard physical labor, sports or physical fitness.

In a couple of days, the car was running well. Mr. Horton liked the car so much that he offered to buy it for double what George had put into it and let him repeat the process. After they purchased another vehicle, George wrote a letter to Jose's wife telling her that Jose was sober and working and would love to come home. She wrote back that she had forgiven Jose long ago but had not known where to find him. She wanted him back. George showed the letter to Jose and they wept together. George bought Jose a bus ticket home and gave him $50 in cash after Jose swore an oath that he would not spend it on drink. George felt better than he had ever felt in his life and even had a fixed up 1962 Chevy Nova waiting for him to turn sixteen. His parents were very proud of him.

Chapter 4 - Night of the Knowing Dead

The success that George enjoyed due to the memory transfer did not escape Margaret's attention. She had already begun to ponder how the right memory transfer could benefit her. If George could pick up significant skills from a drunken bum, just think what a well-selected memory donor could do for her. Her mother had been a fan of a talented performer and movie star named Rita Hawthorn. During the sixties, Hollywood had a love affair with the young and beautiful. Rita's career in movies faltered when she became too old to play romantic roles and she dropped out of movie-making in her mid-forties. She did not handle forced retirement well and became a heavy drinker, living off the fruits of her earlier work. What made her of particular interest to Margaret was that she lived in nearby Park City, Utah.

Margaret talked to George about her desire to receive a memory transfer. George described the downside of memory transfer and his concerns. "You have to realize, Margaret that you will take on not just the learning of your donor but intimate details about their personal lives. Very personal details."

"It sounds, George like you are trying to keep the benefits of memory transfer all to yourself by talking me out of it!" responded Margaret in a huffy voice.

"Not really, Margaret, I just thought that you should be forewarned. I'm still glad that I did the transfer. I love gaining new skills and information. I just wish that there were not so much personal information. I'm sure that your mind is very pure and innocent. I hate to see it polluted. I was also kind of hoping that you could give me suggestions on how to cope with the inappropriate memories."

"Oh! I just had an idea. When Dad was bishop of our ward several years ago, people visited with him, sharing personal problems and even confessing serious sins. Dad never talked about what he heard in confidence. I once asked Mom how he handled all of the negative personal information and never let any details slip out. She said that Dad had learned to compartmentalize his mind. He sort of kept those memories locked up until he needed them. After he was released as bishop, he managed to let those memories mostly slip away. Maybe you can do something similar."

"That sounds really hard to do, but maybe I can figure out how to compartmentalize my mind. I sure need to do something."

Margaret wrote Rita Hawthorn a letter praising her earlier work and asking for an interview for her school paper. Rita, who craved public attention, readily agreed. Margaret arrived for the interview at 4:30. Rita had already begun drinking but was not yet seriously impaired. Margaret asked her questions about her career and took careful notes, knowing however, that if the transfer worked she would not need any notes to report on Rita. After an hour-long interview, Margaret concluded with, "Miss Hawthorn, I have appreciated very much your sharing of your personal history with me. A young woman such as myself could benefit greatly from your wisdom and experience. I wonder if you would mind participating in a little experiment that would greatly benefit my education."

"But of course, Margaret, but what do you want me to do?" By now Rita's voice was becoming slurred.

"Would you mind sharing all of your memories with me?" Margaret knew that Rita had no idea that she was talking about extracting cranial fluid, but this was as close to the truth as Margaret was willing to go to get permission.

"Sure. What do you want to know?"

"Everything." Rita continued with her life history becoming less and less coherent until she eventually passed out. Margaret pulled a kit from her purse and performed the extraction. She covered Rita with a blanket and went outside to wait for her mother to pick her up. Her mom had dropped her off and gone shopping in Park City.

When she got home, Margaret called George and asked him to help her develop some pictures for the school paper. George came over and they entered the darkroom. They decided to give Margaret a smaller dose of chloroform than what George had received. After the injection, Margaret came to much faster than had George after his injection. They exited the darkroom much sooner than during George's earlier visit, much to Margaret's mother's relief. Margaret was so anxious that she went to bed an hour early. However, sleep was slow in coming.

The next morning she awoke and stood in front of a mirror. She looked at herself as if through the eyes of Rita Hawthorn. Rita had been considered an attractive actress with tremendous sex appeal early in her career. In reality, Rita lacked raw classic beauty. However, her mother had taught her that beauty was as much a thing of the mind as of the body. How a woman perceived her own appearance had a great effect on how others saw her. Rita had learned to project beauty. As Margaret looked at herself with Rita's memories influencing her perception, she saw that she had a near-perfect oval face. Rita would have killed for such a well-shaped face. Her eyes were large and her irises had beautiful coloring and form. Her nose was straight and just the right size for her face. Her teeth were naturally straight and white. Her face contained good symmetry. Her body was tall and slender with gentle, subtle curves. She was not buxom, but that had never been a requirement for beauty or even sex appeal.

Rita knew how to augment Margaret's natural beauty. Margaret did not want to wear a lot of makeup but just enough to enhance and highlight. She realized that she also was in serious need of a perm. At breakfast she asked, "Mother, may I have a perm?"

"Have a perm? I have been trying to interest you in a perm for years. You are a young woman now and need to start looking like one. I will make an appointment with Betty right now." With that, Margaret's mother went to the phone and made an appointment for that very afternoon. On the walk to school, Margaret began to sing songs that had previously been unfamiliar to her. She heard herself sing better than she ever had before. She would have to try out for the Viewmont High Madrigals next year. She also knew from her position as a photographer and writer for the school paper that casting was starting for a school production of The Music Man. She decided to go to the auditions. Intimate personal details from Rita's life came to Margaret, but thanks to George's warning, she was ready for them. She had already prepared her mind and stored those memories in a secluded part of her psyche.

As Margaret walked onto campus, she stood taller and exerted more confidence than the day before. The heads of boys turned to look at her as if she were a new girl at school. Rather than looking away, as had been her habit, she smiled warmly at each boy and girl that looked her way. Had boys always paid this much attention to her or was this new?

Meanwhile, George was working on a plan for his next acquisition. Like Margaret, he wanted to pick a talented and well-educated donor. He did not want to steal memories from another living donor and had to come up with an alternative. George had an uncle who owned a mortuary. George's uncle, after whom he had been given the middle name of Martin, had no sons of his own and had often told George of the benefits of his profession. George called him and asked for an interview. "George, if you want a job I will not deny you. After all, you have always been a favorite of mine."

"Uncle Martin, I want to win this job on merit, not blood."

"Fine, George, come by tomorrow at 4:45." The next day George arrived in his Sunday best. His uncle had him fill out an application form. Uncle Martin perused the application and gave him a short oral exam that determined his basic skills. George felt that the interview was going well. "So George, are you squeamish? Does the sight of blood bother you?"

"I have done many dissections. I am not squeamish. Do you have any corpses you can show me?" Uncle Martin was not sure if George was bluffing so he gave him the full tour. He had two bodies on hand, one of which had been killed in an automobile accident. George showed genuine curiosity, not revulsion, at the sight of the bodies. Uncle Martin gave him the job without further questioning. Each weekday George walked to the mortuary after school. At first, he mainly cleaned up and worked alongside his uncle. Uncle Martin could see that George was a quick study and soon began giving him more responsibilities. George was assigned the task of initial preparation of the male bodies as they came in. He always brought a carefully disguised extraction kit with him to work.

Meanwhile, George could not help but observe at school that Margaret looked prettier and more feminine. She also seemed to be much more popular now. Many boys started noticing her and going out of their way to talk to her. George's feelings towards Margaret started to change. The memories from Jose had begun to affect his attitudes. Jose would have seen the many wonderful qualities in Margaret that had somehow eluded George's attention in the past.

So far in high school, George had mostly flown under the radar. Most kids didn't pay him any attention. Even the bullies mostly ignored him, contrary to what his mother thought. However, as Margaret became more popular with the boys, they noticed that George hung around her and strangely, she seemed to like him. As George hurried to meet Margaret in the hallway, seemingly out of nowhere, a foot tripped him. He fell flat on his face, books and pens scattering before him. Somehow, this triggered one of Jose's memories and George swore in Spanish. Laughter erupted from some of the boys around him. Embarrassed, George gathered up his things and went straight to his next class.

After months of work at the mortuary, finally, a suitable donor arrived. George had been hoping for an engineer or scientist, but this man would do in the short term. Robert Peters, a locally famous actor and singer, died from a massive stroke and was brought to the mortuary on a Friday evening. Uncle Martin called George and asked if he could do the initial preparations that night. George cheerfully accepted the assignment and performed the extraction. He called Margaret and asked if she could help him develop some photographs the next morning. She readily agreed. George kept the fluid refrigerated until Margaret injected the fluid into him the next morning. Just before bed was the best time for an injection, but George did not want to take any chances on the fluid losing its full potency. The problem with doing the injection with many waking hours remaining was that as memories began flooding into his mind, George might act goofy. He decided to seek isolation for the rest of the day. "Mom, I have a lot of school work and studying to do. I'll be in my room."

"George, aren't you forgetting that we are going boating with the Medefins today?"

"Oh no!" George thought. Why hadn't Margaret reminded him? The family had talked about the trip, but it was only going to take place if it was an unusually warm day, since it was still April and usually too cold for boating. "We are leaving at ten; you had better be ready, young man. Margaret's mother and I have been planning this trip for weeks." George knew that he would have to wear a bathing suit and even though he was not romantically interested in Margaret, he still wanted to look his best for her. George did as many pushups and pull-ups as he could before getting into his bathing suit and pulling up Levis over the top. Despite Margaret's house being within easy walking distance, his family drove there to meet them.

His mother had prepared a large basket full of food for the trip. The Medefins were outside loading their ski boat that was hitched to their Cadillac Deville. The basket went into the trunk and they all got in the car and headed for Pine View Reservoir. The men sat in the front with George in the middle and the women in the back. The dads talked about sports and work.

Out of the blue, George asked, "Brother Medefin, does this have the 472 or the 500 cubic inch engine?"

"The 500, George. I'm surprised that you would know about those options."

"I sure loved that cherry red '66 convertible 472 Deville that I used to own. That was one sweet ride." Suddenly George realized what he had just said! He was confusing Robert Peters' memories with his own.

"What in the world are you talking about, George?" asked his father. George had to think fast. Although in a panic, he tried to sound calm.

"Oh, I was just quoting something that Robert Peters said. He just died, you know. I prepared his body last night at work. He was quite a guy."

"Maybe you are spending too much time around dead people. Let's stick with the living for now," instructed his father, still taken aback by George's comment.

"You're okay, George," said Mr. Medefin affectionately, as he tussled George's hair with his right hand. "You had me going there for a minute." George worked hard to keep his mouth shut the rest of the trip. As the Cadillac and boat wove their way up the steep, winding canyon, George noticed a small white house precariously perched on a ledge just a few feet from the riverbed. It seemed to George to be a crazy place to build a house. It was right in the flood plain of the river.

Once they had launched the boat, George sat next to Margaret. He could not help but notice as he looked at her in her swimsuit that her formally gangly form was transforming into a lovely figure. Margaret and George were close enough in size to share a wetsuit vest between them. Although the air was pleasant, the water was very cold. Margaret was skilled on one water ski, having frequently gone skiing with her family. George had never been water skiing before but was able to get up on the second try with two skis. He was not able to do any tricks at first but was excited to just get up. He then realized that Robert Peters was an excellent skier on water or snow and the memories started coming to life. He asked to try one ski and surprised everyone when he was able to not only get up but jump the wake and do other tricks. Everyone commented on what a fast learner he was. Margaret's parents also skied, but George's parents declined. They were content to just watch.

On the way home, George's mom said that she needed to sit upfront so that she did not get carsick. He suspected that she wanted him to sit next to Margaret, who ended up sitting in the middle. Halfway home Margaret pretended to fall asleep, at least that is how it looked to George, and leaned on him with her head on his shoulder. Being a gentleman, George made no effort to push her away. He had to admit to himself that after the chill of water skiing, her warm and gentle body felt nice leaning against his side. After getting back to the Medefins' house, unloading and unhitching the boat, Margaret suggested that George stay and help her develop the photos she had taken during the outing. Thinking that there was brain business involved, George agreed to stay. They developed the photos and then emerged promptly from the darkroom before Margaret's mother could become suspicious. "Let's go for a walk," suggested Margaret. "I want to talk to you about something." Margaret turned to the kitchen and yelled, "Mom, we're going on a walk. I will be back before nine."

Margaret and George walked out into the pleasant early evening. "I love this time of day," commented Margaret. "Tonight's temperature is perfect, cool but not cold. Thank you for coming with me. There are two things that we need to talk about. First, you have a decided advantage over me with your easy access to memories. Although you started out kind of strange today, the transformation in your demeanor has been dramatic. You carry yourself with much more grace and confidence. You seemed like a twenty-year-old on the water. If we don't take action, the girls will be swarming all over you, and we wouldn't want that to happen, would we?" Into George's mind came the image of beautiful girls, even seniors, fawning over him. He thought that would be really cool, not something to avoid. "Anyway, I need you to help me with my next acquisition. I like the idea of taking memories from someone that has passed on. They have more memories, going back farther and we are sort of preserving them. I want you to call me whenever a woman is brought in that might be a good candidate, someone educated and talented like your Robert Peters but a woman, of course."

"Sure, I can do that." Margaret moved very close to George and slipped her hand into his. He did not pull away.

"Thank you. Now for the second matter, it's important that we maintain the illusion that you are romantically interested in me. You have been doing great so far today, looking at me like you find me attractive and pretending to enjoy it when I snuggled up next to you and now letting me take your hand. Robert Peters was a superb actor and you are rapidly absorbing that talent. I'm very impressed. We both turn sixteen before the end of the month. Everyone will expect you to ask me to the Spring Dance. Now would be a good time for you to ask and get that out of the way. You can practice your acting as you do so."

George did not have a clue, based on his own personal memories, how a boy asks out a girl. Fortunately, Robert Peters had been an expert on romance in his single days. George unexpectedly broke into song, singing adapted lyrics from the song "Sixteen Going on Seventeen" from The Sound of Music. Only, he sang it as fifteen going on sixteen and worked into the lyrics an invitation to the dance. In rhythm, Margaret responded, adapting Leisl's lines of the song to accept the invitation. George thought about how convenient it was that they had both acquired memories from multi-talented actors. He would need to continue to choose memories for Margaret and himself that would enhance their compatibility, all to help them keep up the appearances of a romance, of course.

George walked Margaret home and then walked to his house, whistling a tune for the first time in his life. He felt amazingly happy. He really liked this acting thing. It was wonderful that Margaret accepted that he was just acting, pretending to be romantically interested in her. He did not have to feel guilty that he was being misleading or deceitful. Margaret really was a great girl. He might even tell her so sometime.

Chapter 5 – Brave Margaret

George got a call from Uncle Martin that another body had arrived. "George, this one is a woman. You have never prepared a woman's body before without me. Can you handle this?"

"Please, Uncle Martin, I'm a professional. I can do this."

"You are a professional. Thank you for taking this one. Your aunt and I have a big date tonight; it's our anniversary."

"You go and have a great time, boss. Everything will be just fine." George prepared to jog the half dozen blocks to the Mortuary. He had turned 16, but his parents kept reminding him of the family rule that he could not get a driver's license until he got his Eagle Scout award, something that he had not been working at very diligently. He had made the required rank advancements but had many merit badges to go and had not even thought about an Eagle Project. He would have to get moving on things. It seemed like a sin against nature to be sixteen, own a car and not be able to drive it. At the mortuary, George found that the woman was named Emily Sacks. He did not recognize her on his own, but Robert Peters knew who she was. She was only 52 years old and still looked very pretty. As Robert's memories assimilated into George's on the subject, he realized that she was a local television celebrity and did shows on cooking, health and fitness. Ironically, she had been killed by a sudden, massive heart attack that came without warning. George was sure that Margaret would be interested in this woman's memories; he did not need to call her. He did the extraction and then prepared the body for the funeral. He had things all cleaned up by eight and gave Margaret a call.

"Mag, I have a roll of film to develop. Do you have time to help me with it if I come right over?" Margaret did not care for the nickname Maggie and George had started calling her Mag, which she tolerated.

"Let me ask Mom if it's alright." Margaret put the phone down and yelled the request to her mother. "She says that it will be alright if we are done by nine. She has been kind of protective lately since boys have started to notice me. Hurry on over." George likewise had detected that boys had started to pay more attention to Margaret. He had hoped that Margaret had not made the same observation but obviously, that was not the case. Even though George was just playing a role in which he liked Margaret, he needed to guard his territory. He did not need any complications. He jogged to Margaret's house. George always carried with him a roll of undeveloped film in case he needed an excuse to use the darkroom with Margaret. The roll that he carried tonight was of Einstein doing tricks. He knew that it was lame, but it should do the job.

In the darkroom, as they developed the film, he explained to Margaret about Emily Sacks. Margaret definitely wanted those memories. "George, I want you to do the injection without putting me under. It will save a lot of time and I won't look all groggy afterward like we have been doing drugs in here or something. I have had shots and blood drawn before. I think that I can handle it. I bought a doggie chew toy to bite down on. If I raise my hand, stop; it means that I can't handle the pain."

"Wow, that is really brave of you, Mag. Just don't move; we wouldn't want to damage that wonderful brain of yours." Margaret grinned at the compliment. Not many 16-year-old boys would think to compliment a girl on her mind. She loved it that George liked that she was smart. She refused to dumb herself down for boys.

George had been to a chiropractor once and thought that maybe the technique that he used would work here. He had Margaret rest her forehead on the cushion of the desk chair and he massaged the back of her neck just under the skull. "Take in a deep breath, Mag, and then let it out slowly." When Margaret was halfway out with the breath, George deftly inserted the needle until it bottomed out at the syringe. Margaret did not even flinch. As he slowly pushed in the plunger, he could see Margaret grimace and could see the knuckles on her right hand turn white as she tightly grasped the side of the chair. At that moment, something happened to George. He realized that he truly felt deeply for this tough, clever, freckled-faced redhead that had become his best friend. Why hadn't he realized before what a beautiful, wonderful girl she was? The plunger bottomed out and he quickly withdrew the needle. "Are you alright Mag?" Margaret took a moment to compose herself, stood and turned.

"I'm fine. Good job," she replied cheerfully but with a quiver in her voice. Margaret put on a brave face, but George could see tears in the corners of her eyes. Why hadn't he noticed her eyes before? They were beautiful, green with a golden ring around each pupil like the sun's corona as seen during a full solar eclipse. Before he realized what he was doing, George put his hands around Margaret's slender waist and gave her a gentle, affectionate kiss on the lips. Margaret blushed bright red but did not pull away.

"You are the bravest, most wonderful girl I have ever known." George paused and then whispered, "You should wash your face and then we should get out of here before your mother starts pounding on the door."

As he walked home, George sang a song that he had heard on the radio and that Robert Peters had known well, You're Just Too Good to Be True. He wondered if he were in love.

As Margaret showered the next morning, she felt joy at the wonderful, useful information that was coming into her mind. She now knew how to cook. No, that was understating it; she was a master chief. She could create culinary marvels. As she looked down at her naked body, she felt the need to tone and strengthen those muscles. She was going to get into shape. She would also be more careful about what she ate.

Chapter 6 - Eagle Award

George badly wanted to get his license and be able to drive his car. He met with his scout leaders to go over what he needed to do to get the Eagle. If he took advantage of all of the Merit Badge classes being taught throughout Davis County, he could complete all of his remaining merit badges in a month or two. George needed to select an Eagle Project and get it approved. There was so much to do. He began to feel overwhelmed. Then he got a break; a well-known scout leader, a recipient of the Silver Beaver Award, died and was taken to Uncle Martin's mortuary. George had the great opportunity of extracting memories from the legendary Cleave Burningham. George had only met Cleave a few times, but he remembered that Cleave was very colorful and interesting. He knew an incredible amount on many subjects, from martial arts to chemistry. He was very fun and witty and was extremely well-liked by youth and adults alike. Cleave had a passion for the outdoors and scouting that George had always lacked. George made the extraction and got Margaret to do the injection later that evening. He received the injection while fully conscious just like Margaret had done. On one hand, George was proud of himself for his bravery, but on the other hand, he felt a little embarrassed that Margaret had led the way. He would have to think of some way to re-establish his manhood with Margaret.

The next morning as Cleave Burningham's memories flooded into his mind, George realized that Cleave was like an iceberg, most people had only seen the tip. Cleave had completed a distinguished military career and was a highly trained Navy Seal. Actually, he had helped to establish the Navy Seal program and had been one of their instructors. He also had a career in law enforcement, including ten years in the FBI. He had even worked as a CIA agent. Cleave knew thousands of people by face and name. He had learned in the military and law enforcement a number of techniques for memorizing small amounts of information instantly. These talents acquired over many years of diligent effort now became George's. George also began to understand what was so great about the outdoors and scouting. Hundreds of ideas for Eagle Projects came into his mind. Instead of just wanting to meet the minimum requirements, he wanted to do something extraordinary.

The feeling of dread that George had felt walking to school after acquiring Jose's memories had been fading. Now they were completely gone, replaced by Cleave's memories that gave him confidence. Cleave knew how to fight and had manhandled many men far larger than himself. With Cleave's memories, George took in everything around him. He scanned for threats but found none. Even the biggest, meanest boys did not intimidate him. George now knew not only how to defend himself but how to take a life in a heartbeat, not that George would ever want to do such a thing. Never the less, it was comforting to know how to take care of himself in a tough spot. The boys around him seemed to sense this confidence and cleared a path for him as he walked.

Memories continued to come into his mind throughout the day making it hard to concentrate on his classes. Cleave Burningham had secrets. He was still working on a freelance basis for the FBI and CIA when he died. Unbeknownst to the community and even Cleave's wife, Cleave had money, secret identities and even safe houses around the world. He spoke Korean and Mandarin Chinese fluently and was conversant in German and Arabic. Cleave was extremely patriotic and had done all of these things for his beloved country and not for personal gain. Cleave had been instrumental in foiling terrorist plots and assassination attempts around the world. George felt a sense of stewardship over these memories and the associated assets. He knew that Cleave would want his life's work to continue. He had only been in his sixties when he died and had many unfulfilled goals. Cleave had left his widow in good financial shape and their children were well established in their own careers and families. He would want George to use his secret assets to further his work.

After much pondering, George decided to make major improvements to the nearby Farmington reservoir. For years, there had been talk of building a small wooden boat dock, but the city had never appropriated the funds. Cleave knew all of the city officials and had actually tried to get several boys to take on the project. Most boys were looking for something easier. George would need to get approval from city officials and raise lots of money and donated materials. With Cleave's knowledge of people and the community, George could see how to accomplish his goals. First, he got approval from the Farmington City Council. He did so by getting the project on the city council's weekly agenda and having all of the scouts from his troop attend the meeting. Each boy had previously pledged in writing to donate a Saturday's labor to complete the project. To demonstrate his personal commitment, George pledged to auction off his Nova to start the fundraising. The council was very impressed with his organization and personal commitment. They approved at the meeting $1000 to help complete the project. The next day George got a commitment from a structural engineer in his neighborhood to design the dock free of charge. Within five days, the engineer completed the task.

With plans in hand, George visited lumberyards soliciting materials. He went to bait and tackle shops and other businesses soliciting funds. At his request, local newspapers provided free publicity. Consequently, the car auction was very well attended, and the Nova sold for well above market value. On a Saturday, George, the engineer, his father and Uncle Martin did the preliminary work of setting the support posts. On the following Saturday, a large group of scouts and their leaders went to work under the direction of the designer and a local carpenter. A local fast food vendor supplied lunch. By three o'clock in the afternoon, the structure was finished. Reporters were on hand to record the event and the mayor of Farmington came for an official ribbon-cutting ceremony. George's parents had helped throughout the day and were very proud of him. Once again, his mother congratulated herself on her excellent parenting. Even George had to admit that his mother had been a very powerful influence in his life. He had completed the entire project from start to finish is less than four weeks. An article in a local paper reporting on the construction pointed out that what the City of Farmington had failed to do over a period of years, a 16-year-old boy had done in less than a month.

Although George did not yet have his Eagle, his parents decided to let him get a driver's license a few days after the completion of the Eagle Project. He was elated because the Spring Dance was the following Saturday. Margaret had arranged to double with her girlfriend, Shelly, and her date. George asked his father if he could borrow the family car. "No, I don't think so, Son," replied his father. George looked very disappointed at him. He never begged for what he wanted and was surprised that his father would refuse him. "Son, why don't you drive your own car?" His father held out a set of car keys. "Your car is parked at the mortuary." George remembered seeing a red 1966 Mustang parked at the mortuary. "Son, it was very generous what you did, auctioning off your car. It made the whole Eagle Project come together. Who could refuse a young man who was willing to sacrifice so much? We were and are very proud of you. Sometimes in life, you get to have your cake and eat it too." George hugged his dad fiercely.

During the early seventies, it had not yet become the custom to make a school dance date a twelve-hour event. George arrived at Margaret's door at 6:45 PM with corsage in hand. They went through the usual parental inspections and photo sessions before leaving to pick up the other couple. After picking up Bruce and then Shelly, they went to the Ristorante Della Fontana, located in a former church in Salt Lake City. Fontana served a five-course dinner starting with a salad, followed by soup and then the main course. Cheese and sliced apples were subsequently served to "cleanse the palate". The meal concluded with a light dessert.

Both Margaret and George now had an excellent understanding of traditional dining manners. They were embarrassed that Bruce and Shelly, especially Bruce, lacked an understanding or at least an observance of even the bare essentials of these manners. It was amazing to George how knowledge had changed their attitudes. He could tell that Margaret was annoyed with her friends. In the culture of their community, youth their age were highly encouraged to group date. With their newly acquired adult perspectives, they now understood the wisdom of these social norms. On the other hand, group dating might prove itself very tedious, if tonight's dinner were any indication.

Not only had Margaret and George grown up within blocks of each other, giving them a common background, but they had also been transformed in ways that would make it hard for them to feel comfortable with anyone else. If they were not originally made for each other, certainly George's science was making them right for each other. They were two teenagers with the knowledge and attitudes of mature adults. George wondered if he had made a big mistake, robbing them of what remained of their childhood. But then, George had never really been good at being a child. He had thought like an adult and identified more with adults than with children his own age since he was 12. He suspected that the same was the case for Margaret. Maybe they had only skipped over the awkward part of adolescence. Even though they had adult memories they could still enjoy a good roller coaster ride. They still had young, limber bodies.

The dance was held at the Utah State Capitol rotunda. The slick marble floor provided an excellent dance surface. Margaret and George had an intellectual and mechanical understanding of social and ballroom dancing but had never put their knowledge to the test. As George took Margaret's hands in his, they started to dance the Swing. Their movement was awkward at first, but soon they had the hang of it. They were doing the basic moves smoothly. They successfully executed a few spin moves and then George initiated the Skin the Cat move. The next thing that he knew he was on his back with Margaret sprawled on top of him. Those around them responded, some with laughter, others with expressions of concern and some mocking. The couple untangled themselves and stood. "Are you alright?" asked George.

"Only my pride is injured. Let's sit for a while." George reluctantly walked Margaret away from the center of the floor.

"Wait," he commanded. "When Olympic figure skaters fall, they don't quit. We can do this. We just pushed ourselves too fast. We have to give time for our brains to work out the fact that our bodies do not fit the memories." George realized that there was more to it than just bodily differences. He and Margaret needed to give their brains an opportunity to make dancing an automatic activity like walking or running or riding a bicycle. They continued with the basic step and simple moves. Over time, they worked in more complex moves. Gradually they became more comfortable dancing the swing. Next, they were doing the cha-cha and then a waltz. Each time they started a new dance step they struggled at first but over time became more comfortable. It appeared to those around them that they were extremely fast learners. George knew that with practice and only with practice, they could become as good as their memory donors had been. As the end of the dance drew near, George could feel certain muscles burning, having been exerted in ways that they had never been used before. The last dance was a slow dance and they danced close, barely moving their feet. "Are you as tired as I am?" asked Margaret.

"I don't know if tired is the right word. My legs feel like they are on fire. You may have to carry me to the car."

"I might have been able to a few years ago when I was taller than you, but you have been in a growth spurt." She felt George's right bicep, which he had been vigorously working on since the Robert Peters acquisition. "And it's not just your height; you have put on some muscle." George was delighted that she had noticed. Robert Peters had been very self-conscious about his physique and the attitude had rubbed off on George.

After the dance, dates were dropped off in the opposite order of how they were picked up, with Margaret being the last. George figured that Margaret's mother had probably stationed herself at a window to watch, so he just gave Margaret a peck on the cheek and hurried home.

Having the memories of three mature men mingling with his own was changing George in many ways, some observable to others and some that he kept hidden. The worst part was that in some ways he had lost his innocence. George had knowledge of intimacies that he desperately wanted to forget. He had also become acquainted with the darker side of life. As an alcoholic, Jose had seen terrible things. Cleave had fought in war and seen comrades killed at his side. He had been required to fight and kill others in war and in law enforcement, not to mention CIA actions. Fortunately, Cleave had never let the dark side of life bring him down. He had possessed a perpetual optimism about life and had been known for his cheerfulness. Working in the entertainment business, Robert had seen the infidelity and immorality that are so pervasive in that industry. Fortunately, he had personally been a moral man.

The memories also began to affect little things in George's life. He was much more careful about his dress and grooming. He carried more things in his pockets, a pocketknife, a lighter, a handkerchief, change for a payphone, breath mints. He started wearing a watch but said no to the memories that kept telling him of the convenience of using a coin purse. Fortunately, there had been no urge to wear suspenders. Even George's vocabulary and speech patterns had been changing. Two of his donors had been sticklers about using correct grammar and of course, he now had a vastly expanded vocabulary.

George used to look at girls and think that one was cute and another was not. Now he thought about so many other qualities of importance. He thought about what kind of wife and mother a girl would make. Would she be a good housekeeper, a good cook? He even evaluated their looks differently. Sure, they were cute now, but what would they look like in twenty or thirty years? He had barely had his first date and he was thinking about what kind of grandmother Margaret would be. Sometimes he wondered if he were losing his mind.

In private, George practiced the languages and other skills that he had picked up. He even sang in private and practiced fighting skills, including knife throwing. He practiced shooting with his bee bee gun. He asked his mother if he could take piano lessons. His mother was thrilled. Robert Peters had a moderate proficiency at the piano, enough to play at church but not enough to play professionally. George's teacher and parents were astounded by his rapid progress. Soon he dispensed with the lessons and just practiced on his own on the family piano that hadn't seen much use since his older sister left home.

Margaret's mother was the Relief Society president of her ward, the Bountiful Third Ward, and had a key to the church. Margaret and George were in different wards (congregations) but met in the same church building, just at different times. They met in a large, old church on Main Street referred to as the Bountiful Tabernacle. The chapel portion of the building was built in a previous century but the building complex had at its center a basketball court, officially referred to as the Cultural Hall. Margaret sometimes borrowed the building key from her mother so that she and George could practice dancing on the spacious hardwood floor. The first couple of times Margaret's parents came along and danced with them, but soon they felt outclassed and stayed home.

George thought about how convenient it would be if Margaret shared all of his skills, allowing him to practice all of them with her. At least they could sing and dance together.

Chapter 7 – Dead Secrets

The next week passed without incident until George received in the mail a formal invitation to try out for the school play that was casting before the end of the school year but would not be performed until October of his junior year. His mother hovered over him as he read the invitation. George suspected that the setting was exactly how Mrs. Nelson wanted it to be so that mothers would pressure their sons to act on the invitation. The following Thursday he walked to the auditorium after his last class. Margaret was already there. George had never sung a song or recited a line from The Music Man before his acquisitions, but Robert Peters knew them all by heart, having performed the play many times. George was asked to read part of "Professor" Harold Hill's discourse on the think method of teaching music. He briefly looked at the script and then delivered from memory the monologue much as Robert Peters had in his performances. All present were awed. "That was wonderful. Can you sing any of the songs?" asked Mrs. Nelson.

"I know them all, but I don't know how well you will like my singing." With that, George launched into "Seventy-six Trombones" a cappella. His voice did not have exceptional artistic appeal, but he hit every note and his timing was very precise.

"That will do just fine, George," commented Mrs. Nelson.

Margaret's verbal performance was good, but her singing really had Mrs. Nelson excited. Margaret had a wonderful, lilting singing voice that was very appealing. Mrs. Nelson said that she would let those who tried out know who got what roles, but it was clear to all that George had secured the role of "Professor" Harold Hill and Margaret was a shoo-in for the role of Marian Paroo, the librarian. A week later, the casting was posted on school bulletin boards confirming everyone's expectations for the lead roles.

George enjoyed the ego trip of winning the leading role but was not prepared for the time commitment that was required to rehearse for the production. The Viewmont High School productions drew audiences from all over Davis County and beyond and were better attended than most professional productions in the area. Part of the reason was that Mrs. Nelson was a relentless taskmaster, demanding nothing short of the best that each participant could offer. George had to renegotiate his hours at the mortuary so that he could meet his commitments.

Although his acquisitions had reduced the need for study time, they had not eliminated it. In fact, there were gaping holes in George's scholastic knowledge that he had to fill by his own inefficient study. Consequently, when a professor of physics from Utah State University showed up at the mortuary, George was delighted. Because he extracted the fluid rather late on a Thursday night he kept it refrigerated until the next evening when he paid Margaret a visit. George had called ahead and expected that since he had not been to Margaret's house for weeks he would probably be very welcomed by her mother. His roll of film contained shots taken at rehearsal. Margaret's mother was anxious to see the prints. By now, Margaret could perform the injection in less than a minute. The couple created 35-millimeter size prints, so that they could decide which pictures were worthy of enlarging. They went over the miniature prints with Mrs. Medefin, who could hardly contain her excitement. She was so proud that Margaret had a leading role, something that Margaret had dreamed about since she saw her first Viewmont production as a young girl. She was also proud of George, whom she already thought of as a future son-in-law. George gave Margaret money to make a large print that he would give as a Mother's Day present. He hoped that it would not appear egotistical that he was giving his mother a picture of himself.

When George awoke the next morning, the memories that flowed into his mind were even more shocking than those from Cleave Burningham. Professor Ian Wilson was not just a college professor; he was a member of a secret terrorist group. This hyper-environmentally concerned group believed it appropriate to use acts of deadly violence to hinder land development and to get across their message. As the day progressed, conspiracy details coursed into George's consciousness. The group called themselves "Live Natural or Die" or LND for short. Up to this point, they had only committed a few sporadic assassinations and acts of vandalism. However, they had been planning for months to blow up the Pine View Dam during the height of spring runoff. This event, if carried out, would endanger thousands of lives and cost millions of dollars in damages. From Professor Wilson's memories, George knew the names of all of the conspirators and some of their immediate plans.

George told his mother that he needed to run some errands and would be out for a while in his car. He drove to the Salt Lake International Airport and using a payphone, called the regional office of the FBI. He told the receptionist that he had vital information concerning national security and would like to speak to an agent. The receptionist said that she would connect him with the first available agent. "Hello, this is Agent Cline. How may I help you?" asked a voice that sounded like it belonged to a man not much older than George.

"Through a method that cannot presently be revealed, I have become aware of a radical environmental group that has committed past capital crimes and is planning to blow up a dam in Utah. I can give you names, addresses, phone numbers and the location of explosives."

"May I have your name, sir?" asked the agent.

"You can just call me Big Brain. I understand these men. I know how they think. If you attack them with a frontal assault, they will scatter and go on a killing spree. First, I need to establish my credibility. You will find a barn full of high-grade explosives at the following Logan address." George gave the address. "I suggest that first you verify covertly that I am telling the truth. I will give you one week and then call back." George gave the names and personal information on the conspirators and got Agent Cline's direct number. He then hung up. He drove to Magna, a small town south of the Salt Lake City Airport. This town contained one of Cleave's safe houses. George located the key hidden in a knothole high in the trunk of a tree in the back yard. He let himself into the safe house and verified what he already knew from memory. The house contained a secret trap door to a basement full of weapons, equipment, provisions and money. As George looked over the impressive arsenal, he could not picture himself killing anyone but could envision at least holding bad guys at bay. George left the house and key as he had found them and drove back to Bountiful. He stopped at the library and checked out some books and then stopped at Carr's Stationary to buy some school supplies. He wanted to be able to give truthful answers to any questions that his mother might ask.

As George had become acquainted with his previous memory donors, he learned to like, even love the men. They were good men who wanted to do right and had done great benefit to others. Robert Peters had brought inspirational performances in plays and musical productions that had uplifted many thousands of people. Cleave had served his country with honor, helping to preserve freedom for millions. He had inspired hundreds of young men through the Church of Jesus Christ of Latter-day Saints young men's program and through scouting. He had been a wonderful husband and father. Ian Wilson, on the other hand, was a slimy, small-minded sort of person, devoid of care for his fellow men or even for his own family. He had been married and divorced twice. No woman who came to really know him would tolerate his companionship. He was bitter about life and people. Being part of a radical environmental group was more about teaching others a lesson than really helping the environment. George worried about having the vile memories of Ian in his head. However, his father always said that you could learn from a bad example as well as a good one. From the memories, George could see the negative consequences of inappropriate behavior and attitudes. Hopefully, he would figure out how to avoid the same mistakes.

Chapter 8 – Barn Blast

After a week filled with play rehearsals, George called Agent Cline. Following greetings, he asked, "Have you investigated the barn that I told you about?"

"I'm sorry, Sir, but my management would not commit resources on the basis of an anonymous phone call when no immediate threat is apparent." George was stunned and frustrated. It was evident that he would have to somehow bring this group's activities into the open on his own.

"Mr. Cline, you force me to take matters into my own hands. Your people have not given heed to my words; maybe they will give heed to my actions." George hung up and began to work on a plan.

A few days later Margaret asked George to drop by her house. When he did, she requested a walk. During the hustle of the play rehearsals, he had not seen much of Margaret away from school and was glad to spend time with her. Once they were away from listening ears, Margaret opened with, "George, there is something wrong. Ever since your last acquisition, you have seemed troubled and preoccupied. What's going on?"

"I have been hoping that we would not be having this conversation, Mag. Let me just say that Ian Wilson was an evil man and I am deeply troubled by what I know of his actions and plans."

"I sense that it is more than that, George. You are up to something. You have secrets."

"We both have secrets, Mag. What we do in the darkroom is not exactly public knowledge."

"But you have secrets from me. I can tell. You used to be more open with me. You never tell me how you feel about anything anymore. Please share your feelings with me."

"I can't Mag. What I know is dangerous. I know about men who would kill me if they knew that I know what I know. I don't want to expose you to that kind of risk."

"Okay, let's suppose that I were the one who knew about dangerous people. Would you want me to include you in on my secret?" George could see that Margaret was maneuvering him into a trap. He hated how she could verbally outflank him and yet admired her for it.

"I can see where this is headed. I don't want to endanger your life, no matter what you say. I would never forgive myself if anything happened to you."

"George, I wasn't going to tell you this, but you have already endangered my life far more than you realize. You have greatly endangered both of our lives. Do you realize what diseases you could have exposed us to with direct injections of another person's bodily fluids? We could have or maybe have picked up any manner of horrible diseases!" George was aghast. How could he not have considered this risk? He was so shaken by this revelation that his defenses entirely collapsed. He started apologizing and broke down and told Margaret everything. Margaret did not interrupt or ask questions until he had divulged all. Like someone with severe nausea, George expelled what was inside until he thought there was nothing left and then at the point of tears came forth with more.

Margaret waited until she was sure that he was finished. "So I suppose that this safe house has communication equipment. Couldn't I be your lookout, be your eyes and ears while you go into danger?" George had never thought of that. He would feel a lot safer knowing that someone would be watching his back.

"Well, yes, there are some portable two-way radios. I suppose you could watch from a hidden position and report to me anything that you see."

"So what is your plan?" asked Margaret.

"There isn't much to it; set the barn on fire. The fire and resulting explosion should attract a lot of attention. Agent Cline should take me seriously after that." Margaret added some refinements to the plan but thought that the basic idea was simple enough to pull off. The hardest part would be coming up with a cover that would allow them to go together to Logan. Asking for permission to go together out of town seemed out of the question. Margaret's parents would never go for that. Then an idea came to Margaret. "They would probably let you take me to Lagoon." Since the amusement park was only a 15-minute drive from her house, Margaret assumed that her mother would approve.

"That's almost a great idea, Mag. They would expect us to spend all day there. The problem is that this time of year Lagoon closes at seven. We need the cover of darkness and a couple of hours to get back from the barn near Logan."

"Then let's just sneak out at night after our parents are asleep. We won't have to make up any stories because they won't know a thing."

"I guess that can work, as long as they don't check on us in the middle of the night."

"My mother checks on me just before she goes to bed, but I have never seen her check after that," Margaret responded. "I can leave pillows under the covers to look like I am there, just in case."

"My mother is a very heavy sleeper. She usually is asleep before I am. My dad never worries about me. But, I'll do the pillow thing to be on the safe side."

A few days later George took Margaret to the safe house in Magna to show her what resources were available. She was delighted and excited that he would share this secret with her. She recognized many of the things in the basement that would have baffled most girls her age. "I feel like a high tech Nancy Drew," she commented. Later, they made a couple of spare keys. It looked suspicious going to the tree before opening the back door.

On Monday night at 11:53, George picked up Margaret a block from her house. Margaret quietly slid into the car and held the door without shutting it until they were out of the neighborhood. She was dressed in dark, long sleeve clothing, as was George. They excitedly drove to Logan going over their plans on the way. After an hour and half of driving, they reached the farmhouse and barn. George drove by at normal speed without slowing while Margaret carefully looked for activity. There was a light on in the farmhouse and a vehicle parked next to the home. George drove another tenth of a mile down the road and pulled off into a small clearing among some large cottonwood trees. The couple wordlessly exited the car and opened the trunk. George had prepared two backpacks with equipment, water and food, in case they had to run for it and hide out. He handed Margaret her small backpack and helped her put it on. He then handed her a two-way portable radio and helped her put the earphone in her ear. George donned his backpack and tested the radio. "Red Angel, do you read me?"

"Loud and clear, Big Brain." George pulled from the trunk a black plastic garbage bag containing an insecticide sprayer that he had filled with lamp oil. He had determined by testing that gasoline would evaporate too quickly and besides it would leave a strong odor on his clothing and the car. Lamp oil had its own strong odor but was more easily contained, being less volatile and thicker than gasoline. His tests showed that double bagging with plastic garbage bags could sufficiently contain the odor. George and Margaret silently walked through the fields back to the farm wearing the backpacks and carrying the bag encased sprayer. There was enough starlight and moonlight for them to navigate through the open fields. The only cover for Margaret was a small clump of bushes. She had to keep very low to stay hidden. George stayed with Margaret for a few minutes while they carefully looked for guards, sentries or anyone else that might be about. All was quiet and clear.

George silently crept towards the barn. He moved to the side of the barn where the explosives had been stored. He took off the backpack and pulled from it an old-fashioned brace and bit. He inserted the drill bit into the chuck of the brace and tightened it into place. Four feet up the side of the barn, he drilled two one-inch diameter holes. Through the hole on the right, he inserted a small flashlight. He put his right eye to the hole on the left and turned on the light. George could see large boxes covered with a canvas. He could not see the box labels but felt confident that the boxes contained the explosives. He put the brace and bit and flashlight back in the backpack and removed a pair of rubber gloves like his mother used when cleaning the toilets. He donned the gloves and positioned the pack on his back again. He removed the sprayer from the plastic bags and stuffed the wadded up bags into a large knothole in the side of the barn. The barn was not oriented square with the house. One corner pointed directly at the small home. Thus, two sides of the barn were in full view of the home and two sides were hidden from the house. Starting from the point closest to the house on one of the hidden sides, George sprayed the lamp oil on the barn wall creating a strip about three feet high. He continued until he had spayed the two walls of the barn that were not visible from the farmhouse. After he had finished the three-foot-wide strip, he moved to the corner farthest from the house and continued spraying, emptying his bottle of oil on the walls.

George pulled some newspaper out of his pack, crumpled it and placed it against one of the walls. "Red Angel, is the coast clear?"

"The coast is clear," responded Margaret. George lit the paper on fire and watched until he was confident that the wall would keep burning. He removed a new plastic bag from the backpack. After sealing the sprayer in the bag, he removed the gloves and threw them against the burning wall. He removed a second bag from the pack and double bagged the sprayer. He quickly and silently returned to

Margaret, leaving nothing behind that was not burning. They paused for a minute to watch the fire spread along the strip of oil. The wood was beginning to crackle in places. George and Margaret hurriedly headed back to the car. After returning the equipment to the trunk, they headed out. George resisted the temptation to drive past the farm again or to wait for the explosion. He departed in the same direction that they had come, moving farther away from the farm. When they were a mile down the road, they heard a horrendous blast! They knew that at that range it had to be an enormous explosion for them to hear it so loudly. George just kept driving. For a while, they were silent. Then Margaret started talking breathlessly. "That was the most exciting thing that I have ever done! This is so cool! We foiled a terrorist plot! Too bad that we can't tell anyone about this." Margaret went on exuberantly for nearly an hour. Finally, she ran out of talk and went quiet.

George had many second thoughts. He wondered if anyone were hurt. Would they get in trouble with the law somehow? He silently pondered on what he had done this night. He had committed arson, a felony. If anyone were killed by the fire and subsequent blast, he would be guilty of a capital offense. Was he out of his mind? Had he let the memories drive him crazy? To make matters worse, he had involved a juvenile in his delusional schemes. He could not see any way out except to keep things a secret. However, that could mean a life of deception and regret. How could he look his parents in the eyes in the morning? In one night, he had gone from being a highly law-abiding citizen to a felon. As the adrenalin dissipated from his system, it was replaced by exhaustion. George had not done much physically but the lack of sleep, the tension and now the self-recrimination left him physically and emotionally spent.

He kept his concerns to himself. After many minutes of silent driving, they arrived back in Bountiful. George pulled into the parking lot of the church where the 26th Ward met and disposed of the sprayer in their dumpster. George dropped Margaret off a block from her house and then drove to his house, parking along the curb in front of the Horton home right where the Mustang had been parked before the trip began. As quietly as possible, he returned to his room via the back door. He undressed and got in bed. To his surprise, he almost instantly fell asleep. George awoke sweaty and cold around five o'clock. He rolled out of bed and onto his knees. He began pleading to God with all of his heart. Even though he knew that God already knew everything, he went over all of the details of what had motivated him to set fire to the barn. He explained about the lives that he hoped to save. George examined his own heart for evidence of selfish motives. Finally, he asked, "Did I do the right thing tonight?" A feeling of warmth started in his chest and radiated throughout his body. George felt a peace such as he had never felt before. He had done the right thing and he would never again second-guess himself about burning that barn.

The next morning the explosion was a big local news story. There had been someone in the house. When his photo was shown in the TV news story, George recognized him as one of the conspirators. That evening he drove to Salt Lake City and phoned Agent Cline from a phone booth in a hotel. "Do you take me seriously now, Mr. Cline?" he asked.

"I take you seriously for arson and attempted murder, you misguided vigilante!" George was not expecting this kind of response. Memories of Cleave's resentment and anger towards do-nothing agents like Cline boiled up inside of George. The memories caught hold of him and temporarily took over.

"Listen to me, you pencil-necked, good for nothing paper pusher! I should have never bothered with you in the first place. I should have known that you would screw this up, just like you did the Franken case. Yes, I know all about you and your pathetic, ineffective career. I should have called Marks in Denver. The man I injured is responsible for the assassinations of Philip Carson in `67 and Wade Walker in `69. If you had done some real detective work you might have figured that out." At that point, Agent Cline hung up. George was astounded by the words that had come from his mouth. Even his voice had sounded different. He sounded more like Cleave than himself. George wondered what to do next. Without consciously thinking, he picked up the phone again and dialed Rex Marks. He answered on the sixth ring.

"Hello."

"Hey Rex, I have some important information for you. Have you got a minute?"

"This sounds like someone who I thought was dead."

"Well, you know the old saying about 'rumors of my death have been greatly exaggerated.' It's best if we leave me dead for now. I can work much better this way. Just call me Buck for the time being. Have you ever heard of Live Natural or Die, LND for short?" George asked in Cleave's voice.

"I have not heard the name, but I have been tracking several underground radical environmental groups. They may be one of them. Tell me about them." George told Agent Marks all that he knew and mentioned the explosion without taking credit for it. Rex promised to fully investigate.

That night George pondered on how Cleave's memories seemed to have affected him radically differently from the others. The more he thought about it the more he saw a common thread. When he tried out for a part in the play, Robert Peters seemed to take over his actions. Without conscious thought, he did what Robert would have done under similar circumstances. When George spoke Spanish or worked on cars he acted and spoke like Jose Martinez would have in similar circumstances. When he did the things that he had always done, he was just himself. George began to worry about whether he would do evil things if he got into some pattern that fit Ian Wilson.

George did not think that he would but decided that he would have to stay on guard. Being able to act without having to think first was an advantage, but he did not want past personalities somehow taking over.

The first chance that George had to be alone with Margaret he brought her up to speed and warned her about how acquired memories could almost take over. She had observed to a lesser extent what George had experienced. "I don't think that I want any more acquisitions," commented Margaret.

"I don't blame you with all of the dangers and weird side effects. Do you regret what we have done?"

"Not for one minute! My only regret is that I only watched you set fire to that barn. I wish that I had lit the match myself. You may have saved hundreds of lives. And thanks for telling off Agent Cline; he had it coming, big time. It looks like Buck will be taken more seriously than Big Brain. Hopefully, the FBI will take things from here."

"Don't count on it. I have a tool that none of them have and the knowledge and equipment to carry out important missions."

"I think that you are getting a superhero complex. Just remember, a bullet can kill you just like one of us mortals and I wouldn't want some Neanderthal fist messing up your cute little face."

"Really, you think that I'm cute?"

Margaret took George's face in her hands and kissed him on the lips. "What do you think, Big Brain?"

Chapter 9 - Instant Quarterback

At an eagle court of honor held in May, George received his eagle award. Never in the history of his community had so many non-family members come to see a single individual receive this award. The mayor and the entire city council of Farmington attended. There were actually reporters covering the event. George had always dreamed about receiving public accolades, but when it actually happened, he felt more embarrassed and humbled than anything else. If ever "standing on the shoulders of giants" applied to someone, it applied to him. He decided that the most appropriate thing was for him to say as little as possible. In these kinds of circumstances, humility can often appear to be false humility or fishing for compliments. After the ceremony, when people congratulated him, George merely said, "Thank you," although in various ways. He thought about 1 Samuel 18:14 that says, "And David behaved himself wisely in all his ways; and the LORD was with him." He was certainly no David, but he could behave himself wisely. The eventual fall of David from righteousness had been a great heartbreak to George from the time that he first read of his affair with Bathsheba. Cleave also had harbored very strong feelings on the subject. It is always so easy for highly accomplished and popular people to lose perspective. George vowed to himself that he would remain humble and meek.

At school, George had never been part of the "in" group, but now the most popular kids at school frequently invited him to associate with them in various ways from eating lunch with them to attending their parties. He tried to treat them like everyone else. George sometimes ate with them, but he also sought out those that appeared to be friendless. He thought that Margaret would want him to sit with her as much as possible, but she seemed to be pleased with his efforts to befriend the lonely. She sometimes joined him with whatever forlorn soul he was visiting and other times herself sought out the lonely. She highly approved of and encouraged his efforts to be a friend to all. For most of his life, George had been very self-centered, absorbed in his scientific curiosities without much concern or regard for others. Although he had been a loner, he had never felt loneliness and certainly not despair. With his new perspective, George saw that many craved friendship and moral support.

As George associated with the popular kids, he was surprised when several members of the football team encouraged him to try out for football that summer, even though he had never participated in sports. George was baffled. He was not fast and although he had shot up to six-one, he still only weighed 165 pounds. He guessed that he looked fit. Those inviting him could not know that he possessed the memories of Robert Peters who played quarterback in high school and college. Nor did they know that he had acquired the football savvy of Cleave Burningham who played safety and was a consensus All-American. Maybe it was his recently gained reputation for being a fast learner that garnered the invitation.

George talked to his parents about it. His father was thrilled with the idea. His mother was torn between her desire for George to be an athlete and her fear of permanent injury. In the end, they gave enthusiastic approval. Tryouts did not begin until July so George had some time to prepare. He approached his father one Saturday morning. "Dad, would you toss the football with me?"

"Son, I have been waiting 16 years for you to ask me to play catch with you. I would be delighted to help you in any way that I can." George had recently purchased a football and they took it out into the street in front of their house. They lived on a wide and lightly traveled street with a 25 MPH speed limit. It was an excellent place for throwing a football. Being over six feet tall, George had hands with long fingers that could easily grasp the ball. At about the same height as Robert Peters, it felt very natural for him to throw and catch. As they threw the ball back and forth, George quickly became more proficient than his father. "Son, I may not be quite as smart as you, but I know that something is going on. You must have cooked up some formula in that lab of yours that has made you and Margaret smarter. No one suddenly starts picking up skills as fast as you have without some gimmick or something. You're like Jerry Lewis in the Nutty Professor or something. It's okay; I won't tell your secret. A lot of boys your age are drinking alcohol to make themselves stupid. You apparently are doing the opposite. I wouldn't mind being smarter myself. Someday you will let me in on your little secret. I can wait. I just hope that you are not doing something dangerous that will leave you an idiot in the end." George just smiled but did not say anything. Soon his mother joined the practices, which allowed George to throw and catch against a defender. Not surprisingly, she was very skilled.

George started doing serious weight lifting and conditioning exercises. By July, he had gained four pounds of additional muscle and was in excellent shape.

On the first day of tryouts, George noticed a line of boys trying out for quarterback. Wanting to take the road less traveled, he decided to apply for the position of safety. Most of the practice session time was spent doing grueling exercises such as wind sprints and jogging in place and going down on all fours when the whistle was blown. George had known what to expect and had been preparing himself over the past six weeks. He definitely had an edge in the conditioning department over most of the boys. During specific position practices, George had a hard time keeping up with the faster receivers but still managed an impressive number of interceptions. The coach noticed his perfect spirals throwing the ball back to the passer. Coach Reid approached George. "Come to the sideline a minute, Horton. I would like to talk to you." Reid guided

George to the sidelines with his right hand on his left elbow. "I thought you said that you have never played football before. There is no way that anyone picks up a sport this fast."

"I have never physically played on a team, not football or any other sport. My parents are super athletic. We have played catch and I have watched some professional games with my dad. I have a vivid imagination and I have played out some games in my mind in great detail." George was struggling to sound plausible without actually lying.

"I don't know what you are hiding, but no one on this field, including me, can throw a better-looking pass than you. Can you read defenses?"

"I expect that with my lack of speed or size, that may be what I'm best at."

"The best safeties are all fast, but some of the best quarterbacks are slow. You'd have to be a drop-back passer, not a scrambler. Let's see you throw some passes to a covered receiver." He walked George back onto the field and asked the passer to trade places with George. The former passer seemed shocked but complied. The receiver easily got separation from the covering quarterback wannabe. George tossed relatively soft, easy to catch passes into the receiver's hands over and over. After 10 catches, Coach Reid played defender and covered the receiver very tightly. George threw the ball where only the receiver could catch it and put more zip on the ball. The receiver caught less than half of them, but there were no interceptions. Coach asked the player whom he had replaced to join him. George threw a couple of passes to the receiver that he dropped. On the third pass attempt, the receiver was totally covered. George scrambled out of the imaginary pocket and threw the ball out of bounds.

"What was that?" asked Coach Reid.

"That was living to fight another day. You didn't want me to throw an interception, did you, Sir?"

"No, I didn't. But in 20 years of coaching, I have never seen a quarterback do that during this drill. Come to my office after practice. I have something for you." George did not know what to think. He was sure that coaches did not give you a pink slip if you failed to make the team. What was Coach Reid going to give him? George went back to practicing as a safety and did the closing wind sprints with the team. After the final whistle, he headed for the coach's office. Coach Reid was sitting at his desk when George entered the room.

"Sit down, Horton. Last year I had a quarterback with an arm like a cannon, but he could not read defenses to save his life. You walk on the field out of nowhere and show more practical understanding of the game in five minutes than the last quarterback did in a full season. You must be some kind of genius or something. I looked up your transcript and you got straight A's last term but didn't do all that well before that. I don't know if this is some kind of Invasion of the Body Snatchers or what, but I'm not going to turn down a chance for a winning season. Do you have any problems playing quarterback instead of safety?"

"No, sir."

"Here is a copy of the playbook. Learn as much of it as you can as fast as you can. We will hold a scrimmage in two days. I want you to play quarterback on the red team."

"Yes, Sir. I will have the playbook memorized by scrimmage time."

"That's all, Horton. You may go."

"Thank you, Sir." What had George been thinking, saying that he would memorize the playbook in two days? He was the guy that had a hard time memorizing. That must have been Cleave or Robert speaking. George had put his foot in his mouth this time, cleats and all.

As George studied the playbook that night, he realized that he, through Robert Peter's memories, already knew all of these simple plays. George only needed to memorize the name for each and that was a simple matter easily performed in an hour. The next morning George arrived at practice a half-hour early and suited up. He went to Coach Reid's office to announce that he knew all of the plays. He found the coach sitting at his desk going over the roster. "Hi, Coach. You got a minute?"

"Sure, Horton. Have a seat." George sat down in one of the chairs against the far wall of the small office.

"I wanted to return the playbook. I have memorized all of the plays. I didn't know if you wanted me to keep this copy or not." George stood and placed the playbook on the cluttered desk.

"You're kidding, right?"

"No, Sir. I have seen all of these plays before in games that I have watched on TV. I just didn't know what you called them. All of your names seem logical except for maybe the 'Hail Mary' play. I didn't get that one." Actually, George did get it, thanks to the memories, but when he said, "I didn't get it", he meant his old self.

"Yeah, I suppose a Mormon kid like you growing up in Bountiful might not understand that one. If you make sure that we have the lead in the final seconds of the game, you won't have to worry about that one, unless of course you are playing safety and the other team tries it. Well, you must be some sort of genius or something to have picked up all of those plays from watching a little football."

"Actually coach, I pick some things up really quickly, but I can be pretty slow about other things, like girls."

"I don't know about that. You seemed to have corralled the cutest, smartest and most popular girl on campus. I wish I had been that slow at your age, not that I have any complaints about Mrs. Reid, mind you."

"By the way, Coach, I'm no prima donna. I will play any position that you want me to play, although I would not advise offensive lineman."

"No, you're a little lean for that. Well, you better get out of here before anyone catches you in the coach's office and accuses you of brown-nosing." With that, George headed out to the playing field to loosen up. That day they practiced some simple plays and George got to practice the quarterback position with an offensive line and multiple receivers. The team had one receiver who was fast and could catch tolerably well and one that was slow but had great hands. The latter caught almost everything that he could touch. In a real game, the fast receiver would probably be double-teamed most of the time. George figured that he would throw many short passes to the slow receiver. There were other receivers, but most of them could not catch reliably. Fortunately, the fullback could catch well if the ball were thrown softly to him. Missiles went right through his fingers or bounced off him.

The scrimmage was very informal. It provided a way for the coaches to get a rough ranking of the players and in some cases see the players in multiple positions. George started as the quarterback on the red team. His team won the toss and chose to receive. George marched the team down the field throwing to the open man on pass plays and eventually scoring. On running plays, George just handed off, but thanks to the memories and Robert Peters acting skills he pulled off the deception part of play-action pass/run amazingly well. Often the gold team was totally fooled, looking for the ball in the wrong place.

Playing quarterback in this first scrimmage, Robert Peters seemed to be totally in charge. For him, playing in high school again was like a dream. The defense was so much smaller, slower and less physical than the ones in college had been. On the other hand, the supporting cast on his team was not very skilled and that was frustrating for a perfectionist like Robert. Since it was all new to George, he was just enjoying the ride.

The gold team had the best running back. He was not big, but he was fast and elusive. He carried the ball on over half of the gold team's offensive plays. The gold team methodically worked their way to the red team's 42-yard line and stalled. They punted, downing the ball inside of the 10-yard line. Again, George dissected the defense, moving his team down the field. By halftime, the red had a 17-point lead. In the second half, George played safety. In the third quarter, he managed to intercept a pass that was thrown a little short. After that, the gold team's quarterback threw long every time he threw in George's direction. The red team's second-half quarterback threw one interception that was returned for a touchdown. The final score was 24 to 14 in favor of the red team. George had established himself as the leading quarterback for the Viewmont Vikings.

Chapter 10 – Busted

That fall was the busiest time of George's young life. In addition to playing football and being a lead member of the cast in a Viewmont High School production, he found himself being invited to join the Spanish Club, the Drama Club and an honor society. Never having been popular before and enjoying the attention, George did not know how to say no. However, by far football and the play took the most time. It was a good thing that George did not need to spend a lot of time studying. He found that the acquired knowledge formed a well-organized framework in his mind for adding new knowledge. That, combined with techniques that Cleave had developed, made it easy for him to learn new information and recall it. George's quest to improve his memory had finally found fulfillment.

Because George was totally unknown as a football player, the opposing teams at first had no idea what to expect from him. On the other hand, Coach Reid had a player who looked great during practice, but how would he perform during an actual game? George was very nervous before the game began. What if the memories somehow failed him and Robert Peters failed to take over when he was on the field as quarterback? The team didn't have much in the way of a backup quarterback. Scott Simmons was a capable runner but not much of a passer.

During the first offensive play, Coach Reid called a running play. It went nowhere. The second play call was a short pass to Randy Spanner, the good-hands receiver. It was right on target and Randy picked up eight yards. The third play was a pass to the fullback. Just as the ball left George's fingertips a helmet slammed into George's back, knocking the breath out of him and leaving him sprawled on the turf gasping for air. Robert Peters seemed to leave him as he lay there in pain; he was on his own. Into his mind replayed the conversation he had with his father the night before. "Son, your mother and I are pleased and excited that you are playing football, but remember, when things get hard and they will get hard, remember that playing was your choice and because of your choice there is a whole team and coaches counting on you. The whole school is counting on you to perform. You have a track record of dropping some things when they get tough or you don't find them fun anymore. You must not do that to your teammates. You have to hang in there for your team." George thought about when he had talked his parents into buying him a violin and lessons. He got bored with practicing and dropped the violin after just a few weeks. His mother was very upset with him.

Voices were calling to him and hands gently helped him to his feet. He was guided to the sidelines and Scott Simmons came in. The pass to the fullback had picked up a first down. Scott picked up three yards on a quarterback keeper.

"I'm ready to go back in, Coach," George plead but without much vigor.

"Are you sure, Horton?"

"Yes, Sir, I just had the breath knocked out of me. I'm fine," he replied with greater confidence and enthusiasm. "Alright, go get em." Coach Reid sent him in with the play, a pass play to Eddie Ricks, the fast receiver. The opposing team smelled blood and blitzed. The coverage was one-on-one and Eddie easily got separation from his defender. George dropped a soft pass right into his arms. No one could catch him and he ran for a touchdown. George received several more hard hits during that game but only after getting rid of the ball. With Robert Peters in charge, he had an excellent start, completing a high percentage of his passes and leading the Viewmont Vikings to a 28 to 3 lead at halftime. In the second half Coach Reid put in Viewmont's running quarterback, Scott Simmons, to confuse the defense and run time off the clock. When the Vikings were on defense in the second half, George went in as a safety. He sacked the quarterback during a blitz and on another play intercepted him. The next game the opposing team thought they knew what to expect, but Coach Reid confused them by sometimes alternating quarterbacks and sometimes having both of them in the backfield at the same time. Sometimes Scott and George even passed or handed off to each other. When George got a handoff, he then passed the ball. The other team had never seen anything like it. The pair of quarterbacks kept the other team completely off balance and when Viewmont was on defense, their opponent never knew when George would slip in as a safety.

During the fourth quarter of the second home game, George was playing safety. The opposing team was in a deep hole, thanks to George's offensive performance and had abandoned the run, reverting almost exclusively to passing plays, hoping to catch up before the quarter expired. The defensive coach had signaled a blitz. Seconds before the opposing center hiked the ball, George moved up close to the line of scrimmage. He kept his eye on the ball. The instant that it began to move, George launched himself into the line. The offensive linemen were large but soft, lacking George's hard, sinuous muscles. George had always compared his personal strength to his family members, feeling weak in the comparison. But that was not a fair comparison. Both of his parents, and even his sister, had deceptively strong bodies. Oh, they all looked strong, but they were twice as strong as they looked. The only men that George knew that were stronger than his father were his mother's brothers, who, although lean in build, were renowned for their physical strength.

George easily tossed aside an offensive lineman. Although only a sixteen-year-old boy, George was as strong as Cleave ever was. Cleave's memories were in charge and he saw the other players as mere boys and manhandled them accordingly. Having slipped through the line, George headed for the quarterback, who had started a throw. George, still being directed by Cleave Burningham's memories, leaped into the air and raised his arms to block the pass. As the ball left the quarterback's fingertips George's mind instantly switched and he was completely himself, no stolen memories required. This was just like the drills that his mother had forced on him since he was a young boy. Most mothers had a rule, no throwing in the house but not his mother. Over the years there had been numerous broken lamps and picture frames due to objects that Mom had thrown at George. Here was a throw that he had seen coming and was coming straight at him. The quarterback had underestimated George's long arms. His mother would have a fit if he did not catch a ball under these relatively easy circumstances. Rather than just blocking the ball as taught by his coaches, who considered catching a ball in this situation too difficult, George snatched the ball out of the air. His leaping momentum carried him past the quarterback and there was no one between him and the goal line, which was only twenty yards away. George sprinted across the goal line untouched, scoring a touchdown. The crowd went nuts, cheering as George kept right on running, circling and heading up into the stands. He located his parents and slipped through the crowd to them. He handed the ball to his mother and kissed her on the cheek. George knew who deserved credit for that catch.

As George returned to his team's bench, the refs, who had not followed George's off-field antics, were looking for the ball. This was not the NFL, where players routinely gave away balls to members of the crowd or kept them as mementos. Seeing the situation, George's mother stood, put two fingers in her mouth and whistled loudly. Almost every head turned to look, including the refs. She pointed at a referee standing on the opposite sidelines and threw a spiraling pass across the full width of the field. It hit him right in the chest. He caught it on the rebound. The crowd, including those supporting the visiting team, erupted into wild applause and cheers. Coach Reid turned to his assistant and said, "That, my friend, explains everything."

After four games, George's father clipped out of the paper an article on George's budding career.

Never has high school football seen a player like George Horton of Viewmont High. Although known principally as a quarterback, he also plays safety. Horton claims to have never played the game before this season but plays like a seasoned college player, not a novice high school Junior. He reads defenses amazingly well and picks them apart when playing quarterback. Although tall and in great physical shape, he does not appear to be a natural athlete; he actually appears slow, awkward and clumsy at times, but somehow he gets the job done on both sides of the ball. He not only leads his region in passing yards and passing touchdowns, but he also leads the region in sacks and interceptions, not of himself but of the opposing quarterbacks. Certainly, his numbers as a defensive player will go down as quarterbacks refuse to throw in his direction. It will be interesting to follow the career of this enigmatic young man.

Although the undeserved attention embarrassed George, it was good to see his parents so happy.

George continued to see the memories, patterns of behavior and personalities of individuals whose memories he had absorbed take over his actions at times. Most of the time the results were positive. For example, when he played quarterback, one of the hardest things for his natural instincts was to focus on throwing the ball even though a member of the defense was charging with the intent of flattening him and causing as much physical discomfort as possible within the rules of the game. George's natural tendency was to brace for collision or run for his life. He was often shocked to find himself calmly delivering the ball to a receiver a fraction of a second before being slammed violently to the ground. Margaret and his mother had a hard time with that part of the game, but his dad was so proud of George in those instances that he could hardly contain himself. George did not have the heart to explain to his father that he was a fraud. He was not the tough, brave kid that his father saw on the field. George was just a scared kid hiding behind someone else's talents.

Often George felt guilty about freeloading on the hard-earned skills and knowledge of others. All of this had come too easily for him. He worried that a price would have to be paid for his ill-gotten success. Would he be revealed as a fraud and a cheat? He tried to compensate by being kind and helpful to everyone, but that led to more praise that he felt was undeserved.

Even though most of the time the results were positive, sometimes George's multiple personality disorder got him into trouble. Cleave Burningham had absolutely no tolerance for bullies and he knew how to put them in their place. With the added size and strength that George had been gaining, together with the acquired hand-to-hand combat skills, those impulses could easily vent themselves on fellow students. Bob Wall had been big for his age since the fourth grade and had been a bully ever since. George had managed to stay out of his way most of his life but found himself on a collision course with Bob. As a senior and with years of experience bullying his peers and the younger boys, Bob was at the zenith of his career. George came across him one afternoon taunting a younger boy by playing keep-away with one of his books. Bob was aided by one of his chums. George intercepted a pass of the book and returned it to the boy. Bob glared at him. "Nobody invited you to this party, Horton! Move on before you get hurt. There is no referee to protect you here."

"You have it all wrong, Bob. No one invited you to Jim's party and he wants you to get lost."

"Or what, you'll sing?" With that, Bob and the other boy broke into hysterical laughter. Pretending to walk away laughing, Bob walked towards George while behind George's back his accomplice was moving into position to kneel behind him so that George would trip backward over the kneeling boy when Bob pushed George. Cleave saw all of this coming and deftly slipped out of the way at the last moment giving Bob a gentle forward nudge and rotation so that he fell backward over his kneeling friend. It was all quite fun for the small group that watched the drama unfold, but George knew that he had created an enemy and had better watch his back.

The big payday for Mom was the school play. She had never seen George act or sing before and was dumbfounded by his newly displayed talent. Many of Mrs. Horton's friends called to compliment her on George's performance and to say what a darling couple Margaret and George made. George's mother insisted that she and Vernon attend every screening of the play. She seemed to enjoy it more each time as she found out something else that she loved about her son's performance. Her husband seemed troubled for some reason, more so with each viewing of the play.

A few days after the last performance, George's father talked to him while they were throwing the football. "Son, I have seen the Music Man performed live before and only one man played the role better than you, Robert Peters. He had a better voice than you but acted the part just like you did. In fact, even the inflections of his voice were similar to yours. You mentioned something about him on our boating trip with the Medefins."

"That's true, Dad. The more I learn about that man, the more I respect him. He was a very fine actor and singer. It is a great compliment to say that I performed like him." George's dad gave him a quizzical look with one eyebrow raised much higher than the other. George could see that he was not going to be able to talk his way out of this one.

"Okay, Dad, let's take a walk." George told his father all about his experiments and memory acquisitions and how he had involved

Margaret. He left out the part about Cleave's covert background and Professor Ian Wilson's illegal activities and his resulting actions. His father listened patiently.

"Son, what you have done is brilliant but reckless in the extreme. You have risked exposing yourself to all manner of disease and legal complications. You have put your uncle at grave risk of being sued. He could lose his entire business over what you have done. The public must never know what you and Margaret have been up to. Promise me that you will stop this insanity. I want Dr. Jacobs to thoroughly check you out and immunize you as much as possible."

"Dad, I promise that I will never use Uncle Martin's business again to gain memories for myself or Margaret. But, Dad, what if I could save lives by taking the memories of a criminal or terrorist or enemy invader? Would that be alright?"

"Son, I don't see much chance of that. I have tried to never put you in a position where you needed to lie to me. I don't plan on starting now. But, from what you have told me, every acquisition that you have made was for purely selfish reasons, mainly to get out of studying or to make it easier to get what you wanted. Your mother and I worked hard for everything that we have gained. We haven't taken any shortcuts. If somehow you need to shoot up with someone else's memories it had better be for a very good reason that involves saving lives, not study time." George was stung when confronted with the truth that selfish motives had been the driving force behind all of his research and acquisitions. His fallen countenance revealed his feelings.

Mr. Horton was a very upbeat person and always tried to offset criticism with love and praise. He put his arm around George's shoulders. "Well, I guess what's done is done. I never took significant risks in my life. Sometimes I wish that I had. So far, this huge gamble has worked out for you and Margaret, but there could yet be major negative consequences for each of you.

"Son, I have taken notice of how humble you have been in all of this. Most men would have let this go to their heads. Keep your humbleness. It is a great trait to have. As you well know, many talented athletes and performers are not only lacking in humility but also morality and virtue. You can be an example worthy of emulation."

"Should we tell Mom about this, Dad?"

"I don't think so, at least not yet. This can be our secret for now. Now, tell me about that red Cadillac you used to own."

Mr. Horton was serious about the vaccinations. He had George miss a day of school and they drove to Wendover, Nevada, a gambling town just outside of Utah on Highway 180. He said that doctors in Wendover had more experience with the kinds of diseases to which George might have been exposed. He also wanted to avoid rumors in Utah. It was an interesting drive for George. His dad talked about his mission to the Southern States in his early twenties. There was a lot of opposition to the Church of Jesus Christ of Latter-day Saints in the south and some missionaries had been murdered. Many more were beaten. "I personally was only threatened with violence once. My companion was a short little fellow and I was not about to let anything happen to him. Three men attacked us as we were walking to a teaching appointment. I had never tried to hurt anyone before that day and had never studied fighting. Somehow, the Lord gave us the strength and skill to repel the attack. We bloodied some noses and cracked a few ribs in the process. Strangely, that seemed to earn us the respect of the town's people and we had some success there."

They had left early in the morning and arrived at the doctor's office before it even opened. Mr. Horton planned it that way so he could talk privately with the doctor. A nurse arrived first and unlocked the front door. She was a large woman, tall and voluptuous. The Hortons waited in the car for the doctor to show. An

Oldsmobile pulled up and a large, heavyset man exited, smoking a cigarette. He tossed it on the pavement and ground it out with his left foot. Apparently, he was the doctor. George was shocked that he smoked. George knew that many people smoked but a doctor! The Hortons followed the doctor and his stifling tobacco odor into the office. George's father spoke up, "Doctor Wilson, I am Vernon Horton. May I have a word with you in private before you examine my son?"

"Certainly, come into my office." George remained in the waiting area while they spoke for several minutes. While they were still talking, the nurse came up.

"George, come back into the exam room so that I can take your vital signs." He followed her into a hall where she had him remove his shoes and stand on an antique scale. George stood on the platform and the nurse shifted the ten-pound marker to 16. The scale did not tip. She moved it to 17 and then slid the one-pound marker until the scale was level for a total of 174 pounds. She then extended the height bar until it just rested on his head. The rule read six-feet two. George had shot up in weight and height. "My, what a strapping young man you are. How old are you George?"

"I'm sixteen." The nurse made a notation on a chart. She then directed George into a small exam room where she took his temperature and blood pressure. Dr. Wilson joined them and he and the nurse began a series of tests and examinations. "Gilda, would you please draw blood for a CBC, BMP, cultures for hepatitis A, B and C, gonorrhea, syphilis, herpes, malaria, ..." George lost track of all of the diseases that the doctor rattled off. George knew that a bunch of them were sexually transmitted diseases. What had his father told this doctor? Dr. Wilson listened to George's breathing and his heart. He looked in George's mouth, eyes, ears and after Gilda left, he looked other places. He thumped and prodded George.

He left and Nurse Gilda came back carrying a tray loaded with an array of needles and vials.

She sat George in a chair with armrests and had him roll up his left shirtsleeve. She tied a rubber tourniquet around his upper arm and examined the veins that swelled. She cleaned an area with an alcohol-soaked cotton ball. She deftly inserted a needle that was supported by a cylindrical shell into one of the veins. She pressed a glass tube into the shell and against the back end of the needle. The needle pierced the tube's rubber stopper and a vacuum rapidly sucked blood into the tube. "You have excellent veins, George." The nurse withdrew the glass tube, careful not to disturb the needle and inserted another glass tube. In all, over a dozen tubes of various sizes and colors were filled with George's blood. He wondered if he would need a transfusion to make up for the blood taken from him. After finishing and removing the needle, Gilda taped a cotton ball over the puncture wound.

"I'm sorry George, but this next part may not be as pleasant as the exam."

"How could it be worse?" thought George.

"I have never had to give this many vaccinations at the same time to a single patient. You may feel like a pincushion before this is over. Oh, well, you have had your fun and now it is time to pay the piper." What had his dad told these people? "You will need to take off your button-up shirt. You can leave on the t-shirt." George removed his shirt. "Let's start with the right shoulder." As George pulled back the sleeve, the nurse wiped a spot with an alcohol-soaked cotton ball and then jabbed a needle into his right shoulder. That was not so bad, George thought. Then she pressed hard on the syringe to inject an apparently viscous fluid into the shoulder. His shoulder burned at the point of injection.

"There. Now let's do another vaccine in the left shoulder." This fluid must have been thinner because it was less painful and flowed faster. Then Gilda picked up a syringe with an attached needle that was significantly larger than the previous two. "Now the right cheek. You will need to loosen that belt and drop your pants." George undid his belt and lowered his pants. He pulled his briefs down a couple of inches on his right cheek. "My but you are modest for a boy of your experience. I need more to work with than that." What had his father told these people? George pulled his shorts halfway down, feeling humiliated. George was shocked out of his embarrassment by the thrust of a large needle into his right buttock. He winced with pain as another noxious fluid was pumped into his body. Gilda moved to his left buttock poking him with another large needle and then back to the right shoulder. Around and around she went, thrusting the larger needles into George's posterior and the smaller ones into his shoulders.

Finally, she ran out of vaccinations. "You can put your shirt back on now. We've finished until the test results come back in." She opened the exam room door and pointed the way back to the waiting area. Apparently, a receptionist had arrived during George's torture session. His dad was counting out a large sum of cash to her. George dared not try to sit, so he gingerly limped his way over to his father. He finished payment and they walked back to the car.

"Dad, I don't know if I can sit."

"I know, Son. Dr. Wilson said that I should let you walk around the block a time or two before we get in the car. I am sorry, Son, for what I had to put you through back there. I am sure that your experience was painful as well as humiliating. I was humiliated. I did not lie, but I did deceive Dr. Wilson into believing that you had been a very promiscuous and wild young man. I hated to do that. It pained me greatly, but I felt that it was necessary. I had to convince the doctor that you needed all of those tests and vaccinations and I couldn't very well tell him the real reason. We came here so as not to cause embarrassment at home." George had been ready to unload on his father for humiliating him when in truth George had caused his father incredible distress, not to mention a significant expense.

"I'm sorry, Dad. I know that my recklessness has caused you great pain. I am so sorry." His father put his arm around George's shoulder. George tried not to wince.

"Son, that was hard, but it would have been infinitely harder if you were really guilty of all that Dr. Wilson thought that you had done."

After walking a few blocks, the pain and stiffness in George's buttocks eased and he felt like he could sit. His dad took him to a buffet for lunch. They had to walk through a casino to get there. George had never been in a casino before. There were no windows and the stifling odor of tobacco filled the air. He was surprised to see many older people at the slot machines, inserting coins and pulling the levers like zombies. Women wearing immodest uniforms carried around drinks. George found it all depressing and disgusting. He was relieved when they finally got to the restaurant. The buffet had a good variety and most of the food was tasty. With his appetite, the restaurant made no profit from the Hortons that day.

On the way home, his dad must have decided that it was a good teaching moment. "Son, you are a fine young man. You care deeply about other people and try to help everyone. You try to do what's right. Sometimes, a really good person like yourself will end up marrying someone because they feel sorry for them or think that they can help them or maybe feel that they owe it to them. Trust me, it seldom works out well. I know that we are taught to be unselfish, but in choosing a wife, be very selfish and with your eyes wide open. Once you're married, then be unselfish and if needed, keep your eyes half shut.

"Your mother has pushed this relationship with Margaret and now you seem to genuinely like her. I like her; she's a wonderful girl. However, if you lose interest in Margaret, don't feel like you have to eventually marry her because of all that she has done for you, or because people expect it of you. You would not be doing her or yourself any favors. Besides, there are probably at least a dozen young men who would love to have you make Margaret available."

George talked later to Margaret about his experience in the doctor's office. Margaret wanted to see a doctor, but since neither of her parents knew about her brain activities, it would be hard to explain why she would need such tests and treatments. She came up with a solution, but unfortunately, it required her to lie to her parents. She concocted the story that she was running barefoot in the park and stepped on a needle that apparently a drug user had left behind. She even had George stick her in the foot with a sterile needle to make the story more convincing. The story worked and she got the works at her family doctor's office. At least she was spared an embarrassing trip to Wendover.

Chapter 11 – Great Season

As expected, it became harder and harder for George to continue scoring on defenses like he had during the first few games. The teams that they played each Friday night had scouted their games to prepare for Viewmont's unique style of play. George had an advantage. Viewmont was one of the first high schools in the state to have a video studio. They sent photographers to upcoming opponent's games to record the action. These recordings were amateurish and in black and white but provided a huge advantage to the Viewmont team. George studied these films diligently to get every advantage that he could. One of the quirks of his original memory was that George had always been able to remember well movies that he had seen. If he watched a movie twice within a short time period, it was burned into his memory and it was hard for him to ever enjoy that movie again because he knew it too well. Consequently, after viewing the films of an opponent several times, George practically had them memorized. Often during a game, it was like watching the film again; he knew just what the opposition would do next.

In addition to intense study of the opponents, George began to think in terms of what Cleave might do if he got to play quarterback and what he himself would do with just his own understanding of the game. As a result, George continued to exploit defenses not only because he understood them so well but also because he was always doing new things. He became less predictable. Sometimes he even ran with the ball. It did not take long for the defenses to catch him, but he got many first downs that way and even scored a running touchdown. George got even more sacks and interceptions than at first because he understood the offenses intimately.

Without the distraction of the play, George began to live and breathe football. He even took the offensive line out to lunch a couple of times at Chuckarama, a local buffet. George had more money now that Uncle Martin had increased his hourly rate due to his proficiency at the job. He was also working increased hours as Uncle Martin relied more and more on him. George applied his full intellect to football, studying the game constantly and watching all of the college and pro games that he could. He even asked the track coach to help him run faster. The coach gave George pointers in what exercises to perform and advice on how to run more efficiently. George did not think that he would ever be a speedster, but he did get significantly faster. George disguised his increased speed on the field so that the competition did not expect it. By the end of the regular season, the Vikings had only lost one game and that was to the eventual state champion who was outside of their region. They went on to win one and lose one during the state playoffs. It was the best season for Viewmont football in many years.

On the social front, George was asked to two girls' choice dances. Margaret and George had agreed that it would be best if she did not ask him. Their parents had strict rules forbidding going steady in high school and thought it best if they date other people. The first girl was fun but of no romantic interest to George. The second was smart, cute, and cheerful. She had a wonderful smile that graced her face much of the time. George ended up asking her out a few weeks after the dance. They had a great time together. Had Margaret not already stolen his heart, George might have fallen for Nancy Whitmore.

George had been watching the local and national news and searching the newspaper since the barn explosion. There was no mention of LND until a story exploded into the news about a coordinated bust of Live Natural or Die. Most of the conspirators that George knew of were captured, but the ringleader, Leonard McCormick, had not been captured and was put on the FBI's most-wanted list. A 10-year-old photograph of him was shown in newspaper articles and on the national news. There was no mention of any anonymous tips.

Chapter 12 – Environmental Activist

On a December Saturday morning, while George was shoveling snow from the sidewalk in front of his house, he noticed a neighbor across the street changing the oil in his pickup truck. After draining the oil, he carried the catch pan to the storm drain on the street corner, intent on dumping the oil. At the time there were no national or Utah laws against dumping motor oil. Without thinking, George dropped his snow shovel and ran to intercept the neighbor. As he approached the man breathing heavily, he called out, "You shouldn't dump that oil in the storm drain, Mr. Barnes. It will end up in the Great Salt Lake."

"Well hello, George. Quite the season you had on the football team. Very impressive. I can't argue with your point, but what can I do with my oil if I don't dump it. Nobody wants it that I know of." Ian Wilson's memories had gotten George to this point, but his group had not applied itself to positive solutions to environmental problems. Fortunately, George's innate interest in science and technology kicked in.

"Your point is very well taken. I'll work on a solution if you'll give me your used motor oil. I will bring over a container to put it in." George ran home to their garage and located an old gallon can that had originally had paint thinner in it. His father had kept it to use as a gas can. He ran back to Mr. Barnes' house and they transferred the oil to the can.

With Ian Wilson's knowledge of physics and George's naturally inventive mind, he began brainstorming for solutions. He even talked to his parents about the issue. His dad had an idea. "George, this may not sound like an ideal solution, but it is practical, makes economic sense and I'm confident is doable. We could develop a low-emissions oil-burning water heater. We can build a small one for our house to test the idea. Then we can convince the city to install a unit to supplement the natural gas fired heaters for the city pool."

"That actually sounds like a really good idea, Dad."

"Don't act so surprised. You don't think that you inherited all of your smarts from your mother, do you? Besides, I originally wanted to become an engineer, but the required calculus scared me off." As George thought about it, he realized that his dad understood how most things worked. He had always enjoyed reading Popular Science, a layman's science and technology periodical. He liked to talk about scientific principles and had helped to inspire George's interest in science.

"So would you be willing to help, Dad?"

"Sure, in fact, I can tell you right now how this thing will probably have to work. We will need to preheat the oil and spray it out of a nozzle into a fine mist. Somehow, we will need to mix the vaporized gas with the right amount of air. Since we will have natural gas available, we can use it to start the process. I once helped tend the tar kettle on a roofing crew. The kettle ran on kerosene and used these principles, except that it did not have a natural gas starter. I had to build a little fire with cardboard to heat the coils. I will draw a picture of what the heater looked like." George's father crudely sketched the device. They discussed ways to develop the oil burner for hours that night.

The next afternoon when George got home from school there was a horrid looking thing parked in the driveway. It had originally been painted orange but was covered with tar. It had two wheels and a trailer hitch. His dad was still at work, but George found his mother in the kitchen. "Mom what is that thing in the driveway?"

"Isn't it hideous looking? That is what your father calls a tar kettle. It belongs to a friend of your father who has a roofing company. He recently bought a new propane-fired kettle and doesn't use this one much. At your father's request, he dropped it off this morning. When Dad gets home you two need to wheel it around to the back yard, out of sight."

"But I need to get to work."

"Dad called your Uncle Martin and arranged for you to have the day off. No one died today." His mother made George a sandwich. "Once your father gets going on something like this he doesn't like to be interrupted by anything. It is unlikely that you will break for dinner, so eat what you can now." George had become a voracious eater, trying to keep up with a growth spurt and muscle building weight gain. His dad got home earlier than usual from work. At his mother's suggestion, George changed into old work clothes. His mother said that she would not wash anything that got tar on it since tar in the washer or drier could ruin any clothes subsequently washed or dried. His father changed into the grubbiest looking clothes that George had ever seen him wear. They went into the yard to move the tar kettle around back. His father lifted the tongue of the tar kettle and George pushed from behind. Once they started it moving, it rolled with minimal effort on George's part and they quickly moved it into the backyard where the fence hid it from the neighbors. His father pulled the burner out from a chamber beneath the main compartment that held the tar. As George studied it, he realized that his father had described it well.

"Grab some newspapers from the back porch, George," commanded his father. Normally his father was very laid back and soft-spoken, but he had now entered his "El Commando" mode as George's mother affectionately called it. In this mode, he could bark out orders like a drill sergeant. If you were not used to it, he could sound very annoying, but George and his mother had learned that if they went along with him without arguing, they could get a lot of work done in a short period of time and get through the toughest jobs.

When George returned, his father was working a hand air pump that was built into the kerosene tank. He pulled out and pushed in the plunger repeatedly to build up pressure in the tank. "Wad up some papers and build a small fire." His father paused his pumping to toss George a book of matches. He got a small fire going. "Hold the coil section over the fire," commanded his father. As the coil heated, the unique smell of kerosene became more prominent. "That smell brings back lots of memories of working on the roofing crew. It was good, hard work." His father stopped pumping and turned a valve on the arm of the burner a quarter turn counter-clockwise to let a little kerosene flow into the coils. The nozzle began to sputter a mixture of liquid and vaporized kerosene that caught fire. After half a minute or so of sputtering, the flame became constant. His father opened up the valve more and the flame grew and produced a soft roaring sound. As George studied the device, he figured out how it worked. The burner was designed so that the flame shot through the center of the coil, heating the coil and the kerosene inside of it so that the kerosene exited the nozzle as a hot vapor. The velocity of the vapor drew in air from the open back end of the coil, allowing the kerosene to burn cleanly, with little, if any, smoke.

"Any questions or tests that you want to perform, George?"

"No, I think I understand how it works. What do we do next?"

"I don't know how an engineer would approach a problem like this, but here is my idea. Let's first see if we can duplicate the mechanism. Then we can start adapting it for used motor oil."

"Sounds good to me." His father opened up a toolbox that contained wrenches, calipers and thread gages, among other tools. They relieved the pressure in the tank and began disassembling the parts. His father took careful measurements and made detailed notes, explaining each step to George.

"I am going to call around now to see where we can find these parts. We will have to bend copper or brass tubing to create the coil. I will look into what kind of tools we will need for that and where to buy them. You can listen and learn if you want or take a break." George followed his dad into the house and his father began looking through the yellow pages. There was a lot of waiting for someone to talk to but he persevered. George brought in his books and worked on some homework. After hanging up the phone, his dad turned to him. "I'll have to make most of the calls tomorrow when the specialty stores are open. I've already arranged to take a day off work."

"Wow, Dad, I really appreciate all that you are doing to help me. You really know how to get things done."

"I'm doing this for myself as well as you, Son. I have wondered for years if I should have stuck with trying to learn calculus so that I could become an engineer. Accounting has provided a good living for us, but it is not my dream job. I want to see what it feels like to engineer a new device. I'm actually having fun." George gained a new appreciation of his father that day. His dad cheerfully went to work each day and worked hard at a job he didn't even like and yet never complained. He quietly served his family.

Over the course of the next several weeks, Mr. Horton and George first copied the tar kettle's kerosene heater and then began modifying the design to work with filtered used motor oil. After two months, they had the most expensive residential water heater in town. After several months of testing the unit in their home and noting the reduction in natural gas consumption, they created a formal report of their work.

Margaret and George took photos of oil slicks on the shores of the Great Salt Lake where storm drains empty into the lake. The Hortons got on the agenda and made a presentation to the Bountiful City Council. They had contacted some of the reporters who had covered George's eagle project to help get the public behind the movement.

George proposed that Bountiful City pass a law outlawing the dumping of used motor oil and provide collection bins around the city. He showed how the oil could be used to heat the city pool and some city buildings, saving thousands of dollars a year in fuel costs. The Hortons offered to design the boilers and space heaters free of charge to the City. In the end, their presentation was overkill. The council unanimously passed a resolution to support the idea and draft the appropriate legislation and executive orders.

George had harbored grave fears about how the memories of Ian Wilson might affect his life, but so far, the effects had only been positive.

The Hortons and Margaret returned to the city council on the night that the new legislation was to be debated and opened for public comment. Most comments were positive, but some expressed concern over the added inconvenience. One man sternly rebuked those that had opposed the law. As he was speaking, he looked right at George, who suddenly recognized him as a fringe member of Live Natural or Die that Ian Wilson had only met once. George hoped that the recognition did not show on his face. The man, Arnold Swanson, kept staring at him the rest of the meeting. Could he possibly have deduced that George was involved in the bust of his organization? George tried not to stare back or become preoccupied with the man.

After the experience with Arnold Swanson, George was on edge and jittery. The first day after the city meeting that he worked, he kept looking in the rearview mirror as he drove to the mortuary. He saw nothing suspicious. A week after the council meeting a car backfired near him and he almost soiled himself. Several times after dinner, he peeked through the curtains of the front window looking for anything unusual but saw nothing. Finally, after a few weeks, he began to relax.

Chapter 13 – Kidnapped

George was leaving the mortuary after a long evening's labors when out of nowhere a blunt object struck him in the back of the head causing him to lose consciousness. When he awoke, he discovered that he had been bound, gagged and blindfolded. George deduced that he was in the trunk of a moving vehicle. He immediately suspected that Arnold Swanson was behind his abduction. The car seemed to drive for hours. From subtle clues, George recognized that the car was driving through Logan, a town in northern Utah. It was cold in the trunk and Logan is typically about 10 degrees colder than Bountiful. Traffic is funneled through Logan's main street that has many lights and it is typically slow going through the lights. George felt each stop and wait. Later, George was tossed from side to side and could hear the churning of a river. He could hear and feel the engine work harder as the car ascended a steep incline. It felt like the way to Bear Lake. He had been there several times for summer scout camp and family vacations.

The car slowed and turned left. George could hear the familiar sound of gravel popping under the tires. After about ten minutes the car stopped. George could hear two car doors open and shut. The trunk opened and one person grabbed him by the feet and another by his shoulders. The man who grabbed his shoulders had large, powerful hands and was very rough with him. From the brief conversation between the two, George could tell that neither of the men carrying him was Arnold Swanson. George was hauled into the front room of what seemed to be a rustic cabin. The men roughly dropped him into a sturdy, unpadded wooden chair. They bound his hands behind him to the back legs of the chair and his ankles to the front legs of the chair. After he was secured, he could hear the two men ascend creaking wooden stairs and eventually heard the creak of bedsprings as each man retired for the evening.

George strained to test the strength of the chair. It felt rock solid. He could wrap his fingers around the chair legs. They were thick and impossible to wiggle. He had no chance of pulling the chair apart and his bounds were tight and very secure. Further straining against his bonds might wake his captors and was unlikely to free his arms or legs.

That was the longest night of George's life. It was impossible to sleep and his wrists and ankles became very sore and began to swell. The gag was the most unpleasant part of the ordeal. The two men arose the next morning and without speaking to George, prepared breakfast. The men smacked their lips and slurped their coffee, apparently to make sure that George knew how much they were enjoying their breakfast. Finally, the table was cleared and carried over to George so that it rested against his chest. He could see through the bottom edges of the blindfold enough to notice that the table was long and narrow.

"We are going to remove your gag so that you can answer some questions. Although there is no one within miles to hear you, we will punish you severely if you cry out. Do you understand?" spoke one of the men. George nodded in the affirmative. He felt the gag being removed and took several deep breaths. George remained blindfolded. That was good. If they kept him blindfolded, they had not concluded to kill him. "Tell us about yourself." George told his name and about his family and a little about his life. He figured that they already knew these things and that there was no point in withholding any non-vital information. "How do you know Arnold Swanson?"

"You mean the man that spoke at the Bountiful City Council meeting?"

"Yes, how do you know him?"

"I had never seen him before that night. I have never seen or heard anything about him." George avoided saying anything that was an actual lie. He suspected that the men would sense if he were lying.

"Why did you look at him the way that you did?"

"He was very rude; I thought that he would do more damage to the cause than good. And then he kept staring at me all night. Every time I looked his way, he was glaring at me. It creeped me out! Why do you care how I looked at him?" Something wacked George on the right side of his face.

"We will ask the questions!" The flash of pain seemed to put Cleave Burningham in charge of George's actions. George released control of his body and let Cleave take over. Cleave knew how to handle such a situation. He began to whimper.

"Please don't hurt me. I'm sorry! I'm sorry! I don't know what I did to offend you men but I'm sorry," George blubbered like a baby.

"Big, tough football player," mocked the bigger man in a deep voice.

"Let's talk a minute," suggested the first man and they walked outside. George had exceptionally acute hearing, not having dulled it by listening to loud music like many of his peers. He could hear enough to deduce that the men did not think that he knew anything but that they would torture him just to be sure but without leaving major marks on his body. It appeared that they were expecting Arnold Swanson to arrive that afternoon and wanted to have information by then if possible. They came back in.

"We think you know more and we're going to have to get it out of you one way or another. We're going to start with bamboo shoots. We'll try not to mark up that baby face of yours." George could feel his right hand being untied and moved onto the table in front of him. He started to sob again.

"What a baby. I am going to get some wood before he starts pissing his pants. What a momma's boy." George heard the large man exit the front door. George could see just enough through the blindfold to see that there was a pencil in his interrogator's shirt pocket. As the man thrust a slip of sheet metal up under one of George's fingernails, George jerked his hand back, pulling the man, who held tightly to George's wrist with his left hand, towards him. George came down with his head using the crown of his head to break the man's nose. George wailed as if in pain to mask the sounds of the struggle. The man let go of his wrist and George snatched the pencil from the pocket and drove it between the man's ribs on his left side, collapsing his left lung so that he could not scream. The loss of a lung incapacitated him. George ripped off the blindfold and tried to untie the bonds holding his ankles. The rope was tightly knotted and only came loose after tedious effort. As soon as his feet were loose, George stood and walked, with the chair still bound to his left wrist, to the kitchen side of the room where he pulled a knife from a wooden knife block that was sitting on the counter next to the sink.

Before George could cut the bonds that secured his left arm to the chair, the other man entered the cabin. Without hesitating, George threw the knife at the man as he gawked at his companion on the floor. Cleave had aimed for the throat, but the man straightened and the knife, which was in the horizontal orientation with the blade edge pointing down at impact, stuck between his ribs with the blade cutting into the lower rib but not penetrating enough to do major damage. An oval-shaped spot of blood appeared on the man's shirt growing outward from the knifepoint. The man looked more angry than injured. He yanked the knife from his ribs and came at George with it. George snatched another knife from the knife block and waited for him as if he could not move. The large man crossed the room and thrust at George with his knife. George parried the thrust with his knife and with great exertion, in a single fluid motion, simultaneously lifted the heavy chair with his left arm over his head. With a squatting motion, George brought the chair crashing down on the man. The man partially blocked the blow with his right arm. Surprisingly, the chair broke and not the man's arm, leaving a thick wooden leg still tied to George's left wrist and forearm.

George used the leg as both a club and a shield. He came at the man with such furry, battering him with the leg and stabbing at him with the knife, that the man slowly retreated. George tried to back him into the table, but he anticipated the move and slipped around it so that the table was between them. The man began pushing the table towards George using his left hand. George blocked it with a raised right foot. The man clenched the knife in his teeth and used both hands to push the table. George planted both feet and pushed back with both hands while awkwardly holding the knife in his right hand. With his greater weight and strength, the man planned to pin George against the wall. George pretended that this plan was working and gave only token resistance. Before the wall pinned him, George used his arms and legs to catapult himself up onto the table and slashed his knife across the inside of the man's right elbow, severing the tendons. As he lost the use of his right arm, the brute fell forward against the table but quickly regained his balance and backed away. His right arm hung limply at his side. The handle of his knife was on his right side making it awkward for him to remove the knife from his teeth with his left hand. George jumped off of the table, facing the man. As his opponent reached across his body to grab the knife by the handle, George stabbed him in the left lung by sliding the knife between his ribs.

The man did not go down and now grasped his knife in his good hand. George had to evade a couple of thrusts before the man fell to his knees and eventually onto his side. George kicked the knife out of his fallen captor's hand.

After freeing himself from the chair leg, George found a roll of duct tape in the kitchen and used it to bind and gag each man. He removed the contents of their pockets to determine their identities.

Both had wallets containing driver's licenses. The smaller man, Richard Morison, had an Idaho license. Burt Harmon had a Wyoming license. Being guided mainly by Cleave's memories, George memorized the important information, removed the cash and threw the wallets into the fire. Each man had carried a set of keys to the white Studebaker Lark parked in the driveway. Each key ring also contained what appeared to be house keys. George stepped outside and observed the Idaho license plate on the Lark. He opened the trunk. Inside was a 30-caliber Remington Rifle with a scope. He removed the rifle and ammunition and cached it in the forest 150 feet from the cabin.

Returning to the cabin, George evaluated the resources there. It was as if Cleave were doing the thinking for him, but George was listening in and making suggestions. George located a downstairs closet and dragged the men into it. A quick check of each man's pulse indicated that they should live unattended for hours. George moved to the backdoor and studied escape routes.

Having explored the cabin, George relaxed and fried up what was left of the bacon along with some eggs. He did not want to have to confront another attacker on an empty stomach. His personal instinct was to take the Studebaker and get out of there, but Cleave knew that Arnold Swanson would just send someone else after him, probably an assassin. It was best to end this thing before the sun went down. After a satisfying breakfast, George washed and dried the dishes and put them away. He fed the remains of the chair to the fire and cleaned and straightened so that there was no evidence of a fight to the casual observer.

George found a heavy coat and headed out the back door. He retrieved the rifle and ammo. He walked up a slope and positioned himself behind some brush and rocks so that he would be hard to spot from the road but could easily see an approaching car. The bushes hid him but were thin enough to allow George to peer through them. The rocks would partially shield his body from gunfire. George made himself as comfortable as possible and began his lonely vigil. He was uphill from the cabin and could easily look down on the driveway and structure. George dozed off for several hours. The sound of tires on gravel startled him to consciousness. A blue Ford Ranchero was approaching. It stopped behind the Lark and both doors opened. George had not been anticipating that Arnold would bring company. His passenger was a tall woman. George had planned to shoot Arnold in the knee and tie him up like his cohorts. Now he had to rethink everything.

He watched the two walk to the cabin. The woman walked with feline, feminine grace. Arnold knocked on the door and shouted. Apparently, he did not want to barge in on violent criminals. Finally, he opened the door and inserted his head, barking, "Anyone in here?" He and the woman entered and looked around. George moved down the hill closer to the cabin so that he could hear their conversation. George was not too worried. He had the rifle, not them. They walked out the back door and looked around. "What could have happened to them?" questioned Arnold. "That's their car in front." Arnold had one of those voices that carries a long way and could be tediously loud if you were close to him. At the city meeting, he had not needed a microphone to be heard by all present.

"Maybe the boy got away and they went after him on foot," suggested the woman in a smoky voice, with a touch of Latin American accent.

"I don't know. The cabin is clean; the dishes are put away, even though I can smell the lingering aromas of breakfast. I know these guys; they are slobs. It looks like they were abducted by a maid service. Let's look closer for evidence inside. Something just doesn't add up." The two reentered the cabin and walked up the stairs. "See what I mean; the beds aren't made. They're slobs. Look in every closet and storage space." George could hear doors slamming and frustration building. George heard them descend the stairs. After a moment, George heard Arnold burst out with, "What the hell?" George moved to the cabin wall adjacent to the closet they inspected.

"I don't think they can talk," suggested the woman. "Look at the bloodstains and holes in their shirts. They probably have punctured lungs. It looks like the work of a real pro."

"You might be right, Francesca. They look barely alive. Find some paper and a pen." It was quiet for a while. "So who did this to you?" demanded Arnold. After another long pause, "What do you mean, 'the kid'? Are you trying to tell me that some snot-nosed kid that you already had tied up beat the crap out of you guys? What a couple of losers! Good thing that I didn't pay you in advance. Come on, Francesca. Let's torch the place and get out of here." George moved back up the hill to his safe position. After some thrashing around, the two exited the front door. They were going to leave the men to die in the fire. George took aim and shot Arnold in the left knee. Arnold collapsed to the ground and the woman dove onto her side behind the Studebaker. George ran down the hill shouting, "I don't want to hurt you, Miss. I'm just trying to get out of this alive. Come out with your hands up and I won't shoot you. You stay down, Arnold, and put your hands behind your head."

"I'm coming out," shouted the woman with fear in her voice. "Don't shoot." She stood and walked away from the car. Her clothes were torn and soiled on her left side.

"Put your hands on the car with your feet spread and as far from the car as you can reach." George walked around behind Arnold and clubbed him unconscious with a sharp thrust of the rifle butt. He fell limply to the ground. "You can stand now. Come help me drag the men out of the cabin." The woman obeyed and George gestured with the rifle for her to take the lead. As she opened the cabin door, a burst of heat and smoke assaulted them. "Stop!" George commanded. "It's too late. They are already dead by now." George simultaneously felt a stab of pain in his right upper arm and heard a gunshot. The rifle fell from his right hand. Francesca moved with remarkable swiftness and agility, snatching up the rifle before it hit the ground. To George's surprise, she whirled around and shot Arnold three times in rapid succession. He got off another shot after her first shot but it went wild. George lifted his left arm in surrender. "Who are you?"

"You don't need to know my name. I'm an undercover agent. I have been investigating a ring of terrorists. We need to clean that wound and stop the bleeding. I have a bottle of coke in the car. It will be more sterile than any water we can find nearby."

"I'm George Horton from Bountiful. The men inside the cabin kidnapped me last night." Francesca walked to the back of the Ranchero and opened up a cooler. She removed a 16-ounce bottle of Coca Cola and popped the lid off with an opener. "I don't know if this will sting or not. I have never done this before. Come sit on the tailgate." She lowered the tailgate and George eased gingerly down onto it. Francesca raised her left foot up onto the tailgate. She reached down, lifted up her pant leg and pulled a small but wicked looking knife from a scabbard on her calf. The knife had a flat handle so that it had been almost invisible next to Francesca's slender leg. She cut away the right sleeve of the coat that George was still wearing and then cut away his shirtsleeve. She saved the shirtsleeve and cut it into strips to use as bandages. She washed the wound with the soda. Fortunately, the bullet had exited George's triceps cleanly without damaging bone or tendons. Within minutes, the bleeding was contained and he was good enough to travel. "We should get you to an emergency room as soon as possible. Get in the Ford." Francesca removed the keys from Arnold's right front pocket. She hid the rifle under a tarp in the cargo section and got into the driver's seat. She backed away from the cabin and onto the gravel road.

After a few minutes on the road, Francesca asked, "I know from Arnold that you were kidnapped, but how did you manage to get the upper hand in this situation?" George explained what had happened, trying to make it sound more like luck than skill. "Most highly trained agents cannot collapse a lung as slickly as you did and you did it twice. I'm glad that you are alive, but now I have lost my only connection to the organization."

"I could maybe help if you want me to," George offered. "But we have to go back now. My arm can wait." Francesca pulled to the side of the road.

"What can you do?"

"I know that this sounds crazy, but I can extract information from a dead man. Please don't ask me to explain; this has to remain my secret. If you don't believe me, fine, but I really can help you."

"I'll let you have a séance, read his palms or whatever you want if it will help."

"You must promise to never tell anyone about this ability that I have. I'm already in enough trouble."

"Look, George, as an undercover operative I know all too well that lives depend on secrecy. You can trust me."

"Okay. Let's go back." George fell asleep during the short ride back. Francesca gently nudged him as they approached the still burning cabin. It was fortunate that the forest was cool, green and wet from a recent rain or the fire might have spread.

"Stay in the car, and please don't watch," George requested. He walked around behind the Lark. He looked around to verify that he was out of Francesca's sight and pulled from his pocket what looked like a fat ballpoint pen. Inside was a slender syringe and needle. Although George had promised his father that he would not do any more extractions at the mortuary, he had continued to carry his disguised extraction kit. He had daydreamed of somehow saving the world or maybe just his country using his discovery. George used the syringe to make the extraction from Arnold, using his body as well as the car to shield view of his actions. George backed up to the Lark and reinserted the syringe into the pen body. He returned the unit to his front left pants pocket. He walked back to the Ranchero and dropped into the passenger seat. George was exhausted. Francesca just looked at him incredulously, wondering what he had just done. George was soon back asleep.

Francesca first drove to a phone booth and called the agency about what had happened at the cabin. She requested an investigation and cleanup team. George sat up when she got back to the car. Francesca turned to him. "We will devise a cover story for the day's events. The agency has experts on creating plausible explanations for bizarre events while minimizing public scrutiny of victims like you. Unless, of course, you want to be known as a hero and be a media darling. We can't cover those types. Do you want us to keep the facts out of the papers or do you want to be a hero, who, admittedly, you seemed to be?"

"I want you to order me not to discuss what happened or the ongoing investigation with anyone but the FBI. The agency can hold a press conference and give their cover story and I won't have to explain anything to anybody."

"You're okay with that? Most young men your age would love to brag about taking out two hardened criminals like you did?"

"I would be dead without your help. I would prefer to bury this incident rather than brag about it." Francesca took George to the hospital emergency room in Logan and did all of the talking. Somehow, she got him promoted to immediate attention. George's wound was again cleansed and he received a few stitches to close the two holes in his flesh. He was given a tetanus shot and a prescription for antibiotics. Francesca filled the prescription at a local pharmacy. She then called from another phone booth for further instructions.

As they headed home, she explained. "Your parents have already been notified that you were kidnapped and driven to southern Idaho. They have been told that your kidnappers are dead but that you were wounded by kidnapper gunfire when agents rescued you. We have told them and the press that there may be other accomplices and so the investigation is ongoing. I am ordering you not to talk to anyone outside of the FBI about what happened. The local police, press and your parents know that. Do you have any questions?"

"No. I just say nothing. I'm good at that."

"I don't know about that. The press seemed to know a lot about you. I was informed that you have made presentations to two different city councils and gotten everything that you asked for. There are even rave reviews of your performance in a school production of The Music Man. And, if that were not enough, you have had more articles written about you than any other high school athlete in the state of Utah. Last year no one had even heard of you. After this incident, you will be the most talked about young man in Utah, if you weren't already." Francesca paused and looked at George. "I will not be taking you straight home. I will drive you to a rendezvous point and a uniformed FBI agent will take you home. I need to preserve my cover."

"Now, what did you learn from Swanson?"

"Nothing yet. It may take me several weeks to get information out of what I did back there. Please don't ask me to explain."

George fell asleep again and woke when the car stopped in a market parking lot in Layton. He was quickly moved to a marked agency vehicle and made the short trip to Bountiful. As they approached his house, there was no place to park due to all of the vehicles around the house. It seemed that a crowd was there to support the Horton family in their time of crisis. The agent double-parked in the street in front of the house and escorted George to the front door.

Chapter 14 – Protective Silence

Before they could reach the door, it flew open and George's mother rushed out. Not only did his mother wrap her strong arms around him, being careful not to touch his right arm, but she actually lifted him off of the ground with her embrace. People poured out of the house like ants from a disturbed anthill. Before George's mother could release him, his father wrapped his arms around both of them. For a moment, George could hardly breathe. Everyone began welcoming him and peppering him with questions.

"Are you alright, George?" sobbed his mother, overcome with emotion.

"I'm tired, hungry, have a nasty bump on my head and a shot-up right arm, but other than that, I'm fine."

"Son, the FBI called and said that you had been kidnapped. Is that right?" asked his father anxiously.

"Yes, I was hit over the head and taken as I left the mortuary. That is all that I can tell you right now. I was given a strict charge to remain silent on any other details due to the ongoing investigation."

"But why, George, why did they abduct you?" asked his mother.

"I can't tell you. We will just have to wait for the FBI to figure things out." His parents parted to give George some room when Margaret emerged from the throng and threw herself at him. Her eyes were even redder and more tear-streaked than his mother's. She just hugged him, too filled with emotion to speak. Her tears moistened the front of George's shirt as he gently held her there with his left arm. During his ordeal, George had not taken time to think about how his parents or Margaret would be affected by his disappearance. Had he been self-centered or was it part of Cleave's training? Before George realized it, they were inside and he was sinking onto a sofa with Margaret still clinging to him.

Mrs. Horton politely thanked people for their support and ushered them out the door. Her boy, her only boy, was tired and hungry. In spite of the fact that the kitchen was full of food that neighbors had brought, she flew to work to make a ham and cheese omelet. It was one of George's favorite foods and she could whip one up in less than ten minutes. The activity helped calm her nerves and gave her a sense of purpose after many hours of feeling helpless. She wondered what she would do with all of the food that the neighbors had brought. Unfortunately, most of it fell far below her high standards of nutrition.

George's father fidgeted while Margaret clung to George on the couch. "Can I get you something to drink, George? Cold water, milk, juice?" he asked.

"Milk, please." His father rushed off to fill his order, leaving George alone with Margaret.

"Oh, George, I was afraid I would never see you again."

"You're not getting rid of me that easy. I handled the situation."

"Tell me all about it."

"I can't Mag. It's like I said already, I am under strict orders not to talk about it. If I tell anyone anything I will open up a can of worms that I can't handle right now." Although Margaret seemed to understand, it was obvious that she was not happy with his concealment of the details. His father returned with a tall glass of cold milk.

Soon they were sitting down at the table. George's mother started frying sliced potatoes while an omelet was cooking and had cleared most, but not all of the neighbors' food from the table. George inwardly smiled to himself. His mother detested Jell-O, which the neighbors had brought in abundance. His mother sat and they all bowed their heads as George's father asked a blessing on the food. He gave thanks for not only the food but also the safe return of his son. George deduced from the prayer that his parents had been fasting since they first realized that he was missing. With tears of gratitude, his father closed their fast in the prayer. It appeared that Margaret had also been fasting. Everyone ate with vigor. The rush of protein and calories had a soothing effect on all. Soon they were even laughing and joking.

George thought that it would appear unnatural for him to want to develop photographs right after being kidnapped, so he froze the cranial fluid. The next morning he had his mother take some photos of his wounded right arm. A week later, George called Margaret to see if he could come over the next evening to develop the photos. He needed to plan ahead so that he could thaw the fluid just in time to preserve freshness. The next evening, once they were in their inner sanctum, the darkroom, Margaret wanted to know who the "donor" was. "I'm sorry, Mag, I can't tell you. It relates to my kidnapping."

"I thought that we were partners, George. Now you keep everything from me," she pleaded in a pouty voice.

"I'm sorry, Mag. What else can I do? I couldn't very well ask the FBI to exclude my girlfriend from the nondisclosure order, now could I? They don't know about our little acquisition business. To them, you and I are just ordinary 17-year-old kids. They have no idea of the mature woman that lies behind that cute little freckled face." George stroked Margaret's cheek with his left index finger as he said the last part. To his dismay, she sharply turned away.

"Let's get this over with, boyfriend," she said with a mixture of contempt and sarcasm in her voice. She performed the injection with none of her usual bedside manner. They developed the photos in silence. George was dying inside. He hated how Margaret was handling this but could not see a way out. He had given his word to the FBI. He was not going to break his oath just to appease a teenage girl that was, well, acting like a teenage girl. At least she had not cried yet. George decided to give Margaret her space. She was a wonderful person; she would get over this.

George had never personally used frozen memories before, so he did not know quite what to expect. The next morning memories did not flood into his mind spontaneously, like with other injections. They had to be triggered by associated sensory inputs, just like how a certain smell, sound or other trigger brings back natural memories that are acquired through experience. Some of the memories greatly concerned George. Arnold Swanson spoke Russian fluently, a great thing for George to add to his acquired memories. What concerned George was Arnold's motivation for learning Russian. He had deep ties to the Soviet Union and was secretly working for the communist nation. Arnold was a traitor to his country. Greed and spite motivated him rather than politics or ideology.

After a few weeks of absorbing memories, George called the FBI office to report that he had important information to share. They sent a car to pick him up at his home the next afternoon. The driver informed George that he would interview with several agents at the branch office. George became uneasy; he had not triggered before that moment, knowledge that the organization that he had penetrated, and it was much larger than LND, had a mole in this branch of the FBI. George was hoping that he would know when he saw an agent if he were the mole. The driver escorted George to an interview room and asked him to sit and wait for someone to talk with him.

After a few minutes, a tall, spindly young man entered the room. "Hello, George. I am Agent Cline. How are you today?" he greeted enthusiastically. To George's shock, he realized that this was the agent that he had talked to when he initially called the FBI. If George spoke, Cline would most likely recognize his voice, causing serious complications. George said nothing. "It's natural to be a little frightened. Take your time. We are in no hurry. We have all evening." George remained silent. "You have had quite an ordeal. Have you figured out yet why you were kidnapped?" George nodded in the affirmative. "Good. Maybe we can start there. Did you know something that they didn't want you to know?" George nodded again. "Now we are getting somewhere. Did you know about something illegal that someone had done?"

George decided that if he continued answering questions in this way, Agent Cline might figure out who he was, without him ever speaking. George reached across the table and took the note pad that Agent Cline had been poised to write on and reached for his pen. George wrote, "There is a mole among you. This room may be bugged. I will only speak with the agent who brought me in. She called herself Francesca." George pushed the notepad and pen back to Agent Cline. He read the note and looked around the room with a worried expression on his face.

He wrote, "OK" and pushed the pad back to George. Cline left the room and did not return for over 20 minutes. He stuck his head back in the room and in a low conspiratorial sounding voice, as if he were talking to a four-year-old with a vivid imagination, said, "We can't get a hold of Francesca right now. We will take you home and call you." It was all that George could do not to call Agent Cline a pencil necked paper pusher who couldn't find his butt with both hands and a search light, but he refrained.

A couple of female agents took George home as if he were a child who would feel safer with women. They prattled on like two sisters that had not seen each other for half a lifetime while George sulked in the back seat. By the time he got home, George was seriously frustrated and there was no one that he could talk to about it.

A couple of nights later Margaret called him. "George, I'm sorry I acted like such a creep the other night. Let me make it up to you this Friday night. I will pick you up at seven. Is it a deal?"

"Sure Mag, I'd love to spend some time with you."

Friday night Margaret pulled up in her dad's Cadillac. George saw her through the window but let her come to the front door. His mother always liked to greet guests and invite them in, so George hurried off to his bedroom to let Mom do the honors. George let the women chat for a while and then sauntered forth from his room. "Hello, Margaret. You look cute tonight, as always."

"Watch out for him, Margaret. He can be a charmer when he wants to."

"Don't worry about me, Sister Horton. I can match wits with George any day of the week. And don't worry, I'll have him back by the agreed-upon time."

"Well, you two have fun and be good." With that, the couple escaped out the front door.

After they were in the car with Margaret in the driver's seat and George buckled into the center position, he leaned over and kissed Margaret on the cheek. "It is so good to be alone with you. Things went horribly wrong at the branch office last week. There are some things that I can tell you without violating my promise to the agency. Guess who tried to interview me?"

"Well, I only know the names of two agents, Cline and Marks. Was it one of them?"

"You are one smart girl. It was Agent Cline. I didn't speak in his presence. I was afraid that he would recognize my voice. He tried to ask me yes or no questions like I was a frightened child. He is such a jerk but kind of an innocent, naïve one. Anyway, I finally wrote on his notepad that there was a mole in their office and the room might be bugged. I said that I would only speak to the agent that brought me in. After that, he treated me like a delusional child. I wanted to ring his skinny little neck."

"Do you think that they will let you talk with the agent who brought you in?"

"I hope so, but I don't know. The problem is that she is an undercover agent."

"She?" Uh-oh! George had made a serious slip. "You were rescued by a woman?"

"Well, sort of. But, I kind of rescued myself. But I can't talk about it," George replied in staccato bursts. Margaret could always verbally outmaneuver him and he knew that he was in trouble. George tried a different approach. "Look, Margaret, I really need someone right now that I can talk to who won't try to get information out of me. I need your support."

"Okay. I'm sorry. I'll be a good listener and won't probe."

"Thank you. Anyway, if they don't call back in a few weeks I will call Agent Marks. He will know what to do.

"So what are we doing tonight?" George inquired.

"I am taking you to the drive-in. There is a basket full of dinner in the backseat. It's a double feature and I convinced your mom to let us stay out till one-thirty. I promised your mother that we would behave ourselves. The gate opened at six and the first feature should start around eight. I want to be able to park in a good spot. I don't want to get there when it's crowded. Even with my acquisitions, I'm still not very good at parking, especially with a car this large." There were only a few cars when they arrived. Margaret parked near the center so that they had a straight-on view of the screen.

"Now what?" George asked.

"We eat in the back seat. The only way that Dad would let me do this was if I covered the backseat with a blanket and we ate over the blanket."

"Isn't it a little unusual for a dad to encourage his 17-year-old daughter to get in the backseat of a full-size car with the boy that has the hots for her?"

"We have known each other our whole lives and in my parents' eyes been star crossed lovers for over a year and you have only kissed me once on the lips. My parents are more worried that we'll fall asleep and not wake up till morning. Dad even made me bring his Big Ben alarm clock. Can't you hear it ticking?"

"Yea, I thought that this Caddy had the loudest clock in car history. Well, before we go back there, would you like kiss number two?" Without speaking, Margaret slipped her long slender fingers around the back of George's neck and pulled him in for a long, delightful kiss. She held George to her lips for a long time before releasing him. Not wanting things to get out of hand, George got out of the car, walked around to the driver's side and opened the door. "Shall we proceed to the dining room, Madam?" Margaret slid out gracefully and he opened the back door for her. After she was seated and he had closed her door, George walked around to the opposite door and let himself in. George figured that the basket between them would help keep things from getting overheated. Margaret had prepared a wonderful dinner. Knowing that George was not a big fan of cold lunches, Margaret had brought hot lasagna, fresh-baked whole wheat bread, and a hot apple pie. From a large bag on the floor, she extracted wicker trays that had a one-inch high railing that kept things from sliding off. She removed china plates and crystal glasses from the basket. Cloth napkins and real silverware added the finishing touches.

"This is absolutely amazing, Margaret."

"I'm sorry, but we have to drink water. My dad refused to let me bring any other beverage. I know that you like grape juice, but it stains horribly."

"Water will be fine. You are really amazing." The two teens enjoyed their delectable dinner while making small talk, catching up on the little things in their lives.

"My mom made the pie crust. I still haven't quite learned to make a crust like hers. Hers are so flaky. But I made everything else." Margaret had been surprised that in spite of Emily Sacks' reputation of being a master chef, she could not make a pie crust as good as her mother's.

"You know, I can help you learn to make crusts like your mom makes. It wouldn't be hard."

"No thanks. I don't want to remember giving birth to myself. That would be too weird."

"Okay, but if you change your mind you know where to find me." The food was delicious and George ate far more than he should, especially on a date. After dinner, George transferred the basket and accessories to the trunk and Margaret shook out the blanket.

The first feature was Butch Cassidy and the Sundance Kid. George and Margaret had returned to the front seat and Margaret snuggled at George's side with a blanket over them to ward off the chill. They had to roll the windows down a little to keep from fogging up the windshield. The second feature was some goofy B-rated science fiction movie. George used to love these movies, but on this night, he fell asleep shortly after the opening scene. The next thing George remembered was Margaret gently shaking him to his senses. The movie was over and cars were leaving the lot.

"Sorry, Mag. I really conked out there. I guess I wasn't the hot date that you were hoping for."

"Oh, I don't know. You kiss pretty well in your sleep."

"You didn't? I have been violated in my sleep!" George cried out in mock horror.

"You act about as well as the characters in the second movie. I'm going to get you home before Dad comes looking for his beloved Cadillac."

Chapter 15 – Moody Margaret

A couple of weeks after their date, Margaret joined George in the cafeteria. "Hey, tough guy, I need you to help me develop some film. Can you come over tonight?"

"I don't know. Do you think you can behave yourself in the darkroom?"

"I can try, but I'm not making any promises. I just can't seem to control myself alone with you in the dark." George was happy that Margaret seemed to be over her frustration with him. He had hated her aloofness during that awkward time right after the kidnapping.

That evening George walked to Margaret's house and rapped on the door with his signature knock. A few seconds later, the door opened to reveal a smiling Mrs. Medefin. "Why, good evening, George. Come on in. Margaret is waiting for you."

"Thank you, Sister Medefin." George found Margaret waiting in the darkroom. As they developed some film, he inquired about Margaret's new acquisition.

"So how, and from whom did you obtain this new fluid?"

"I'm not saying," she responded with both a flirtatious and mocking voice. "You have your secrets and I have mine."

"That's fair enough, I guess." George wasn't about to rekindle her ire towards him by trying to justify a double standard. They finished the photos and proceeded with the injection. After injecting the cranial fluid, George helped Margaret to her feet and gave her a quick kiss on the cheek. She responded with a long kiss on the lips. As they left the darkroom, George asked Margaret if she wanted to go on a walk. She declined due to unfinished homework.

The next day George tried to talk to Margaret several times at school, but she avoided him. When she did return his glances, she did so with a peculiar expression on her face. What was going on? The next day went no better nor the next. After two more weeks, she was still avoiding George, refusing to talk to him. It was as if her new acquisition completely changed her attitude about George. He decided to give Margaret her space until things returned to normal. George ended up asking Susan Bennett to the spring dance. Susan had been showing a great deal of interest in him lately. George wanted the end of his junior year to be a fun time, not a romantic tragedy. Besides, Susan was cute and fun. They had such a great time on the first date that George asked her out again and then again. They started sitting together at school lunch and calling each other. Susan came from a very nice LDS family, and her parents seemed very enthusiastic about their dating. Neither set of parents wanted the two teens to go steady so they tried to cool things down a little and date other people.

Meanwhile, Margaret's personality seemed to be changing. She spent a lot of time with the athletes and started lifting weights. By now Margaret was six feet tall and intimidated most of the boys. Her newly muscular arms added to the intimidation factor. She became popular with the tall, athletic boys. Some of the guys that hung around her were huge. George tried to talk to Margaret's mother once, but she seemed even more mystified than he was. George still really liked Margaret, maybe even loved her, but he didn't have a clue as to how he could get back together with her. George was very practical and brooding was not what he did, not when there was a Susan Bennett to fill the hole left by Margaret's emotional departure.

The strangest thing happened the last week of school. Bob Wall had grabbed Jim's yearbook and wrenched it from him. He was threatening to rip out a page. Margaret came upon the screen. "Give the book back, right now, or I will shake you so hard that that hideous lump you call a head will nearly snap off that pencil neck of yours!" commanded Margaret, not with a loud or angry voice but a cold and deliberate voice, ringing with confidence that she could back up her words. At first, Bob was too stunned to respond.

Realizing that he would never live it down if he followed that command he lifted the page and replied, "Yea, right freckles, like I care what ...." Bob could not complete that sentence. Margaret had seized him by his long, curly hair and had started shaking his head with both hands. Saliva flung from his open mouth as his head experienced G forces greater than from any rollercoaster ride. Margaret's right knee flew up knocking Bob's butt right out from under him. Margaret pushed down with her might causing Bob's posterior to accelerate towards a hard concrete floor with unnatural swiftness. The inevitable, sudden, painful landing quickly followed. She then jerked Bob's head around as if she were going to break his neck, stopping suddenly, just short of inflicting permanent damage. She rotated Bob's head back so that he was facing straight up looking into Margaret's angry eyes.

"Don't ever mess with me or my friends, Bob," she said in parting as she finally released Bob with a shove that toppled him from a sitting position to lying on his right side. As she slowly walked away, Jim snatched up his yearbook and ran after Margaret.

"Margaret, Margaret, wait up. That was awesome. Will you sign my yearbook?"

Chapter 16 – Game Over

George was becoming very frustrated with the local FBI office. He had called half a dozen times and had just gotten the runaround. Finally, he drove to Ogden to place a call to Rex Marks. He stopped at a phone booth adjacent to a service station on Washington Boulevard. He inserted the coins and began to dial the number, facing the phone with his back to the door. Suddenly, George saw motion in the corner of his eye as the folding door was forced open, slamming him against the phone! Some kind of wire or cable came over his head and pulled tight against his neck. George started to struggle, but a voice said coldly, "Resist and I will break your neck." There was no doubt in his mind that the massive form pressed up against him could do just that. George relaxed. The last thing that he remembered was a prick in his left thigh.

When George awoke, he found himself chained to a cinderblock wall in a windowless room. His arms ached from supporting his body weight. His body was stretched into an "X" shape with his feet being pulled down and spread by chains. George was not blindfolded and the two men in the room wore no masks. That meant one thing, they were planning to kill George after extracting from him all of the information that they wanted. The jig was up. George's brief life would soon be over, probably after excruciating torture. He thought about what information they might force out of him. These men already knew what he knew concerning LND, but he knew something that they did not. They did not know how George knew what he knew. He had to come up with a plausible explanation for how he got the information that he possessed. George had never lied in his life and would have no talent for it. Fortunately for George, Arnold Swanson had been a superb liar. He took great pride in his ability to deceive. George now possessed this ability. He felt confident that the crying-child trick would not work in this situation. It was obvious that these men considered him dangerous and skilled.

His attackers were conversing softly about his capture and how easy it had been. He didn't know what hit him according to their report. In a very calm, almost jovial voice George began, "Gentlemen, may I congratulate you on your excellently executed abduction. You make Richard and Burt seem like amateurs. And the chains, a very nice medieval touch. Do you have a rack for the torture? That would be choice indeed. Obviously, you must be highly trained professionals or very devoted to your cause." The two men turned to face George. "Well, well, Rico and Stuart, my apologies. I did not recognize you from the back. It is nice to know that Mr. C. has sent his finest." The men were dumbfounded at what George knew and volunteered to them. "I hate to disappoint you, but we are on the same side. I work directly for K.T. I'm part of the new youth sleeper-cell program. I live a double life, outwardly living the life of the ideal young man while secretly training and preparing to commit acts of terrorism. Obviously, you can't take my word for that. You have to keep me chained until you get verification. I just ask that you offer me the same courtesies that I would offer you if our positions were reversed."

"Okay, kid," began Rico, a short, muscular man with an intelligent air about him. "But first answer a few questions. Why did Swanson hire Richard and Burt to kidnap you?"

"Good question. I don't know for sure, but Swanson spoke at a city council meeting in favor of a bill that I was pushing. He wasn't helping much, by the way. How did that guy ever make it as a lawyer? Anyway, we made eye contact and he perceived that I recognized him. He figured that he had been made. I guess that he wanted to know what I knew."

"Makes sense, but how is it that Richard and Burt and even Swanson ended up dead and you come out looking like a hero?"

"Another great question. Richard and Burt were morons. They took me to a cabin up near Bear Lake. I could see signs everywhere that the feds had the place under surveillance. I figured that after we were captured Richard and Burt would tell all, causing irreparable damage to the organization. Not only that, but my cover was in danger of being blown. I had to take out Richard and Burt. What amateurs."

"Now you got me interested. How did you take them out?" George related the whole thing, exactly as it happened. Then he continued with the fabrication.

"After I rendered them harmless, I slipped out unobserved by the feds and hid in the woods. Swanson showed up and set the cabin on fire with Richard and Burt still in it. I came out of hiding to warn Swanson, but he shot me. I had to kill him or be killed. The feds showed up and took me home like the nice boy that I am. End of story."

"That's quite a story, kid. I have never been good at puncturing lungs. You'll have to show me that one. Look, like you said, we need to play it safe until we get confirmation on who you are. We will give you another injection and when you wake up you will be in a much more comfortable arrangement."

"That sounds great, guys." When George awoke, he was sitting up in a wrought iron bed with fluffy pillows behind his back. His hands and feet were chained to the bed, but he was much more comfortable than he had been hanging on the wall. Rico and Stuart were eating pizza. "This is so much better, gentlemen. Thank you."

"Would you like some pizza, kid?" asked Stuart, addressing George for the first time.

"That depends on whether I will be allowed bathroom breaks. I don't want to hasten a messy situation, if you catch my drift."

"Yeah, sure kid. We'll find a way to let you take a dump," replied Rico. "We've got Canadian ham and pineapple or pepperoni. Choose your poison."

"Canadian would be great."

"I know that this is embarrassing for both of us, but I will have to hand feed you," offered Rico.

"That's fine guys and we don't need to tell anyone about this, do we?" The men chuckled. George could see that he was winning their confidence. So far his risky approach was working.

After the food and some root beer, the boys were ready for some R&R. "You play cards, kid?" asked Rico.

George had never played a game of face cards in his life. Grandma Ruth, his mother's mother, consider face cards to be tools of the devil. George had played a little Rook and Uno, but that is all. Nevertheless, because of the memories he responded, "Sure, pinochle, bridge, twenty-one, poker."

"You got any money on ya?"

"There should be about twenty bucks in my wallet." Swanson had been quite a card shark and the idea of using his knowledge and bluffing skills appealed to George. Surely, Grandma Ruth would make an exception when his life was on the line. "You guys could have robbed me so I guess if you clean me out, I'm still ahead. Besides, even losing money sure beats the rack you had planned for me." The two men laughed.

"You're alright, kid. I know we are supposed to be tough guys, but quite frankly, I don't like torturing." He leaned close and said conspiratorially, "Now Stu, I'm not so sure about him." George grinned. They commenced playing poker. At first, they tried playing with George totally chained. They gave up and unchained his right arm. George did not even think about trying something; being chained by both feet and one arm, he would be forced to shoot these guys to defeat them. Even if he could get a hold of a gun, he liked these guys; he didn't want to kill them. George let them break even for a while and then he went to work. After a couple of hours, both men had exhausted their cash. Stuart was out $352 and Rico was out $511. Stuart wasn't the better player; he just had less cash to lose.

"Hey, look, guys. You need your operational capital for the mission. Just hold onto your money. I don't need it. I've got dough stashed all over the place. Besides, I took advantage of you. You just thought that I was a dumb kid. You didn't know that I was a card shark."

"No, no, kid," objected Rico. "A man has to have his honor, even in this business. We've got our resources. You know, you really got a lot on the ball, kid. In ten years, you could be running the whole outfit. I wouldn't mind taking orders from you, even now."

"Me neither, George," added Stuart. "Yeah, it doesn't seem right to call you kid when you're smarter than both of us put together. I suppose that you have a lot of skills, more than just being good at cards."

"Well, I don't mean to brag, but I do have a thing with languages. I'm fluent in Russian, Spanish, Korean and Mandarin Chinese. I'm conversant in German and Arabic."

"No kiddin. How do you say 'Hey baby, what's your name?' in each language?" asked Stuart.

"'Hey gatita. Como te llamas?' That's Spanish, of course." George proceeded to loosely translate the line into each of the other languages, not translating the line literally but using the typical jargon of an area speaking the language.

"That's amazing," added Stuart who seemed to be warming up to George. "What do you say, Rico, shall we unchain his other hand and put him on a leash?" Before Rico could respond, George jumped in.

"Wait guys, are you sure you want to do that. What if Mr. C. finds out?" George was playing the bluff. Swanson knew every con trick in the book. Make sure you really have them hooked before you reel them in.

"Yeah, let's just chain his feet. If this kid isn't on our side, we need to get him there." While Stuart held a gun on George, Rico unlocked the manacles on his ankles and installed a new device that effectively hobbled George's feet so that he could walk but just barely. Stuart opened up a small trap door in the floor and pulled out a heavy chain. Rico locked the chain to the hobbling device. It gave George enough slack to be able to move from the bed to the bathroom and back. "I wanna to show you something, George," explained Rico. "It takes two keys to unlock the shackles from your ankles or the chain from the hobble. The locks are spring-loaded so that it takes two hands to turn the keys. These locks are impossible to pick. Don't even think about it. The other end of the chain is welded to a heavy steel bar embedded in a ton of concrete. It's not going anywhere." Rico then unlocked the manacle from George's left wrist.

"Now, how about showing me how to puncture a lung," requested Rico. George carefully slid off the bed and experimented with taking small steps.

"Do you have anything thin but harmless like a crayon or some spaghetti?" George inquired. Stuart left for the kitchen and came back with a small, wilted carrot.

"Are you out of your mind, Stuart? I have killed men with carrots!" Stuart looked as though he thought that George was serious. He actually started to turn and head back to the kitchen. "Just kidding, Stuart." They all had a good laugh. "Okay, here's the deal; you puncture a lung to do two things. You want to make it impossible for the victim to scream and you want to disable him. There are some advantages over slitting the throat. Besides not killing him, you can always do that later, there is much less blood and you don't have to reach as high or as far, which in some instances can be the difference between life and death, your life and death." George showed the men how to find the gap between the ribs in an instant, just before the final thrust. He demonstrated the all-important twist of the blade or cock of the ice pick, pencil or whatever, to let air pass. "If you stab with a knife and pull it straight out, the wound may seal itself without deflating the lung," George explained.

Before the night was out, George had also helped them improve their garrote technique and weaponless killing. He may have found his calling in life. George was a natural-born teacher.

They called it a night well past one. George had been having so much fun that he had not realized how tired he was. He collapsed into bed. George awoke the next morning to the smell of cooking eggs and hash browns. After a stop at the bathroom, George wandered towards the kitchen, dragging the heavy chain behind him. "That smells great, guys. Thanks for letting me sleep in. I'm still a growing boy who needs his sleep."

"Anytime, George," responded Stuart. The two men grabbed the table and pulled it close enough for George to sit at it. Stuart brought him a chair. They had a great breakfast, stuffing themselves and reminiscing about the previous night's activities. After breakfast, Rico broke the bad news.

"Sorry, kid, but we have to shackle your wrists again. Boss's orders." George pretended to meekly go along while contemplating how to gain the upper hand. These were powerfully built, well-trained men. Overcoming them would not be easy. Rico handcuffed George while Stuart covered him with his pistol. Then Rico unlocked the chain from the hobbling device. They walked, while George shuffled, to the dreaded wall. Stuart kept a gun on George the whole time. Rico chained his hands and feet to the wall as at first. George did not resist. There was a palpable expression of relief on the men's faces once George was secured to the wall. George was convinced that they did not want to kill him any more than he wanted to kill them. He was sure, however, that his ruse had been exposed. He would have to come up with a new story.

Rico looked George in the eyes. "Kid, K.T. never heard of ya. You got some explainin to do."

"Well, I should have known it was just a matter of time. I guess I should have killed you when I had the chance. I was hoping that it wouldn't come to that."

"When did you ever have the chance to kill me, kid?" asked Rico indignantly.

"Oh come on, Rico; you, me and the carrot." Stuart snorted.

"Look, kid. I don't know how you stay so calm. You know that we are going to have to torture you now. We may even kill you. Aren't you just a little scared?"

"Well, maybe a little. However, before you start the torturing, let me come clean on my own. I know you will have to make sure that I am telling the truth and that may still mean torture. Here's the deal. I am a Live Natural or Die wannabe. I have been spying on you guys for years. I bugged the places where you congregate, not just with microphones but with hidden cameras. That's how I recognized you. That's how I know all about you. I'm a genius with electronics. I have financial resources that no one knows about. I've been disguising myself and making a killing at Wendover playing blackjack for years. School is boring so I use you guys as a diversion. Maybe I'm not on your side yet, but I really want to be."

"I believe you, kid, but I still gotta torture you," responded Rico.

"That's okay. I understand. I won't hold it against you guys. I still want to be friends after we get past the unpleasantness." George knew that Cleave had been highly trained in how to withstand torture. He was hoping that Cleave's training would get him through this ordeal, but he had no illusions of it being easy. George was facing something harder than anything that he had ever had to do in his life. He needed to act as if he had no training in enduring pain yet maintain the lie that he had just put forth. Stuart had brought over a tool bag from another room. Rico pulled out a pair of pliers and lightly clamped it on George's left little finger. Rico was positioned to clamp down on the finger but could not bring himself to apply full pressure.

"Let me see that!" growled Stuart. He grabbed away the pliers and after clamping them on George's finger, gave a hard squeeze. George felt a bone crack and screamed at the top of his lungs! He heard a crash coming from the living room! Both men turned towards the sound while drawing their firearms. The men rushed to each side of the room's open door. Rico signaled to Stuart to hang back and he moved into the doorway. In instant succession, there was a click, a muffled explosion and a thud as Rico fell back, revealing a bullet wound centered in his forehead. The sheetrock wall hiding Stuart from the intruder exploded inward as thunderous high caliber gunfire echoed about the room! Sheetrock skittered across the floor towards the back wall that George hung from and projectiles threw up wood fragments into the air pelting his lower body. George closed his eyes and turned his head in an attempt to gain some protection. The stream of lead took Stuart's legs out from under him. He fell into the hail of bullets. The gunfire stopped and George opened his eyes. A tall, dark-haired woman appeared in the doorway holding a sound suppressor equipped pistol in one hand and an assault rifle in the other. Her skin was dark brown and her hair was long, wavy and black. She wore a savage, desperate expression on her face. Although just rescued from further torture, George felt terrified. He studied this strange woman more closely. She was not just tall but unusually muscular for a woman. She looked quite young. His gaze fell on her face. Her eyes did not fit the rest of her. They were green. Wait a minute; George knew those eyes.

Chapter 17 - Margaret to the Rescue

Margaret was frustrated beyond measure. Since before Jr. High she had liked George and schemed to win his affection. None of her efforts had yielded fruit, but then a miracle happened. Of his own accord, George shared a secret with her, not just any little secret but the secret of a lifetime, of multiple lifetimes. And it did not stop there. George had spent time with her, taken her on dates, kissed her and told her that she was wonderful.

Then it happened! George was abducted and whisked away from her. Somehow, he had survived, but he would not tell her how. He would not tell her anything. She kept telling herself to relax, that everything would work out. Did she relax? No. She got angry and frustrated! Then she got angry and frustrated at herself for getting angry and frustrated. She just could not seem to let it go. She obsessed over George's secrets continually.

Then an idea came to Margaret. A wickedly deceptive idea occurred to Margaret. If George would not share his secrets with her, she would take them by subterfuge. It would be easy, child's play really. George would not suspect a thing. The plan was very simple. Put George in a situation in which he would naturally fall asleep. Make sure that he stayed asleep and then do the extraction.

The drive-in movie date worked perfectly. George fell asleep during the second feature as planned. Margaret knew that chloroform would leave an odor behind that George would immediately recognize. Nitrous oxide has a slightly sweet odor and taste, but George would not detect the faint lingering odor. Of all of his senses, most of which were very acute, his sense of smell was the weakest. During their visit to the safe house, Margaret had noticed a bottle of nitrous oxide with a regulator and mask. She researched the usage of nitrous oxide so that she would be able to give the proper dosage. It was all too easy. The problems began after the injection.

Margaret had taken on not just the memories of one person but of six. And they were not women, they were men. Some of them had evil, filthy minds. All of them, even George, were obsessed with women's bodies. Why are women's boobs so fascinating to men? Okay, maybe Margaret knew the answer to that one; men don't have boobs. Anyway, Margaret was disgusted with men yet she had all of these memories and habits of six men invading her girlish thoughts. Margaret knew that if she spent any time with George he would realize what she had done and hate her for it.

Margaret had chosen a horrible time to take on a crash introduction into the world of men. Although very popular and successful at school, she was never the less at that awkward stage in which she was not comfortable with her body and was very self-conscious. Margaret hated being so big and tall. At six feet and over 150 pounds, she was taller than ninety percent of the boys her age and outweighed more than half of them. And let's not even talk about those things that men are obsessed with. Maybe if Margaret's had been placed on a five-foot-two, 110-pound frame they would look impressive, but on her huge frame, they were mere speed bumps. All of these thoughts and memories were driving Margaret crazy. In spite of the teenage girl body image issues, there were male body image issues. A part of her wanted to be muscular and strong. Every male memory in Margaret's brain wanted to be fit with a muscular build. She was suffering from multiple personalities and most of them were male. Margaret was a mess.

In spite of all of her personal issues, Margaret realized what incredible danger George was in. He was living his happy go lucky life, dating the lovely Susan Bennett, who even Margaret liked, as if he did not have a care in the world. Margaret was trying to anticipate every thought and move of the enemy. She was getting herself into shape so that she could protect George. Margaret made several trips to the safe house. She verified the location of the bugs and tracking devices. She put a tracking device on George's car and others in his shoes. Margaret already understood the use of the weapons available to her, but she drove to a desolate area west of Magna on the other side of the Oquirrh Mountains with the weapons and practiced. With the memories, she quickly became an excellent marksman.

Margaret knew that George was frustrated with the FBI and was ready to call Rex Marks. He would not call from his house. He would drive to a payphone somewhere well away from Bountiful.

Then it happened; George headed north. Margaret dropped what she was doing and followed. Her parents had bought her a silver '65 Cutlass. Margaret had installed the tracking equipment in a foldout panel under the dashboard for easy use. She stayed well behind George, knowing that he would quickly realize that he was being tailed if she got within sight. When George finally stopped in Ogden, Margaret parked several blocks away but with a clear line of sight. She watched from her observation point with binoculars. As expected, George went to the payphone to make a call. Margaret had always been good at anticipating what George would do, but now, with his memories, she sometimes knew what he was going to do before he did. With her limited field of vision, looking through the binoculars, Margaret did not see the approaching men until they were at the phone booth. She was afraid that they would just kill George on the spot, but they overcame him in the booth. Then they supported him between each other as if they were walking arm in arm to the black Cadillac that they had driven to the scene. They deposited him upright in the back seat.

One of the men drove George's car while the other man followed. Margaret had not been able to see the men's faces well enough to identify them. She forced herself to wait a minute before starting the engine. The tracker had a range of ten miles. Margaret wasn't going to lose them. She drove to the service station and inspected the crime scene. There was no blood. George had been limp when carried to the car so the men must have drugged him. The Mustang got back on I-15 and headed south. Margaret stayed a safe distance away. The car exited on Antelope Drive and headed west. It drove a few miles and turned onto a side road. The cars finally pulled into a driveway at a home on a large lot.

Since Margaret was unarmed, she drove past the house and headed to Magna. Cleave always said that it was better to arrive late and well equipped than early and lacking what you needed to do the job. On the way to the safe house, Margaret stopped and bought supplies. At the safe house, there was a white van in the single-car garage marked up like it belonged to the phone company. Margaret knew from Cleave's memories and verified on one of her visits that the van was filled with electronic equipment for tracking and bugging. She loaded it with guns, ammunition, food and miscellaneous supplies. She showered, figuring that it might be days before she could bathe again. She died her hair black and coated her body with the kind of tan lotion that gives you an instant, dark tan, no sun required. She put on several coats. Margaret applied heavy eyeliner, mascara and eye shadow. She dressed in a tight black miniskirt.

She put on a highly padded pushup bra. Margaret knew what distracted men and was going to take full advantage of it. She wanted to turn her speed bumps into stop signs that would keep men's eyes from noticing other details. Not only would no one recognize her, but men would not be thinking about shooting her. Margaret put on a white, long sleeve blouse and left the top three buttons undone. She finished with a pair of sturdy heels that she could actually run in, if required. Margaret called her parents from a payphone. Fortunately, no one was home and she left a message on the recorder. The Medefins owned a very early model of magnetic tape based message recorder. Margaret's father loved gadgets. Margaret said in the message that an urgent matter had come up and she might not be home for a few days.

Margaret calmly drove back to the house where George was detained. On her earlier drive-by, she had studied the phone line routing. This time she pulled up to the pole that supplied the home. She slipped from the front directly to the back without having to exit the van. There Margaret put on coveralls and changed into work boots. She strapped lineman spikes to her lower legs, donned a white hard hat and headed out wearing a tool belt. She climbed the pole and installed a phone tap transmitter that would transmit to a receiver in the van any phone conversations on the house line. She returned to the van and tested the equipment. The van equipment allowed any phone conversation to be recorded as well as listened to live in the van or via radio transmission using a wearable receiver with an earpiece.

During the drive-by, Margaret had noticed a house on the street that had the porch light on during the day and several free advertisement newspapers on the front porch. There were no major newspapers on the porch as if the subscription had been canceled for the week. Margaret pulled into the driveway and drove around behind the house. By now, it was around seven in the evening. A red light went on in the van, indicating that the phone receiver had been picked up. The electronic screen showed that someone was calling the local Pizza Hut. A man ordered a large ham and pineapple and a large pepperoni. This was perfect. The van was supplied with bugs that looked just like those little plastic devices that keep the lid from collapsing on the pizza. Margaret figured that it takes at least 20 minutes to make a fresh pizza.

She raced to Pizza Hut and pulled around back. Only one delivery car was parked in back. It probably would not be waiting for the order that Margaret wanted to intercept, but she put a tracker on its bumper just in case. Five minutes later a young man carrying a large stack of pizzas departed the building and left in the car. Six minutes later a different delivery car pulled in and the driver rushed into the building. Margaret ran over to the delivery car and hid low in the back seat. Within two minutes, the driver returned with a stack of pizzas. Margaret let him drive to his first delivery. He delivered the top pizza first. While he was gone, Margaret sat up to check the addresses on the pizza boxes. The bottom two had the desired address. Since the top pizza on the stack was not for her destination, she slunk down again. After the second delivery, only two boxes were left. Margaret waited for the driver to return and start the engine. As the engine was cranking she slowly sat up. Then suddenly she grabbed the driver's hair with her left hand, pulling his head back. She simultaneously used her right hand to apply a chloroform soaked gauze pad to his mouth and nose. He was quickly out. Margaret reached over the seat and grabbed the two boxes of pizza. She installed a bug and left the boxes in the back seat. She laid the driver over into the passenger seat and moved around to the front seat. Margaret shoved the young man's thin body over to make room to sit. She placed his hat on her head and drove to the small house where the boy she loved was being held captive. She carried the pizzas to the front door and rang the doorbell.

A very large man opened the door. Margaret recognized Stuart immediately and almost called him by name. She had to cover the expression of recognition on her face. She improvised. "Well hello, tall dark and handsome," she said with a thick Latin American accent. Stuart was surprised and delighted by what he saw on his doorstep. As he ogled Margaret's body, she moved the boxes out of the way so that he could get a full view. "Now it's my turn," she said. At six-four and well over 270 pounds, the man was impressive. "You are quite a man." Margaret reached out and felt his large upper arm muscles, deftly depositing a bug on the backside of his shirtsleeve. The bug's Velcro like surface clung well to any coarse fabric. "Most men are intimidated by my height and strength, but a man like you wouldn't be."

"I think not," he replied in a cocky, self-assured voice.

"Great. Well, here's your pizza. That will be nine ninety-five." Stuart handed her a twenty.

"Keep the change, senorita."

"Gracias, Senor Grande." Margaret walked away knowing that Stuart was checking her out all the way to the car. As she got to the vehicle, she turned and sure enough, the man was still in the doorway watching her every move. She gave him a little wave and drove off. The other man must be Rico, she thought. Stuart and Rico almost always worked as a team. Now Margaret knew whom she was up against. She drove back to the Pizza Hut and parked. She stuffed one hundred dollars into the delivery boy's shirt pocket and a note that said, "Sorry for the inconvenience. I hope that the money adequately compensates you for your discomfort. I needed to help a friend in trouble. Don't worry, I delivered the pizzas." Margaret had also kissed the note leaving a heavy coating of red lipstick. She figured that most guys would be delighted to have the money and a great story to tell their friends. Margaret drove the van back to the home whose yard she was using. She set up the electronics so that she could remotely switch the earpiece to either of the microphones that she had planted. The one on Stuart's arm was giving the best reception.

Margaret heard Stuart say, "I like the kid. He has style and guts. I don't know how in the world he could not be who he says he is and know all that he knows about us. Do you think that we did the right thing taking him down from the wall?"

"Yeah, sure," replied Rico. "That looked mighty uncomfortable hanging spread eagle like that. He'll be secure enough on the bed." Margaret could not believe what she was hearing. George had been hanging from the wall and now he was in a bed! He must have done some great storytelling. It was growing dark. Margaret put on a dark coat to be less visible and left the van, still following the conversation with the remote receiver. She took a very long way around to the back of the house. Meanwhile, the men kept talking about how much they liked George. It sounded like Margaret did not need to rescue George at all.

The house was an older home and had cinder block walls on all sides. All but the back wall had windows. Margaret looked closer and observed that there had been two windows that had been filled in with cinder blocks. George had probably been fastened to this rear wall. It sounded from the conversation as if George were waking up. They must have drugged him again for the move. These guys were very careful.

After a while, it sounded like the men were hand-feeding George. Margaret headed back to the van taking a different but no less indirect route. She made herself comfortable in the van. Now it sounded like they were playing cards with George. Margaret dozed off for a while. She could not tell for sure, but from the conversation, it appeared that George had won all of Rico and Stuart's cash in a poker game. He was offering to give it back and they were refusing. Margaret had never known George to be such a smooth operator. Having obtained his acquisitions one at a time he must have been able to more fully take advantage of them. He must have been drawing on Arnold Swanson's memories. He was a smooth operator, sly and deceitful and worst of all, a seducer of women. George was seducing these seasoned thugs as if they were two lovely women. Margaret wondered if she should just go home and let George handle the situation. He seemed to have everything under control. The van had a very comfortable built-in bed, so Margaret caught some sleep.

Margaret had left the receiver on all night and had fallen asleep to the soothing sounds of George teaching Stuart and Rico fighting techniques. She slipped in and out of sleep, but if she were not mistaken, George's hands were unshackled. The rattling of a heavy chain indicated that he was somehow tethered. Margaret was startled awake around seven the next morning by lights and alarms in the van alerting her that there was an incoming phone call. She snapped to attention. The caller did not give his moniker, but he seemed to be the man known as Mr. C. Apparently, Mr. C. had checked with the figure known as K.T. and K.T. had never heard of George. Why hadn't George tried to escape during the night? He had won the men's trust and had not made his move. Maybe he was getting overconfident. Now he was likely to be tortured and killed if Margaret did not intervene.

Cleave Burningham had lots of rules of thumb and maxims that guided his decisions. One was, if you are going in with force, go with full force. In a life or death situation, you go in with both barrels blazing, shooting to kill with no hesitation. Margaret packed all the heat that she could carry without overly encumbering her movement. On a belt hung tear gas grenades and concussion grenades as well as spare ammunition. In one hand, she carried a silencer-equipped Glock 17 TB pistol and in the other hand a fully automatic M16. Slung over her shoulder was a battering ram for breaking down doors. Margaret wore the receiver and earpiece so that she could follow the conversations. The sun was already up so she would have to use speed and stealth to avoid being spotted while armed to the teeth. After leaving the van, Margaret ran from cover to cover until she reached the back of the house. She had to wait there for over an hour while George, seemingly oblivious to the danger he was in, slept like a child and then enjoyed a hearty breakfast with Stuart and Rico who were still treating George like royalty.

Eventually, the subject of the phone call came up. Stuart and Rico explained to George that they had to return him to the wall. Margaret could not believe the calm and skill that George displayed with this setback. He had a ready and very plausible explanation of why K.T. did not know him. Stuart and Rico seemed to be buying George's story. However, they had a job to do and would do it but only after apologizing to George for that which they would do. And George was so understanding. Did he think that he could survive torture and not betray himself and her? Using a portable tracking device that hung from her neck, Margaret had followed the travel of George's right foot. She could detect that George's right foot was now elevated above the floor. The conversation confirmed that Rico and Stuart had chained George to the wall. She moved back to the front of the house.

As Margaret heard Rico and Stuart prepare to torture George, it was as if a switch flipped in her mind. Cleave seemed to take over. However, he was not moving to just stop some evil men. It was as if he were acting to protect his own son. Margaret moved to the front door and readied the battering ram. She heard George scream. She flew into action, swinging the ram, putting her body weight behind it. The door burst open. She shucked off the battering ram and rushed in raising both weapons. A head popped into view. Time seemed to slow down. Rico looked to the open doorway. Instinctively, Margaret had moved to the right knowing that Rico's attention would first be drawn to the door. Her pistol was already pointed at the doorway that Rico occupied. As if in slow motion, she refined her aim and squeezed off a shot. Rico had seen Margaret from the corner of his eye and had started to swing his gun to her position. Margaret saw a red dot appear on Rico's head and his head jerk back from the momentum of the slug. Knowing that Stuart would surely be hiding at the side of the door from which Rico had emerged, Margaret moved closer to the wall and holding the M16 high and pointing downward, let loose with a line of fire back and forth along the full width of the wall, starting where she suspected Stuart to be hiding. By shooting downward, she minimized the risk of hitting George, who was chained high on the back wall. She stopped firing before expending the entire clip of ammunition. She wanted something to fall back on. Expended shells clattered as they hit the floor and bounced about. One shell continued to spin long after the others had stopped. Then there was total silence. Margaret rushed to the doorway, not sure of what to expect. She searched the room for threats. She found only two mutilated bodies on the floor in a dark pool of blood and George hanging from the wall.

His work done, Cleave seemed to leave Margaret. The awful awareness that she had just violently taken the lives of two fellow human beings suddenly hit her. She fell to her knees and convulsively vomited and continued to vomit until nothing was left in her stomach. Then she convulsed with tears until she thought that she could weep no more. Meanwhile, George patiently hung on the wall without making a sound. Finally, Margaret looked him in the eyes. His expression was inscrutable. Surely, by now he had figured out what she had done to him. Was his dominant emotion anger at her betrayal, relief at his rescue, fear or disgust at the slaughter before him of men of whom he had actually become fond? His eyes looked to a desk in the corner. Margaret saw a key that appeared to match the wall cuffs. She grabbed the key and set George free from his captivating chains. She helped him to a chair. He seemed wobbly and unstable. Margaret took his cute baby face in her hands, looked into those puppy eyes of his and said, "I'm sorry. I had no right to steal your memories."

George waited for what seemed to Margaret to be an eternity but must have only been a few seconds before replying. "I stole the memories of Jose Mario Martinez, a man I came to love and respect. Because I stole his memories, I was able to rescue him from a life of addiction and degradation. You stole my memories because you already loved me and feared for my life. You used the knowledge gained to save me from torture and death. In the process, you lost your innocence. You did what you had to do. I would have done the same for you if our places had been reversed. I'm sorry that my recklessness forced you to follow such a painful path. It is I that should be apologizing." Margaret started to weep again. George pulled her down into his lap with his long, powerful arms. Together they wept themselves dry.

"We need to leave now, George, and do so without evidence tampering. I have broken enough laws in the last twenty-four hours to last a lifetime." Margaret was wearing thin cloth gloves to prevent leaving prints. "Let's just leave the Mustang. It isn't safe now anyway. I'll take you to the safe house until we can figure out what to do."

"It's kind of spooky hearing you say just what I would say. When it comes to these matters, we both have the same voice in the back of our minds instructing us as to the best course of action. You have sort of made yourself into my female clone. By the way, that's a new look for you, isn't it?" Margaret was still wearing the heels, miniskirt and white blouse. Embarrassed, she buttoned all but the top button on her blouse.

Margaret drove the van back to the safe house while George stayed in the back. They did not want to risk anyone spotting George. The safe house had extensive medical supplies and Cleave Burningham had emergency medical training. In addition, Arnold Swanson had attended almost three years of medical school before being forced to drop out after being caught cheating on an exam. Only the influence of his politically powerful father prevented public humiliation and expulsion. Using the supplies at hand, Margaret was able to rig a splint for the broken finger. The damage to the flesh was minimal and did not require dressing.

She then fixed lunch that included sirloin steak, baked potato and salad. Margaret had purchased things that were easy to fix. It felt almost like they were married. They had their own home and she was fixing a meal for her man after a hard day, a very hard day. After lunch, George did the dishes and cleaned while Margaret showered and attempted to return her flesh and hair color to normal, although getting rid of the black was more challenging than she had anticipated. She changed into her regular clothes. It was good to be back to her modestly attired self. Margaret found George in the living room where he had her join him on the sofa.

"Mag, I will have to go into hiding. If I return home, I endanger all of our lives. With the safe houses, I have food, shelter and money. The hardest part will be moving around the country. I don't know where I will go first or when. Don't return here unless you have to. You probably will be followed for a while." George handed Margaret a folded note. "Give this note to my father soon but discretely. I don't want anyone but the three of us knowing that you have been involved. You don't need to say anything. The note will tell Dad all that he needs to know. It is not safe for us to communicate right now. Wait for me to make the first move. I'll have to become a ghost, leaving no sign of my passing. You should go home now. Your parents are probably worried sick about you."

Margaret kissed George goodbye and headed home in the Cutlass. One of the advantages of having lived for most of her life as the near-perfect daughter was that her parents rarely worried about her getting into trouble, or so Margaret thought. Her dad was still at work when Margaret got home. She found her mother in the kitchen. As she looked up from her shopping list that she had been composing, she seemed more angry with Margaret than worried or alarmed. "Don't ever go off like that again, young lady! Your father and I have had no idea where you were. We appreciate that you left a message, but you could have given more detail and then called us. You're grounded for a month. No car, no dates, nothing."

"I'm sorry, Mom." With that, Margaret burst into tears and buried her head on her mother's shoulder.

Chapter 18 – Biker Buck

George was safe for the moment, but he had very little time to distance himself from the area. If his father followed his instructions, George would soon be on the missing person's list. He had to change his appearance but not in obvious or expected ways. George had not shaved in a day and a half. Both the police and his enemies would be looking for a clean-cut young man traveling alone. He could not do anything about the alone part, but he could work on the clean-cut part. George walked to a nearby pawnshop. There was a corner of the shop devoted to biker related items. He found a well worn, sleeveless, leather jacket that fit and some boots and pants. The boots were black leather with squared-off toes. The pants were dark and looked to George like something a biker would wear. He found a helmet that looked like a human skull. He also purchased some silver looking chains and a duffle bag that could be strapped on the back of a motorcycle. George carried his supplies back to the safe house and dropped them off. He walked to a local supermarket and perused a biker magazine to see what additional apparel would be appropriate. He returned to the safe house and got out of his old clothes.

Cleave had a whole room devoted to disguises. The supplies included kits for applying temporary tattoos that would last for at least two weeks. You just peeled off a plastic liner, pressed the kit onto the skin, and held it there for thirty seconds. Then you peeled off the backing paper leaving behind the tattoo. The system worked best for small tattoos. George applied a knife and a snake to each arm.

He located the key to the garage that resided on the back of the property and used it to unlock the swinging doors. Inside were a racing motorcycle and a chopped Harley. George wheeled out the Harley, turned on the gas and the ignition and thrust down the starter lever with his right foot. The engine leaped to life on the third kick. The bike was well equipped for travel with lockable hard case side bags and a rack on which to tie down additional luggage. George packed the bike with supplies for the trip and drove to a Harley dealership. He found some sleeveless biker shirts with various decorations and sayings. All were dark in color. He drove to a gas station and after gassing up, changed into one of the new shirts. He had previously donned the boots and pants.

Since Utah did not have a mandatory helmet law, George rode with the helmet strapped on the back, ready to be slipped on at the border of any state requiring helmets. He took the back roads, avoiding I15, the main north-south highway through Utah and headed for Arizona. Because George had no personal experience riding a motorcycle, he had to let Cleave take over. Unfortunately, Cleave was not as conscientious about keeping the speed limit as George was. George had thought that while traveling on a motorcycle the speed would seem faster than going the same speed in a car. For some reason the opposite was true. Going twenty-five on the motorcycle felt like going less than twenty to his original, untrained senses. Consequently, when Cleave was going thirty-five in a twenty-five mile an hour zone, George did not notice the excess speed. A police officer passed the bike going the opposite direction. In the rearview mirror, George saw the brake lights go on. Before the police car could turn around, George cut through several businesses and got out of sight. It turned out that the policeman was responding to his radio and not to the bike's speed. After turning, he started the siren and flashing lights and took off for an unknown destination. George really needed to get a new driver's license that did not have George M. Horton on it. In the note to his dad, George instructed him to report him as missing so that no one would come after his parents looking for George. At this juncture, George could not risk being hauled back to Bountiful by the police where he would be a sitting duck for an assassin.

George could have easily gotten out of Utah that day, but he wanted to be able to hear the local news. He drove to Ruby's Inn outside of Bryce Canyon and rented a room for the night using cash. There was a brief news story about George. Since he had been abducted once before, the police naturally suspected that he had been abducted again. The story showed a picture taken at his Eagle Court of Honor. Perfect. No one would be looking for an unshaven biker. The story also described his Mustang and invited anyone seeing it to report it to the police.

After the news, George tried to sleep, but the events of the last two days haunted him. He mourned the deaths of Rico and Stuart. He had not known their hearts but had actually grown to like his captors during their short time together. George felt incredibly guilty that his carelessness had required Margaret to kill them. There was no telling the psychological damage to Margaret. Taking on all of those male memories had already driven her nearly to insanity.

George's schemes to improve his memory were reckless enough for him alone, but he had dragged Margaret into his machinations, with no regard for her safety. He had seen an opportunity and callously used her for his own ends. Cleave's voice seemed to come into his mind. "Snap out of it kid. What's done is done. There is no point in counting the dead bodies. If you made mistakes, learn from them. It's time to move on. Your family and your country need you."

George managed to eventually fall into a fitful slumber. He dreamed about the rescue, only this time the dark-haired woman continued to shoot as she entered the room, spraying him with bullets as he hung from the wall. He awoke with a jerk.

Since he could not sleep, George dressed and drove to Moab, another tourist destination in southern Utah. He figured that in tourist towns people do not pay any attention to strangers, except to try to sell them something. That night the news told of someone locating the Mustang and the discovery of the carnage in the house.

The story made it clear that George had likely been a prisoner and that he had been rescued or kidnapped by a third party. That night George was not racked by guilt like the night before, but he really missed having someone to talk to. His family had vacationed in Moab several times and being there made him miss them even more.

So far, he had been zigzagging through Utah. On the third day of being on the road, George meandered into Arizona. He traveled for several days, sleeping at campsites and cheap motels. He had the money that he won from Rico and Stuart plus he had borrowed a couple of thousand from Cleave's cash reserve, to which he had earlier added the money from Richard and Burt. It seemed strange borrowing money from a dead man.

George had never been on his own before his flight. During the last few days, he had hardly spoken to anyone. He felt intense loneliness. He needed to hear another person's voice in the worst way. It was like a deep hunger in the pit of his stomach.

On the sixth day, George pulled into a rest stop. By now, he had become comfortable driving the bike without the help of past memories. One of Cleave's habits that had become second nature to George was to closely observe every new place for hidden dangers and to scope out escape routes in case things required a quick exit. In accordance with this habit, George observed in a glance all of the vehicles parked at the rest stop. Only one caught his attention, a beat-up looking motorcycle with a swastika crudely painted on the gas tank. George killed the engine and let the bike coast into the parking area. He spotted a girl about his age trying to start a bike similar to Cleave's. She did not appear to fit the motorcycle at all. She was very modestly dressed with no visible tattoos. She was wearing tennis shoes and white slacks. She appeared to be very uncomfortable with the bike. The only biker equipment that she wore was a long sleeve, black leather jacket that was much too big for her. A scruffy-looking man wearing a faded Levi jacket with a swastika sewn on the back approached her. George could see an even rougher looking guy, similarly dressed, lurking just out of the woman's sight on the other side of the restroom. George immediately suspected a plot to take the bike from the young woman.

The restroom had an entrance and an exit at each corner, men's on the south side and women's on the north side. George entered the men's west door acting oblivious to the drama unfolding nearby. He exited the east door and circled around to come up behind the waiting accomplice. While passing through the restroom George had removed from a plastic bag in his left front pocket a chloroform soaked gauze pad. He smoothly wrapped his right arm around the much shorter Nazi wannabe's neck, placing the gauze over his nose and mouth using his left hand. After subduing one member of the duo, George dragged the man into the men's room and placed him on a toilet. George circled back around and approached the second member of the inbred white team. He was offering to help the young woman get her bike started while simultaneously sneering at her obvious lack of pure Arian blood. George decided that this was definitely not a time to be himself. Those searching for him were looking for an Eagle Scout. He would be a different sort of character. He let Arnold Swanson's personality take over. It was kind of fun.

"Hey Sergeant Schultz, back off," George commanded, calling the man by the name of the famous character from the TV series Hogan's Heroes. "From the looks of your rattle trap bike, you would be hard-pressed to fix anything." At first, the young man was totally confused and shocked at George's lack of respect for his obvious physical prowess. A switchblade seemed to magically appear in his right hand and the blade flicked out. "Good idea, those fingernails of yours really could use a good cleaning. Have you ever heard of toilet paper?" The man lunged at George. In a smooth, continuous motion, George both disarmed and tripped him. He fell flat on his face and then rolled over grasping his now broken right index finger. "Didn't your mother ever tell you not to run while carrying knives? You could really hurt yourself." The man sat in the dirt looking around for his partner who should have backed him up. "Your boyfriend is on the can taking a nap. I suggest that you join him." The man slinked off in the direction of the men's room.

George turned to the young woman. "I apologize, Miss, for that display of violence. When I drove up, I could see that the Neanderthal addressing you had a companion who was hiding just out of your sight behind the restroom. They only have one sorry bike between them and were looking to gain another, much better motorcycle. It is unlikely that you will be able to get your bike started without some minor adjustments. I would like to help you, Miss."

"Keep riding buster. I'm not the girl you're looking for."

"Oh, what girl is that?"

"An easy one."

"You're not easy?"

"I'm impossible." As a spy, Cleave had learned to quickly identify the nationality and background of any strangers that he met. George looked at the girl more closely. She had high cheekbones like an Asian. Her height and the relative fairness of her skin would indicate that she probably had some northern European blood. Her accent sounded Midwestern.

"Well then, we should get along just fine. In spite of looks to the contrary, we may be more alike than you think." George lowered his voice. "I'm on the run, just like you, but I'm much better prepared than you are. For example, I have a convincing disguise."

"How do I know this isn't just a new pickup line?"

"Ask me a scientific or mathematical question?"

"What is the value of Pi?"

"Pi is an irrational number and cannot be represented exactly. Its value is approximately 3.14159."

"Okay. What's a noble gas?"

"A noble gas is a gaseous element that doesn't easily combine with others. Examples are helium and argon."

"All right, so you're smart, but you're still a biker."

"Are you a biker?"

"Well, no."

"Neither am I. I'm just traveling incognito. I'm running from bad guys that want to kill me. How about you?" Suddenly the girl burst into tears. George wanted to comfort her but knew that he dare not approach her closer. He waited for her to regain control.

She blurted out, "I'm running from my abusive stepfather." Then she fell back to sobbing. George looked more closely and noticed a bruise on her left cheek.

"Is that his bike?" She nodded again.

"Look, I have money and I know what I am doing. Unfortunately, I am terribly lonely. I can help you, and you can help me. I promise to be a complete gentleman." She stopped crying.

"How can I help you?"

"Those who are looking for me expect me to be alone. Also, you could shop for me so that I don't have to show my face so much."

"That's all you want from me, to shop for you?"

"That and pretend to be my biker babe. But just pretend."

"I guess I could do that."

"I must warn you that traveling with me could be very dangerous, but traveling as you are is even more dangerous. It's best if I not tell you my name. Just call me Buck."

"You can call me Luanna."

"It's nice to meet you, Luanna. Now, about your bike; do you think that it has been reported stolen?"

"Probably."

"Then we need to ditch it. I know just where to leave it. But first, let me fix it. It looks like you accidentally snagged one of the spark plug wires and yanked it loose. I just need to plug it back on." George reinstalled the wire on the spark plug. "Would you like me to start it?"

"Would you please? My leg is killing me." George started up the bike and then held it upright while Luanna got on.

The couple rode to the next town and stopped at a park. "Here is the plan," George said. "We drive to the police station and you park in the first empty stall that you can find that is reserved for someone important. Park the bike and leave the key in the ignition. I'll be waiting just out of sight." After dropping off the bike, Luanna jumped on the back of Cleave's Harley and they headed out of town. Luanna did not put her arms around George to hold on. George was not sure how she was staying on the bike so he drove as slowly as traffic would permit. He did not encourage her to hold onto him or make any maneuvers that would require her to use him for support.

In the next town, George suggested that Luanna buy some biker clothes. He gave her two fifties and sent her shopping. In addition to the clothes, she bought another duffle bag. George gassed up at a station and Luanna changed into her new clothes. Now she looked the part, that of a hot biker chick. With her long black hair, she was quite striking. George was very careful, exercising great restraint not to gawk at her. As they were cruising slowly, still within city limits Luanna breached a delicate subject.

"Buck, where are we going to sleep tonight?"

"I have been camping and sleeping in cheap motels. I guess we can rent a couple of rooms."

"You have already spent a lot of money on me today. I am not a high maintenance girl. One room will be fine. I trust you to continue to be the gentleman that you have been so far. It would look totally wrong if we rent two rooms. It will arouse suspicion." Luanna then lightly placed her hands just above George's hips. He drove a little faster.

They drove until sundown and then stopped at the first little town. George pulled into the parking lot of a small motel. After they got off the bike, George held out to Luanna $300. "Luanna, the most dangerous thing for a woman on the road is to be broke. If anything goes wrong just run. With money, you can at least supply your basic needs and buy a bus ticket. Hopefully, it won't come to that, but just in case, I want you to always have at least a couple of hundred on you."

"Buck, I can't keep taking your money."

"Look, Luanna, a wealthy man gave me that money to use to help people just like you. He would be very upset with me if I didn't." George stuck the money in her coat pocket. "Now, go rent us a room." Ten minutes later Luanna returned with a key.

"It's number five." George parked and carried in his stuff. Luanna had already grabbed her things and lugged them to the room. There were two double beds.

"Girl's choice," offered George. Luanna dropped her things on the bed closest to the bathroom. "Why don't you buy me a burger and fries at that drive-in across the street and buy yourself whatever you want. You look pretty hungry." George had been brought up on homegrown fruits and vegetables and homemade whole wheat bread. It seemed exciting to eat some junk food for a change.

When Luanna returned, the smell of greasy fries filled the room. It was such a relief for George to have someone to talk to while he ate. He asked Luanna to tell him about her hometown. He figured that subject would be safe and not engender too many bad memories for Luanna. He savored the fries as he listened.

That night George fell asleep first. Before Luanna could get to sleep she heard George mumbling, "Don't shoot me!" over and over. As she silently lie in her bed, Luanna contemplated what horrible things must have happened to Buck to make him so afraid. Buck was the bravest person that she had ever met. Something terrible must have befallen him. He really did need her. Finally, she fell asleep. During the middle of the night, George was awakened by the sound of Luanna's voice.

Luanna had cried out, "Don't touch me!" George pondered on how hard it must have been for Luanna to endure abuse from her stepfather. George quietly rolled out of bed and began to pray for Margaret and Luanna, pleading that each would be able to find peace in their lives, in spite of what they had gone through.

They hit the road without breakfast in the morning. George felt a knot in his stomach and he remembered having experienced similar pain once before when he had eaten a lot of greasy food at a friend's house. Luanna tightly grasped George around the waist as they rode. They stopped around ten for brunch. The humble little café lacked any other customers during their stay. They traveled until sundown, and having traveled for many miles without seeing a motel, stopped at the first that they spotted. They pulled into the parking lot of the crude-looking little inn. Luanna slid off the bike and walked to the office. A few minutes later she returned.

"We're in number two. It's not what I wanted, but at least it was cheap." George parked the bike and brought in the duffle bags. There was only one bed!

"I'll sleep on the floor," volunteered George.

"No you won't!" demanded Luanna. "You paid for that bed and you are gunna to sleep in it! Now sit on that bed and I will go buy us some food with your money." While Luanna was gone, George did some strength exercises. Luanna returned, not with takeout but with groceries. She fixed hoagie sandwiches that they ate along with some apples and oranges. Luanna really was low maintenance.

"Luanna, I want to explain some things about me. I'm not entirely normal. At times I may appear to have multiple personalities. One moment I am the local church going Boy Scout. Something may trigger me like back at the rest stop and I become almost deadly violent. I'm extremely skilled at fighting with or without weapons. Please don't surprise me in the middle of the night. I might hurt you. If you see me go into a combat mode and I tell you to do something, just do it. Your life may depend on it. If I tell you to get on the bike and ride, then you ride, as fast as you can and don't look back." George thought that his little speech would scare Luanna, but it seemed to have the opposite effect.

"Could you teach me to fight?"

"Really? You want to learn how to fight?"

"Very much. I am tired of being afraid all the time."

"I could teach you a few simple things. My skills are the result of many years of training. I guess I could teach you some basics each night. You first need to understand the weak points of the human body. Some are obvious; some are not. When most guys fight they try to hit each other in the face, but there are far more vulnerable places on a man." George went through the key vulnerable strike zones and what kind of blows to apply to each. Luanna hungered to learn what George was teaching and appeared to be very bright.

The next morning Luanna was still asleep on the floor when George awoke. He carefully walked around her to the bathroom. He showered and as he was drying off there was a sharp knocking on the door.

"I have to go. Now!" pleaded Luanna with great urgency in her voice. George wrapped the towel around his waist and opened the door. Luanna slipped in as he moved out. George quickly pulled on some boxer shorts and some pants. The toilet flushed and soon Luanna stuck her head out. "I'm so sorry to kick you out. That is the best night sleep I have had in months."

"Man, you must really have an uncomfortable bed at home."

"The bed is fine. I just haven't felt safe. I feel safe with you. Thank you. By the way, you look pretty hunky for a science guy." George blushed. "Is it alright if I shower now?"

"Go right ahead. Since I quit shaving there isn't much for me to do after drying."

"Yea, we need to talk about your beard." With that, she pulled her head back into the bathroom. Twenty minutes later Luanna stuck her head out of the door again. "Buck, would you please pass me my bag." George grabbed the bag and handed it to her, not looking directly at her to be sure that he did not see something that he should not. After another half hour, Luanna returned from the bathroom looking and smelling fresh and lovely. George did not find Luanna as pretty as Margaret, but the overall package was still very appealing. He would have to be on guard to make sure that their pretense of shacking up together did not turn into the real thing.

"Buck, do you have a plan or are you just drifting?"

"I was about to ask you the same thing. Do you have a plan?"

"Actually I do. It is very simple. Stay on the run until I turn eighteen and then I won't need a legal guardian. I will just get a job and live my life far away from my family. How about you?"

"My situation requires a much more complicated plan. I have to find the identity of the top leadership of the organization that is hunting me and take them out, breaking as few laws as possible."

"Sounds like Mission Impossible. I know you are smart and tuff, but what hope does one guy have against the mafia or whoever it is that's after you?"

"You would be surprised. I have been abducted twice. The score is five of them dead, me, a broken little finger." George held up his splinted finger.

"You killed five men?"

"Actually, no. I didn't kill anyone, but I did disable two thugs and tie them up."

"How did you do that?"

"That is probably lesson twenty or so. If we're together that long I will teach you."

"I loved the lesson last night. I can't wait for the next one."

"We should probably get moving. It makes me nervous to stay in one place too long."

The next morning they hit the road, again skipping breakfast, but at least this morning George's stomach felt fine. As they rode, Luanna encircled his waist with her arms and leaned against him. They were almost like one rider instead of two. George was able to drive at full speed and take curves and corners faster. At times, it was difficult to keep his mind on the driving with a beautiful girl pressed tightly against him. They stopped after a few hours and ate an early lunch at a buffet. They both gorged themselves, not knowing when they would eat again. In the evening, they stopped at another cheap motel. Again, George let Luanna rent the room and do the shopping. She bought some fruit and milk.

"Buck we need to talk about your beard. It doesn't look right for a biker. You look more like Bluto, Popeye's nemesis. We need to remove some whiskers from certain areas at least once a week for the right look. I know just what to do. I will shave you right after you shower. Showering softens the beard, as I'm sure you know. I bought a disposable razor. Don't worry. During my dad's last days, before he died of cancer, I used to shave him. He was too weak to do it himself."

That night they had a great training session. Luanna was a natural and learned with impressive swiftness. She was very strong for a seventeen-year-old girl, possessing relatively thick and powerful arms and legs. Luanna also possessed amazing speed. By the end of the lesson, they were actually sparing.

Again, Luanna insisted that she be the one to sleep on the floor. It got cool that evening. The heat was turned off and the temperature dropped below sixty-five in the room. George was shivering, lying under just a sheet and was sure that Luanna was also cold. Somehow, he got back to sleep. In the morning, he was neither cold nor alone.

Luanna was lying next to him, on top of the sheet with the blanket over both of them. George realized that they were moving into dangerous territory but could not help but enjoy Luanna's body heat as she snuggled next to him. George stayed in bed for a few minutes enjoying the contact, yet feeling guilty. Finally, he slipped out of bed and took a shower. It probably should have been a cold shower, given the circumstances, but it was not. There were few luxuries in his life on the run and a hot shower was one of them. Luanna had showered the previous evening so George made his shower long and hot. He had carried clean underwear and pants into the bathroom and put them on before exiting shirtless.

Luanna was dressed and ready to shave him. She had placed both pillows up against the headboard so that he could lean back on them. George sat with his legs straight out before him on the bed. Luanna sat on the bed next to him and lathered him up. At first, George was afraid that Luanna would cut him, but she did not and as he gained confidence in her ability, the shave became a very pleasant experience. After Luanna wiped George clean and pronounced it good, she kissed him, not a quick peck on the cheek but a long seductive kiss on the mouth. George struggled not to obey the urge to reach up with his arms and press her body against his naked chest as they kissed. And yes, he kissed her back. He probably should not have, but he did and he enjoyed every second of it. After the kiss, George quickly donned his shirt.

"Luanna, that was wonderful, but our arrangement cannot continue with us having a romance. If we are falling in love while living together ... well you know where that could lead."

"Buck, I have very little faith in men. But at every turn, you have done the opposite of what I expected a man to do. Part of me has felt the need to keep pushing you farther to see if in the end, you are just another one of 'those men'. No matter what I have thrown at you, you have done the right and honorable thing."

"If that was just a test you deserve an Academy Award for that performance."

"Oh, I like you, Buck; I like you a lot. I enjoyed that kiss immensely. But this is not the time for romance. This is the time to save your life. You have already saved mine. I was ready to give up and end my life. I was just trying to start the bike so I could go somewhere private to do it. I would give my life to save yours." George was shocked. He had no idea.

"Buck, I don't turn eighteen for six months. I don't see how we can afford to go on renting motels that long. You don't have that much money, do you?"

"Not the way we've been spending it."

"I set up your tent while you were in the bathroom to see how big it is. We could easy both sleep in it, in separate bags, of course."

"I appreciate your desire to conserve our money. However, just because you trust me, doesn't mean that I trust myself to behave while sleeping next to a beautiful girl night after night. It may seem like we have been wandering but there is actually a plan behind our actions."

"You think that I'm beautiful?" interrupted Luanna.

"Well, yeah," responded George, blushing. Luanna appreciated Buck's virtue but inwardly wished that Buck found it harder to resist her advances, instead of easily dismissing them. However, she was pleased that Buck had kissed her back. George continued, "Anyway, back to the plan. I had to distance myself from Utah, but the organization that I need to take down is centered in Idaho. We are taking the long way to Idaho, keeping our distance from Utah where I'm a very public figure. The good news is that I have access to a home in Montana. It even has a supply of non-perishable food. If we have to, we can hole up in it for months."

"You continue to amaze me, George M. Horton. Yeah, I looked in your wallet while you were showering. I have never met anyone remotely like you. You are only 17, yet you seem to possess the knowledge and experience of a mature man. You have the skills of James Bond but the morals of Andy of Mayberry. You kneel in prayer every night; I peek when you think I'm asleep. But you aren't preachy like most religious guys. You look like a Hells Angel, but instead, you're a saint, a Latter-Day Saint, I presume. By the way, my real name is Vicky Lee."

"It's good to finally know your name, Vicky. I think it best though, that we continue calling each other by our false identities. Before we go to Montana, I need to do something illegal, but that won't hurt anyone. I need to get a fake driver's license. I know of a man in El Paso that can make it, but I don't want to deplete our cash enough to pay his normal fee. I may be able to get it on credit or something. I will just have to see."

George sent Luanna to buy some food for breakfast and for the road. He mainly wanted to send her away for some privacy. He was still deeply troubled by the moral quicksand that he had slipped into. George had always been taught to not only avoid morally compromising situations but also the appearance of impropriety. He was masquerading as a very immoral man, traipsing about the country with another runaway, sleeping in the same room and once in the same bed. Cleave's memories seemed to shout out to George to watch his step. George could hear in his mind his own father's words concerning moral purity. He went to his knees to seek guidance. This time George was not filled with peace or warmth. He had crossed a line and needed to get back on the right side. Into his mind came a scripture, "Unto whom much is given, much is required." He had been given much and he needed to live up to the wisdom that he possessed.

Chapter 19 – Kick the Dummy

George had been gone for over two weeks and Margaret had not heard one word from him. Yes, that was the plan, but it still frustrated Margaret to no end. She had to do something or she would go crazy. George had told her not to, but she drove to the safe house anyway. She loaded up some weapons and ammo and drove to the backside of the Oquirrh Mountains to shoot. She was already an excellent shot due to the memories and her naturally steady muscle control. The target practice was more a form of psychotherapy. How could she help George? What could she do? Then a thought came to her. She remembered her first experience ballroom dancing with George. Because of the acquired training, they quickly began to dance complex moves and ended up in an embarrassing tangle of bodies on the dance floor. If she tried to use her self-defense skills, it might end in disaster. She needed a way to practice and allow her knowledge to adapt to her own body, especially since her body was far different from that of Cleave Burningham. Maybe she should start a self-defense club.

She was so excited about the idea that she immediately loaded the guns into her car and returned them to the safe house in Magna. First, she talked to her parents about the idea. She convinced them that they needed to learn how to defend themselves. Then she convinced a few friends to join the club. They had the first meeting in her family's spacious unfinished basement. Her father got a deal on a used wrestling mat that a local high school sold when it replaced it with a newer model. It provided an inch of dense cushion.

They held their first meeting on a Tuesday night. To her surprise, the Hortons attended the meeting. Margaret had set up chairs against the west wall several feet from the mat. She asked everyone to be seated and addressed them. "You are probably wondering who will teach this class. I have obtained a great deal of knowledge on the subject of self-defense or more correctly, the art of hand-to-hand combat. A situation may arise in which you need to go on the attack, perhaps to save another or take on a home invader, for example. However, we will start with self-defense. I understand the theory, but it will take me a while to catch my body up to where my brain is. Brother Horton, you are a large and powerfully build man. Try to drag me away." Mr. Horton looked embarrassed but stood and reluctantly tried to grab Margaret. Fortunately for Margaret, Cleave had taught hand-to-hand combat and knew how to defend without injuring an opponent. Rather than hitting or kicking her neighbor, she used a Judo move to throw him to the mat, using his own weight and momentum against him. She could tell, however, that Brother Horton was holding back. She knew that he was very strong and fast. Never the less, there were oohs from those seated.

"You are probably saying to yourselves that this all looked staged. You are right. In an actual abduction, my attacker would have been rougher with me and I would have been rougher with him. I did not want to hurt Brother Horton and he did not want to hurt me." With help from her parents, Margaret had created a sandman, a heavy canvas man-shaped dummy filled with sand. It hung on a strong rope from the ceiling so that its feet just touched the floor. "Let's say that my attacker is this sandman. I'm not going to wait for him to grab me. I will strike first." Margaret whirled and kicked the sandman so hard in the head that the entire house reverberated with the blow. There were gasps from those seated and Brother Horton looked a little pale.

Now that Margaret had the group's trust and attention, she launched into her prepared lecture and set of detailed demonstration and practice sessions. She taught the most vulnerable areas of the human body and showed how to strike each location. She had each member of the group team up with a partner and go through the motions without making contact. Once they had the motions down, she had them practice on the sandman making full and forceful contact. When the Hortons worked on the dummy, the house rumbled. The group had planned on an hour-long meeting, but it was well over two hours before anyone was willing to leave. They had planned on meeting just once a week, but everyone wanted to meet at least twice a week.

That night as Margaret prepared for bed, she realized that for the first time in weeks she did not feel frustrated or helpless. In her own way, she was doing something to help protect those whom she loved. She slept soundly that night.

Bob Wall unlocked the front door to his father's tire sales and service business. Why did his father insist on him opening the store so early? Hardly anyone came in before nine and here he was at seven in the morning. There wasn't even any work left over from the previous day. The worse part was that it gave Bob too much time to think. For weeks, his anger had simmered over the humiliation that he received the last day of school from that snotty Medefin girl. How had she so totally manhandled him? And being the last day of school, he had no opportunity to redeem himself. Man, he would like to put that girl in her place, but how did you get back at a girl. If he punched her out, it would only make things worse. What made it even more irritating was that he had actually been quite attracted to Margaret. She was one of the few girls that he knew that was both big and pretty. Being very large, Bob figured that he needed a good-sized girl to match up with him. It was frustrating wanting to kiss and punch the same girl.

A bell jingled as the front door opened. I tall, buxom blond walked in. Now here was a big woman. She was only two or three inches shorter than he was and she had arms and shoulders worthy of a bodybuilder. She looked as solid as a rock. She had a pretty face and a gorgeous thick head of hair. "What can I do for you, Miss?"

"For starters, you can fix my right front tire. I picked up a nail and the tire is half-flat. We had better skip over the paperwork and drive it in while we can."

"I'll open a bay door and you can pull it right in." He left the counter and moved into the bay. He opened the bay door and watched as the young woman pulled a '68 red Corvette into the bay. A babe like her in a Corvette. It doesn't get much better than that, he mused. He guided the car into position over the hydraulic lift and then opened the car door to facilitate the woman's exit. She moved with a feminine grace that Bob found very enticing.

"Mind if I watch?" she asked. Bob was under strict instructions from his father not to let customers remain in the bay area, but there was no way that he was going to send this gal to the waiting room.

"No problem, Miss ... ?"

"Flanders, Susie Flanders. And you are?"

"Bob Wall, at your service."

"How chivalrous of you. I like that in a man." Bob raised the lift enough to lift the tires just off of the pavement. He began removing the lug nuts. Susie managed to work in a conversation during the brief pauses in the racket from the air wrench and other equipment. "I'm new in town, Bob. How about you?"

"I've lived here my whole life."

"So, are you a Mormon boy?"

"Sort of but not really. My dad's not a member, but my mother is. She took me to church when I was young, but I quit going in my early teens."

"Too bad."

"Why, are you a Mormon?"

"Do I look like a Mormon?"

"I don't know, contrary to popular belief, Mormons don't have horns."

"Well, I'm from Minnesota and there aren't many Mormons up there, but when I come to a new place I like to figure out what makes it tick. From what I hear, you can't get any more Mormon than Bountiful, Utah."

"Yeah, that's about right." Bob decided that maybe it would be a good time for him to be Mormon. "I was baptized and I do know a lot about the church. If you want to go to church I could take you."

"I don't know. What could a half baked Mormon do for me?" Susie leaned in and sniffed Bob's shirt. "I can smell tobacco."

"I don't smoke, but my dad does. My mom smells of tobacco worse than I do and she is as devoted as they come."

"Well, alright. I won't kick you to the curb just yet. So, I take it that your dad owns the business."

"Yep and I'm his slave until he passes it on to me."

"I know the feeling. My dad's loaded; he bought me the Corvette as a graduation present. I moved to Utah and got a job at the truck stop in Woods Cross just to spite him. The irony is that with tips, I probably make more than my older brother who works for Dad."

"That's cool."

"I get off at ten. You could pick me up and drive me around town; that is if it's not past your bedtime." Did this hot chick just ask him out?

"Sure, there isn't a whole lot going on after ten, but I could tell about things." Bob had plugged the leak and was remounting the tire. He invited Susie back into the office and filled out a receipt with her name, address, phone number and license plate number. He handed her the pink copy. "There's no charge. We only ask that you think of us when you need new tires. Come fall, you will definitely need to put on snow tires. The tires you have mounted are fine fair-weather tires but lousy in snow and ice."

"I'll definitely think of you first, Bob. I'll see you at ten." With that, Susie blew him a kiss and was off. The next fourteen and a half hours were the longest of his life. Bob could not stop thinking about Susie. When he got off work, he went home and cleaned up as thoroughly as possible. He scrubbed his hands raw removing every spec of grease and grime. His fingernails were gleaming white. He dressed up with a dress shirt and tie and dress slacks. He polished his shoes until they almost glowed. He borrowed his mother's Oldsmobile convertible. It had been a hot day, but Bob was hoping that it would cool off enough to make Susie want to cuddle.

He arrived at the truck stop at 9:59. He did not want to be late but did not want to seem too eager. Susie saw him pull up and waved through the large window. She looked very fetching in her uniform. Bob exited the car and walked around to the passenger side. Within a few minutes, Susie was leaving the Café portion of the truck stop and headed to the car. Bob held the door open for her.

As they drove around town, Susie was very curious. She asked about everything. After an hour of driving, Susie asked if they could park somewhere quiet and talk. Bob was hoping that was code for kissing. He was close to Viewmont High so he pulled in and parked facing the football field. Susie unfastened her seatbelt and slide over closer to Bob. Bob wanted to put his arm around her and kiss her but was terrified that it would be too much, too fast. This girl was worth waiting for. He had to play it cool.

"So, did you play football, Bob?"

"No, I wanted to, but my dad always insisted that I work for him after school. Fall is a busy time for us as people get their vehicles prepared for cold weather."

"Too bad, I bet you would have been great. So, did you know the kid that was kidnapped twice and then disappeared?" Great, did she have to bring up George Horton, his nemesis?

"Yea, he was a year behind me in school, but I knew him." Bob could not keep the frustration out of his voice. Why did she have to bring up George Horton? Next, she would be asking about

Margaret. This was not good. Maybe he should have just gone in for the kiss.

"It must have been hard seeing him become a star when you weren't even given a chance to play." She was giving him a graceful way out of his dilemma. It would not look good for him to be resentful of George. Bob had never been very good at diplomacy or even deceit, but he desperately needed both now. He would have to do his best. Bob actually said a little prayer in his heart, promising God that if he could win this girl's affection he would never bully anyone again. He would even start going to church again.

"I don't begrudge George his success. We all cheered him on. Everyone wants to see their team have a great season. If I could have played, I could have been an offensive lineman and helped protect him. I could have given him more time to throw the ball." Well, he could have, he thought to himself.

"So why do you think George was kidnapped?"

"I don't know. I can only guess, but there was this thing about George. If he saw something wrong, he didn't look the other way, he did something. I saw him intervene to stop a couple of bullies from taunting a younger boy. He was fearless." Don't look at me like that, God! Everything that I said was true. Besides, I'm not that bully anymore, starting right now, even if I don't win the girl.

"That kind of attitude would surely rile some people. I heard that his former girlfriend kind of went nuts or something."

"She didn't exactly go nuts, but she seemed to experience a major personality swing. She went from being a bookworm to super jock. She was always tall, but she really bulked up the last few months. She is strong as an ox now."

"Interesting. Some of the guys at the truck stop think that she is the one that rescued George. Do you think that she could handle an M16?"

"Handle one, she could probably eat an M16 and poop out squirt guns. That girl is tough as nails." As Bob talked up Margaret, it made him feel better about having been roughed up by her. He almost felt a sense of pride concerning the incident. He had tangled with Mad Margaret and lived to tell about it. In a year, it might be something to brag about. Thank you, Susie, you just made my day. Susie moved over even closer to Bob.

"So, Bob, will you take me to church this Sunday?"

"Sure, but I will have to check on the time. I remember my mother saying something about stake conference. Mom said that it is going to be held in what used to be the Valley Music Hall. The Church bought it and remodeled it to be used for large meetings. The last time that I was there, it was to hear The Monkeys. I'll give you a call with the details." Bob had memorized Susie's address and phone number.

"I've had a great time, Bob. Thank you for the tour. Could you take me home now? I walked to work from my house."

Chapter 20 – New Wheels

George and Vicky reached El Paso that afternoon. Vicky was surprised to learn from George that El Paso has a Chinatown dating back to the 1880s. George parked in front of a small restaurant with Chinese style lion sculptures on each side of the doorway. "I hope that you like authentic Chinese food, Luanna. I will order for both of us. This place is very traditional. Act quiet and subservient to your man." Luanna put her hands together and gave George a mock bow in the Chinese fashion. They entered the restaurant. It was very small with only a half dozen tables.

A diminutive Chinese woman in traditional Chinese attire addressed them. "Table for two?" she asked with a thick accent.

George replied in Mandarin. "Table for two next to the window, if you please." George was not sure whose face showed more surprise, their receptionist's or Luanna's. The woman left to fetch menus.

Luanna leaned over to whisper to George. "I'm not fussy but nothing too spicy for me."

The woman returned with ancient-looking menus. George glanced at them to make sure that they had not changed and ordered in Chinese from memory, Cleave's memory, that is. "Two egg rolls, white rice, two bowls wonton soup, Kung Pao chicken, Baby Kai Lan, water, no tea."

Luanna leaned over again. "You continually amaze me, Buck. Can you just order in Chinese or are you fluent in Chinese?"

"I speak Mandarin Chinese fluently but not Cantonese or any of the other dialects. However, I am fluent in Korean."

"That's it, just Mandarin and Korean?" Luanna asked sarcastically.

"Well, I am fluent in Spanish and Russian and I get by in German and Arabic."

"You must be a total genius."

"Not really. Let's just say that I discovered a major trick in how to learn things. It is sort of cheating. It's like seeing a copy of the final exam before taking the test. This ability is what has gotten me into the trouble I'm in."

"People know that you cheated?"

"Not exactly. In my cheating, I found out things about evil men and their plans. I snitched on them. Those who are still alive are not too happy about it, especially those in prison. There are plenty on the outside to come after me. That is why I have to be so careful and keep moving for now." The waitress, the same woman who greeted them, arrived with the soup. They ate their meal in relative silence. Even though they were not talking much, George was delighted to have someone with him while he ate. He hated eating alone. Mealtime had always been family time at his house. He yearned for his parents' companionship, but Luanna was a wonderful substitute.

The waitress returned with dessert menus. George ordered Mi san dao. The waitress protested that Mi san dao was not on the menu. George asked to speak with the owner. The waitress nodded and went into a back room. A few minutes later, an elderly Chinese man headed towards their table. George stood and bowed. "Is the weather fair today, Master Lim?" he asked in Mandarin.

The old man replied in remarkably good English, "The weather is always fair when the sun shines. Come." The man turned and walked back the way he had arrived. George motioned for Luanna to follow behind him as he trailed the man.

After they had passed through several doors and down a hallway, they entered a small room and the man motioned for them to sit on a couple of bamboo chairs. He sat across from them. "How may I be of assistance?" he asked.

"Master Lim, I come needing your assistance to obtain a new driver's license. I know that your work is of the highest quality and worth far more than you charge. Unfortunately, most of my cash is in another state. The man you knew as the white dragon died last year. He is like a grandfather to me. He has left me all of his secret resources. I thought that possibly, due to your mercy and benevolence, we might be able to work something out."

"I remember well the man you speak of. Is that his Harley that you drove up on?"

"Yes, Master Lim."

"Did he teach you anything other than Mandarin? You speak it just like him."

"He taught me everything that he knew. I possess all of his wisdom as well as his training." Suddenly a punch was directed at George's head! He easily deflected it with his left arm in the traditional manner and slid his right arm just under Lim's, coming up with an undercut blow but stopping just short of his throat. Luanna leaped to her feet and assumed a defensive stance. "Relax Luanna. This was just a test. You couldn't expect Master Lim to believe all that I claim without some evidence. Everything is fine."

"Why does a young man such as you need a new driver's license? You do not seem like the kind of boy that would get into trouble. Who are you hiding from?"

"Let's just say that I kicked a Russian hornet's nest and I don't want to get stung."

"You said 'I' not 'we'. Why have you involved this lovely young lady?"

"I met her on the road. She is also on the run but not for any crime that she has committed. I am trying to protect her."

"If you met someone else on the road that needed help, would you help them?"

"Maybe, if it seemed like the right thing to do."

"Here are my terms," began Lim. "They are not negotiable. First, I want the Harley for the new license and $700. Second, you will allow my youngest son, Tony Tan, to accompany you. He has a car and will drive."

"You are very generous, Master Lim. My path is very dangerous. Your son could be killed. Can he defend himself?"

"I have taught him my skills and training, as you say. Unfortunately, I have not been able to teach him more than a small fraction of my wisdom. He is impulsive and reckless. Maybe you can teach him wisdom. He cannot be in more danger with you than he will be if he stays here. He stole drug money from a gang with ties to Mexico. The money is burning a hole in his pocket, as you Americans like to say. If he spends it here, he will surely be found out. I have only let him buy one thing, my beloved 440 Plymouth GTX. To outsiders, it looks like he is just borrowing it. I even still hold the title."

"Before we agree to this, may we meet your son?" George inquired.

Master Lim pressed a button on his desk. Soon the waitress entered the room. "Miss Wu, would you please see that my son joins us at once." Miss Wu quickly left the room. Minutes later a young man around twenty years of age entered the room. He was wearing a white apron with food stains on it. Luanna and George stood. He was much shorter than George but of a stocky, muscular build. His black hair was long and straight.

"You wanted me, Father?" he inquired.

"Tan, I want you to go with my new friends on a dangerous mission." Tony Tan looked over at George and then Luanna. His eyes grew large as he took in Luanna. "They are leaving behind their Harley and will need you to drive. Will you do this thing, Tan?"

Tony Tan looked again at Luanna and back to his father. "Yes, Father. When do I go?"

"You should have all you need for the trip by tomorrow afternoon. You may return to your work, Tan."

"One moment, Tan," George interjected. "Can you act as a gentleman around Luanna and treat her as a lady?"

A look of disappointment crossed Tony Tan's face. Finally Tony said, "Yes, Sir." George did not like his hesitation. He looked over at Tan's father.

"Tan will act as a gentleman or he may find one morning that he is no longer a man!" threatened his father.

"I will be a gentleman," affirmed Tan, this time with more conviction.

"One other thing," George added. "No alcohol or drugs. I want you to have a clear head. Our lives, your life, may depend on it."

Tan was quicker to respond this time. Without hesitation and with certainty he responded, "No alcohol, no drugs."

"Thank you, Tan," George said extending his hand. "It was a pleasure to meet you."

After Tan left, Master Lim got down to business. He explained that a driver's license looks suspicious if the photo looks like it was just taken with clothes and hair looking the same as the owner currently wears. Master Lim located a wig among his supplies that was close to George's own hair color. He had George put on the wig and a headband that obscured the fact that he was wearing a wig. He took several photos. "Tonight you change your beard. Shave a little more off. How old do you want to be on the license?"

"Is 21 too much of a stretch?"

"Yes, and it might arouse suspicion. How about 18?"

"Okay, that works, I guess."

"Fill out this form with the name, address and other information that goes on a license. In the notebook are some suggestions that will work well. However, it is best if you know the town that you say you live in." Fortunately, with all of George's memories, he knew many towns quite well.

George had Luanna rent two cheap hotel rooms on the other side of town. The next morning Luanna shaved George again, but this time George wore a shirt and there was no kiss. After the second shaving, George had long sideburns and a goatee. They spent the morning training. Luanna was getting to the point that she almost hoped that some guy would attack her so that she could let him have it with all that she had learned.

At a thrift store, they purchased some additional clothes that seemed more appropriate for teenagers traveling in a car. They showed up at the restaurant around two o'clock. The waitress seated them and then ran back to the kitchen to let Tony Tan know that they had arrived. He rushed out to greet them.

"Mr. Rogers and Luanna, today lunch is on the house. Let me surprise you with some of my favorite dishes. I promise that there will be nothing too spicy." With that, Tony Tan returned to the kitchen.

"Mr. Rogers?" asked Luanna incredulously.

"Not like the guy in the sweater!" George said with exasperation. "My name is Laurence Bradford Rogers. My friends call me Buck; you know, like the space cowboy sort of guy."

"Okay, if you say so, Laurence." George was beginning to second-guess his choice of names. Miss Wu brought them egg drop soup that was surprisingly good. An assortment of tasty appetizers arrived. Then larger dishes started coming. Most of them were not on the menu. Only Cleave had ever tasted such wonderful Chinese food. Their food indulgence made the meal at the buffet seem like a light snack. After two hours, they were ready to lie down and take a nap.

Tony Tan came out again. "How did you like it?"

"It was wonderful," they said in stereo.

"I have parked the GTX next to your motorcycle. Here are the keys so that you can transfer your things from the motorcycle." After

Tony Tan left, George deposited a generous tip and they waddled out to the parking lot. After moving the duffle bags and their newly purchased suitcase into the trunk, George unlocked the rigid sidesaddles and removed from each a form-fitting suitcase that had fit perfectly in the available space. He carefully placed each of them in the trunk of the car. Tony Tan came out and escorted George through the back way to his father's office.

As they entered Master Lim's office, he arose. "Mr. Rogers, here is the driver's license that you lost. I trust you will be careful with it in the future." He handed George an envelope containing the $700 and the license, whose hard plastic surface was scratched and stained. George handed him the keys to the Harley.

"I shall be careful, Master Lim." George bowed and departed, followed by Tony Tan. When they returned to the GTX, Luanna was in the front seat.

Before starting the engine, Tony Tan explained the car rules. "If you ride with me you have to obey the car rules. Number one, call me Tony, not Tan. I appreciate Mr. Rogers that you called me Tan in front of my father, but he is out of the picture now. Rule two, wear your seatbelts. You never know when I may have to take evasive maneuvers. Rule three, no eating in the car. Rule four, nobody messes with the radio but me. We listen to what I want to listen to, when I want to listen to it. Is everyone clear about the rules?"

"Yes, Tony," Luanna and George both affirmed. With that, they were off.

"Mr. Rogers, what is our destination?"

"Head north."

"Luanna, if we are questioned we need to have an agreed-upon surname and place of origin for you. What do you prefer?" asked Tony.

"Why Rogers, of course. Buck and I just got married two weeks ago on June 3. How do you like my ring?" Luanna held up her left hand that was adorned with a modest ring bearing a zirconium stone.

"Mrs. Rogers, we can't have you wearing that fake trinket. I will buy you a real ring at our first stop," offered Tony.

"Why thank you, Tony." Luanna leaned over and kissed him on the cheek. "Now, don't get jealous back there, sweat heart. You know how I have to sit in the front seat so I don't get carsick. In answer to your second question, I grew up in Butte, Montana, same as Buck. We met at Butte High our sophomore year. Buck asked me to the county fair on our first date and he held my hand and kissed me. We went steady and finally got married right after graduation." Luanna continued for two hours, inventing a life history for them. George had thought all along that Luanna was very smart, but the creative talent she displayed convinced him that at least in some ways she was downright brilliant. Amazingly, Tony seemed to enjoy the whole performance. When Luanna would seem to slow down or run out of ideas, he would ask another question. George could tell that he was quite taken with Luanna and not just by her looks.

They stopped in Albuquerque and Tony bought Luanna the promised ring. She had to keep steering him to less expensive rings, arguing that working at the feed store Buck would never have been able to afford an expensive ring. While they were stopped, Tony took them to eat at a very nice restaurant, assuring them that he would pick up the tab. His father had been right about the money burning a hole in his pocket. Luanna and George were too full to have anything other than a light salad. They spent the night at a nice hotel in Pueblo, Colorado. Tony rented two rooms, one for Mr. and Mrs. Rogers and one for himself. The married couple's room was large and had two double beds.

Tony was hoping for a little nightlife together, but Luanna wanted another training session. Tony was anxious to join them, so they all trained together. At first, Tony appeared to be anxious to learn, but it was clear after a while that Tony possessed excellent fighting skills, many of which surpassed George's own skills. During the sparing phase, they added lessons on how to handle two simultaneous opponents. It was a very enjoyable evening.

As Tony returned to his room, George was still uncomfortable about sleeping in the same room with Luanna. "Luanna, would it be alright if I slept in Tony's room tonight? Even though we are not doing anything wrong it would be flirting with temptation if I stay."

"Well, if you are going to talk like that you can just sleep with the hogs for all I care! You get your skinny butt out of here right now!" shouted Luanna. She grabbed George's things and threw them into the hallway. He sheepishly slipped out of the room. Several people in the hall had stopped to listen to the drama before their eyes.

"Women," he moaned. "You can't live with them, you can't live without them." Fortunately, Tony's room was right next door and he had heard everything. He opened his door before George could even knock.

"Problems with the misses?" he inquired. After the door was closed, George quietly explained to Tony that Luanna was just giving the public a reason for her husband not to sleep with her. "Right," responded Tony stretching out the word. "And I'm the one that had to promise that I would be a gentleman."

As they started out the next morning Tony turned on the radio to a pop station. Bridge over Troubled Water by Simon and Garfunkel started playing. Tony had heard it before but not Luanna. Tony sang along with it. An hour later, it came on again. This time Luanna sang along hitting every note, not with perfect pitch but just like the lead singer. She used the same inflections, sounding just like the lead singer but in her own voice. George was very impressed. After Tony turned the radio off, George asked her to sing the song again. She repeated the performance with exactness. George had noticed this quality in Luanna during their training sessions. She could mimic his moves with incredible accuracy and seemed to remember them perfectly after only seeing them one time. Here was a form of intelligence that was almost absent in him. With Luanna's hunger for knowledge and this talent, she could learn almost anything.

They ate lunch in Buffalo, Wyoming before reaching Montana and finally pulling into Butte.

Chapter 21 – Reconciliation

Bob and Susie found excuses to talk daily. Bob bought himself a suit and some long sleeve dress shirts. He started a regular exercise program that included weight lifting. He started reading classic novels, anything that he could think of that would make him more appealing to a classy girl like Susie. When Bob picked up Susie at her home, she was wearing a very modest and attractive dress. His mom would like that. The former Valley Music Hall, now called the Regional Center, was a huge building with abundant parking. Bob's moderately sized stake did not come close to filling the seating. The Valley Music Hall had featured theater in the round. It did not look like a church at all. His mother had saved seats up close and center. She beamed as Bob introduced Susie to her. Bob's mother was especially excited because Elder Marvin J. Ashton, her favorite general authority, was presiding at the meeting. In his younger years, Bob had paid little attention to the speakers in stake conference or other church meetings for that matter, but today he paid rapt attention. He suspected that Susie would want to discuss the meeting and he did not want to sound like an idiot. Bob actually had excellent recall, when he paid attention, that is.

The highlight of the meeting was when Elder Ashton spoke. He told of attending a ball game. A friend showed up late and asked him who was losing. Elder Ashton had replied, "No one." In his mind, they were all winners. Bob thought about all of the times that he had called other kids losers. Why hadn't he realized how wrong that was? He wished that he could relive those years and be nicer. All he could do was try to be better from now on. During the meeting, he looked to the right and looked right into the eyes of Margaret Medefin who was sitting with her parents. To his surprise, she smiled cheerfully. She was such a pretty girl. His former anger was melted by the warmth of that smile. What a contrast from the way that she looked at him last time that he saw her. Maybe she regretted her actions as much as he regretted his.

During the meeting, Susie reached over and took Bob's hand. No girl had ever done that before. Bob was thrilled, a thaw with Margaret and things heating up with Susie. What else had he been missing by skipping church? During the closing hymn, Susie learned over and whispered in his ear. "Is Margaret Medefin here?" Bob pointed her out. After the closing prayer, Susie asked him to introduce Margaret to her. They worked their way through the crowd to Margaret who greeted Bob warmly.

After the meeting, he took Susie to his house for lunch. His dad sat in the Lazy Boy chair listening to a baseball game while the rest of them ate at the table. His mother was full of questions and Susie was generous with her answers. After lunch, Bob took Susie to her house. When he returned home and walked through the front door his dad called out, "So who was the bimbo, Meathead?"

"She's not a bimbo, Dad. She's a very nice and classy girl."

"Well, she's built like a brick ...." Mr. Wall looked up at his wife glaring at him and finished the sentence less profanely. "Outhouse."

"Roger, you be nice. Susie is a wonderful young woman and you missed out on a wonderful treat listening to baseball instead of eating with the family."

Later that week Bob got a letter from Margaret Medefin, of all people. He opened it eagerly.

Dear Bob,

I have been thinking about you and seeing you at stake conference gave me the impetus to write you. I am so sorry for the way that I treated you the last day of school. I totally overreacted to the situation. I embarrassed myself and you. I am so sorry. I hope that you can forgive me. I would like to count you as a friend.

Sincerely,

Margaret

Bob was stunned. Margaret apologizing to him and wanting to be friends. Never in a million years did he expect that. He immediately wrote her back.

Margaret,

Thank you for your kind letter. I was in the wrong and I know it. Even before your letter, I had been examining my treatment of others and regretting my actions. No apology from you is necessary. I thank you for your actions that have helped me to turn a corner in my life. I have vowed to never bully again. If you ever see me being a bully, let me have it. I have never told you, but I have always admired you. You are smart and kind. You are nice to everyone and never stuck up. I would love to be your friend.

Bob

A few days later Margaret called Bob. She told him about a self-defense club that she had created and invited him to come to a meeting and bring Susie if she would like to come.

Susie's phone rang. She picked it up on the fourth ring, a signal to those in the know that she was alone. "How's my Susie Q?" asked the voice on the line. The nickname came from a 1956 song by Dale Hawkins.

"Nana," squealed Susie, using the Russian equivalent of Daddy. Susie continued in Russian. "Everything is going great. I got a job at a truck stop where I hear all sorts of gossip. I have a local boyfriend who has introduced me to Margaret Medefin."

"That's my girl," replied her father in Russian. "Is anyone suspicious of why you are there?"

"I have asked the boy a lot of questions and he may be wondering why, but I have a plan to completely throw him off track."

"Tell me about it." Susie went on to explain her plan.

Susie had invited Bob to come to her house for a home-cooked meal. As Bob pulled up to her residence he wondered if tonight would be the night that he finally got to kiss Susie. She greeted him warmly at the door and led him right to the table. She must have asked his mother about his favorite foods because many of them were arranged on the table. Susie asked Bob to give thanks for the food. He said a short prayer; his mouth was beginning to salivate. During dinner, Susie continued to ask questions about Bountiful and its people. This sort of annoyed Bob. Why did she ask so many questions?

After dinner, she took his hand and led him to the couch. "Bob, I know that you like me and would like to kiss me, but before you do, there is something that I need to tell you." In a deep voice, she said, "I'm really a man." Heat flashed through Bob's entire body as he experienced multiple strong emotions. He thought about how muscular Susie was and remembered that she had always worn very modest tops, exposing no cleavage. She must be telling the truth. Susie erupted in laughter, nearly falling off the sofa. It took her several minutes to regain control. Finally, she said, "Oh, Bob, if you could have seen the look on your face! I was kidding. Here look." She unbuttoned several top buttons of her blouse and gave him a quick peek of generous cleavage. She buttoned back up. Okay, she wasn't a man, but how could she tease him like that? Yea, he had done as bad or worse than that to girls at school, but he expected her to be better than him.

"Here's the deal," she said. "I do have a problem, but I wanted to put it into perspective." In a soft voice she said, "I have a weak bladder and when I get excited or scared or even emotional, I can lose control. In fact, I think I had a little accident during that laughing spree. Excuse me while I change my panties." Susie stood, walked briskly to her bedroom and shut the door behind her. Bob sat stunned on the sofa. A bladder problem didn't sound so bad. He could live with that. Heck, with that body and personality he could live with a lot worse. Maybe she would be more inclined to overlook some of his faults, which he knew were many and serious. The fact was, even with a bladder problem, Susie was way out of his league, yet here he was sitting in her living room on the verge of kissing her. Maybe she asked a lot of questions about the town folk because she wondered how accepting they would be of her.

As Susie reentered the room, Bob stood. She approached him and put her hands on his upper arms. Man, she had big hands for a woman, but they felt just right on his beefy arms. "So, what do you think, Bob? Can you live with a little bladder problem or are we through?" Bob leaned in and kissed her gently on the lips. When he pulled away she whispered, "Good answer." They sat down on the sofa and just held each other for a few minutes.

Chapter 22 – Elevator Attack

It was after eight o'clock in the evening when George and company arrived in Butte. George had Tony drive past the safe house once to provide a chance to check it out. It appeared unmolested. The lawn was freshly mowed and there were flowers growing in the yard. Cleave had contracted with a local family to maintain the property. After obtaining Cleave's memories, George continued sending money to all of those who were maintaining Cleave's assets, as if Cleave were still alive. On the second pass, George had Tony drop him off a block from the house. All of Cleave's safe houses had both a front and a back entrance. There were homes lining the street but just farmland behind the lots. George slipped past the houses and walked across the farmland to approach the safe house. He cautiously walked around the sides and back of the house looking for anomalies. Finding none, he inserted a key into the backdoor lock. This house had locks keyed the same as the one in Magna. George pulled a Smith and Wesson from his ankle holster and went from room to room. After a thorough search, he opened the garage door. Within ten minutes, the GTX returned and pulled into the two-car garage.

George gave Tony and Luanna a quick tour of the house, holding back many of its secrets. They relaxed and watched a little TV before Luanna insisted that they have a combat training class. Luanna was learning Tony's skills much faster than George was. She was as tall as Tony, and with her exceptionally strong arms and legs, she matched up well with him. It was only a matter of time before some fellow got fresh with her and received the surprise of his life.

None of the three was hungry enough for a full dinner so George popped some popcorn and they watched a little more TV before going to bed. There were three bedrooms so there was no need for any awkwardness. The next morning Luanna was up early to do laundry. "I'm running a load in the washer. Can I wash anything for you?" she asked the men. Tony declined, but George gathered up all of his dirty clothes and brought them to the laundry room.

"Thank you, Luanna. You don't have to wash for me but thank you."

"No problem, any time," responded Luanna cheerfully.

Later that morning George took inventory of the house while Tony and Luanna went grocery shopping. He verified the presence of all of the equipment and supplies that should have been in storage. This house was not as well-stocked as the Magna home and George was glad that he had brought some equipment with him.

Tony and Luanna returned with enough food to feed a small army and a new wardrobe for Luanna. While they waited for nightfall, Luanna put on a fashion show. Even with all of his memories, George was no fashion authority but felt that Luanna looked stunning in some of her new dresses. This fact was not lost on Tony, who, acting the perfect gentleman, still seemed to nearly drool during parts of the show. Luanna did not discourage his attentions in the least. On a subconscious level, she was hoping that a little competition would pique George's interest in her. The move completely backfired. George thought to himself that he would have to move fast to get his work done before a full-fledged romance broke out between the seemingly well-matched couple. Since Luanna continued to flirt with George, he saw a potential explosion of jealous emotion on the horizon.

After dinner, George had Tony drive him to a telephone pole near the headquarters of the organization that he was stalking. It was a long drive and George took the opportunity to talk to Tony. "Tony, it is obvious that you are interested in Luanna. That's fine with me. I'm her protector and traveling partner, not her boyfriend. You have kept your promises admirably. If you want to pursue her I have no objections, as long as you continue to be a gentleman and Luanna welcomes your attention."

Tony remained silent until George was done and then responded. "So you don't have the hots for Luanna?"

"Don't get me wrong, Tony. She is beautiful, smart and very resilient. I like her a lot, but I just don't see romance in my near future. It could get us all killed. I really don't want to die. Besides, you are my friend. I wouldn't want to do anything to hurt you." George would see in the coming days that their discussion, rather than accelerating Tony's falling for Luanna actually put the brakes on things. As he would find out, Tony was very competitive and before their discussion was competing for Luanna's attention.

With one pass by the group's headquarters, a large, older home, George had located the telephone pole that serviced the phone that he wanted to tap. They turned around and parked at the pole. George exited the car dressed in lineman attire, including a hardhat. He knew that it did not look right not having a phone company van, but fortunately, there was little traffic. He shimmied up the pole using a lineman's pole strap and lineman spikes. At his destination, he opened up a slender junction box and attached some electronic equipment. The equipment had long slender leads that George spiraled on the main cable until it reached the pole where he nailed the electronics package to the wooden pole. The electronics were encased in what looked like a barn swallow's nest but was made of brown rubber. George tested the device as much as possible without a phone conversation when he got lucky. Someone made a call from the headquarters. George's headset picked it up perfectly. The call did not contain any useful intelligence but did allow him to verify the operation of the device. He closed things back up and shimmied down the pole.

Every thirty miles George had to plant a signal booster, a device that picked up the transmitted signal, amplified it and retransmitted it at a different frequency. He placed the boosters at the top of high points that had good reception of the signal. The boosters were very bulky, with each having a sealed lead acid battery and a small solar panel. The day was dawning before they returned to the safe house. George set up the receiver and recorder to catch all incoming transmissions. They all ended up listening around the clock taking turns manning each shift. Nothing of significance was transmitted that George did not already know. They were getting bored and the combat training sessions provided their only recreation. Tony was getting restless. Now that his interests in Luanna had cooled, there was less to occupy his mind.

Finally, they got a break. Through several intercepted phone calls, they learned of a meeting that was going to be held in a few days involving key leaders of the organization. The Butte safe house lacked a surveillance van but did have a Mercury station wagon. George figured that it would draw less attention than the GTX. They loaded up all of the equipment that they might need, including the two suitcases from the Harley saddlebags. George had a vague memory that the leader, called Mr. C., usually stayed at a nearby Holiday Inn and tended to arrive the day before the meeting. They drove to Idaho and found in a phone book the likely Holiday Inn. George let Tony and Luanna check into the hotel. Luanna explained that her sister was nine months pregnant and due any minute. She said that she would need additional rooms for family that was coming. She asked how many rooms were available on the ground floor. Tony was relieved when hearing that only three rooms were vacant on the first floor. Tony rented all three. They wanted to force Mr. C. to rent an upper room. Tony paid in advance for two days so that they could leave immediately if needed. While Luanna and Tony settled in, George went to work installing equipment, some of which came from his special bags.

After all was set up, they waited for Mr. C. and his bodyguards to arrive. The next afternoon a black Cadillac El Dorado pulled into the registry alcove. The driver, who also doubled as one of Mr. C's bodyguards, stayed in the car while Mr. C. and the other bodyguard registered for three adjacent rooms on the third floor. After fetching the luggage, Mr. C. and the bodyguard entered the elevator. George was waiting on the roof of the elevator car. To his surprise, Mr. C. was mimicking the voice of the receptionist, who had a strong southern accent. Mr. C was doing an excellent job of impersonating the woman. The bodyguard was quite amused. After the elevator had risen a few feet, George detonated a gas grenade that he had placed on the ceiling of the elevator. The device, which looked like a smoke detector, released a blinding flash of light and a burst of knock out gas that instantly mixed with the air. Its explosion was relatively quiet and could not be heard outside of the elevator above the normal elevator noises. The flash of light caused Mr. C. and his bodyguard to instinctively inhale, despite their training. George allowed the elevator to travel a few more feet and then stopped it using controls that he had installed.

While he waited to hear bodies drop to the floor, George donned an air mask. When he heard two thumps, he opened the trap door and dropped down into the car. As George moved Mr. C. into position, his looks seemed strangely familiar, not to the acquired memories but to his own personal memories. He pulled a syringe from his pocket and made the extraction. For good measure, he removed the men's weapons, wallets and watches so that robbery would be a plausible explanation for what had happened to them. George pressed the button for floor two. Then, using his remote controller, he restored the normal operation of the elevator. The elevator reached the second floor and the doors opened. Luanna and Tony had been watching to prevent any patrons from seeing George leave the elevator. Fortunately, no one had entered the hall. Luanna and Tony ran back down the stairs to the basement to remove the controls that George had installed for interrupting the elevator. The elevator doors closed and the unconscious men were delivered to the third floor. George followed Luanna and Tony down the stairs but exited directly out of the building without entering the lobby.

He drove off in the Mercury, headed for Bountiful with Mr. C's memories on ice. This was the first time that George had taken someone's memories by force. Not only that, but he would be absorbing the memories of undoubtedly a very wicked man. Or was he a wicked man? Could he not be a patriot for his country just like Cleave had been and through George was continuing to be for the United States of America? In his earlier years, George had been very quick to judge others. His father was very slow to pass judgment except when quick judgment was expedient. He had tried to teach George to be less judgmental. Cleave had a very practical outlook on judgment, "Judge quick and right on whether to shoot or hold your fire, but leave all judgment on the worth of a man to God."

George had prearranged with Margaret, before his departure from Utah, how to contact her. He would ring twice and hang up. If her mom answered before George could hang up, he would hang up anyway. He was to repeat the signal twice to confirm that it was he and not a wrong number. Margaret was to wait for him near the fire station on the corner of 100 West and 200 South. There were tennis courts there and a small park. If George did not show after an hour, Margaret was to leave a note tucked behind the bark of the largest tree, letting him know anything of importance.

By the time he got into Bountiful, it was past midnight on a Wednesday night. There was a high probability that Margaret would be home. George called from a payphone at Lee's Café on the corner of 500 South and 500 West. He hoped that with his facial hair, no one would recognize him. None of his friends were likely to be there given the time of night and the day of the week. George was able to let it ring twice and hang up before anyone answered. He waited one minute and repeated. Margaret's mother picked up before the first ring was finished. George cut her off before she could even finish "Hello." He waited in the café, taking a full thirty minutes to have pie and milk and then headed for the meeting place. From a block away, George could see Margaret's tall figure, her long red hair fluttering in the wind. Suddenly he broke into uncontrollable sobs. There stood the love of his life, the woman who had saved his life at great personal risk to her own life and sanity. She had been faithfully waiting for him while he had been off traveling with and kissing (well technically being kissed, but he thought that the distinction would be lost on Margaret) another girl. George looked straight ahead and drove on, not even turning his head towards Margaret. He turned left on 100 South and pulled over to compose himself. He dabbed his eyes and cleaned up his face using a handkerchief. George leaned over and rolled down the front passenger's window. He circled back around using 200 West and then 300 South to get back to the same approach. This time he pulled over to the curb next to Margaret.

"Hey, babe, you want a lift?" George called through the open window in a fake voice.

"Beat it, before the guy I'm waiting for gets here and kicks your butt!"

"Mag, is that any way to talk to your best friend?"

"George?"

George leaned across the front seat and opened the passenger's door. "It's me Mag. Hop in." He was on the move before Margaret even had her door shut. George headed for Grand Central, a shopping center just a few blocks away.

"So what happened to the Harley?" Margaret asked anxiously. "I noticed that it is gone from the Magna house. Did you have to hawk it?"

"Sort of. As you already know, this car is from Cleave's Butte safe house. Master Lim wanted the Harley as partial payment for a new driver's license."

"Oh, what was the rest of the payment?"

"I had to take his son, Tony Tan, with me, or maybe I should say, let him escort me since he is the one with the car."

"You mean the little squirt that was always getting scolded by Master Lim?"

"Yeah, that's the one, and he is still getting into trouble." They reached Grand Central and George parked in the middle of its large parking lot. "I need you to help me develop some film."

"That will cost you, Mister."

"What's your price, Miss?"

"I want you to kiss me and then hold me for at least 15 minutes."

"Well, I'm a little short on cash, but I guess I could meet that price." Margaret and George slid next to each other and Margaret reached up and felt his beard.

"I wasn't sure if that baby face of yours could grow a decent beard ... but not bad. It's thick and you did a great job of trimming it." Soon they were kissing and cuddling. George did not dare look at his watch to check on the time. After what seemed to him to be fifteen minutes, but he would realize later was more like an hour (he thought that Albert Einstein had said something about that), Margaret was ready to fill her end of the bargain. She did the injection for George and he returned her to the meeting place.

"Wait!" she commanded. She got out and pulled from behind a tree a brown paper bag. She ran back to the car with it and sat it on the seat next to George. "It's not much, just some fruit and a ham and cheese sandwich and stuff, but at least you can have something fresh without showing your face in town. I assume that you will spend the night in Magna before heading north."

"That's the plan, pretty lady. Love you." George drove off into the night, tears blurring his vision. Despite of the pie, he was starving and the bagged meal was perfect. Hopefully, Margaret and he would live through all of this and, after some more school and a mission, get married. She would make a terrific wife and mother. What had he been thinking, getting serious with Susan Bennett, Margaret was the only girl for him. Susan could never watch his back the way that Margaret did. Along with the sandwich and fruit, George found inside the bag a large Snicker candy bar, his favorite. He savored it along with the memory of his time with Margaret.

George approached the Magna safe house using the rear entrance and left the car parked behind the house. He ignored cautious protocol and walked right in and went to bed. By now, it was well past two. Sunlight woke him the next morning. To his surprise, he could smell pancakes. He surmised that Margaret had ditched school and fixed him breakfast. George got up and showered. After dressing, he entered the kitchen. Margaret was radiant, leaning over the stove. George slid up behind her and kissed the base of her long, elegant neck.

George did not tarry long with Margaret, knowing that the longer he stayed, the harder it would be to leave. They ate her lovingly prepared breakfast, kissed and George headed to the rendezvous point to join up with Tony and Luanna.

Chapter 23 – No Fooling Margaret

Bob picked up Susie to take her to a meeting of Margaret's self-defense club. He could not keep a grim off of his face. He was so thrilled to be with Susie. He did not know what she saw in him. He was happy about the reconciliation with Margaret but still wanted to show her up. Actually, he wanted Susie to show her up. Susie kept revealing hidden talents and Bob daydreamed that she was a big, female version of Bruce Lee. Well, there probably wasn't much chance of that, but I guy could dream. He reached over and took Susie's hand. Like Susie as a whole, her hand was large, strong and yet very feminine. Her fingernails were precisely trimmed and polished. The flesh of her hands was soft and supple. Her hand felt just right in his hand. Bob had learned to shift with his left hand so that he could hold Susie's hand while driving his Ford Fairlane. Shifting left-handed was awkward but worth it.

As Bob parked along the curb in front of the Medefin home, the Horton's arrived on foot. Bob hopped out of the car and circled around to open Susie's door for her. He greeted the Horton's and introduced Susie to George's parents. The Hortons treated Bob like he had been their son's best friend instead of an enemy. He expected them to be self-absorbed with their son missing and possibly dead, yet they were very warm and friendly. Mrs. Horton even gave Susie a little hug. He lived among so many wonderful people and somehow had not realized it. He needed to think more like his saint of a mother instead of like his father who seemed to see and bring out the worse in people.

Bob was amazed by the organization of the club and the quality of instruction. In the few meetings that the club had held, they had covered a lot of material and Bob felt way behind the rest of the class. Fortunately for him, Susie seemed to understand everything and was very good at explaining it to him and helping him to learn the moves.

Towards the end of the meeting, each club member had a chance to punch, elbow and kick the sandman. Susie kept giving up her turn to the person behind her, never touching the sandman.

Margaret watched Susie intently. Something seemed very familiar to her, but she could not quite figure out what it was. After everyone else had multiple turns with the dummy, Margaret insisted that Susie practice on the sandman. She hit and kicked with precision using the moves that they had practice but with little force behind her blows. It was obvious to Margaret that Susie possessed great fighting skill as well as physical strength. She thought of a way to maybe get Susie to show her cards. "I would like to do something new tonight. We are retiring the sandman after tonight as we move from the basement to the recreation center. Before we leave, let's each give the sandman our best shot. Pretend that he is after a vulnerable love one and you need to take him out. Give him your most ferocious and lethal blow. I will go first to give you an idea of what I am talking about." Margaret motioned for everyone to keep clear of the dummy. She approached and leaped into a flying kick, striking the sandman viciously in the throat. The room thundered with the reverberations. It was a good thing that they had found a new place to meet; Mother would never allow a repeat of tonight. Each member in turn struck the dummy with a frightful blow. It leaked sand after the Hortons had attacked it. Bob gave a powerful but untrained punch.

Bob really wanted to see Susie show her stuff. He was sure that she had been holding back. "Come on Susie, rip his head off!" Susie casually walked up to the dummy, but when she was maybe six feet away, with lightning speed, she performed a maneuver that Bob could not fully follow with his eyes. Somehow, Susie had flipped so that her head was down and the heel of her right foot stuck the dummy where his left eye would be. The thunderous blow broke the rope and the dummy flew several feet through the air before slamming to the floor and spewing sand out of its ripped apart head.

At first, everyone looked on in silent awe. Margaret started to clap. Bob shouted, whistled, and clapped. He loved this girl. He would do anything to make her his forever.

The kick provided the mental trigger that Margaret had needed. Cleave had trained a man named Richard Flanders as a navy seal. The kick that Susie used was a favorite of Richard. Richard had joined the church while in the Navy after being introduced to the restored gospel of Christ by Cleave. They corresponded over the years. Like Cleave, Richard had gone to work for the CIA. He had been instrumental in the defection of a Russian agent, Malvina Azarov. They eventually fell in love and married. Cleave had never met Malvina but had seen pictures of her. Susie looked just like her but with hints of her father's features. Susie must have been sent, either officially by the CIA or NSA or unofficially by her father to gather information on the Russian threat that George had uncovered.

As Margaret pondered on this new discovery, she wondered if and when the Soviets would send their own spy to Bountiful to find out what was going on. She would have to stay on high alert, watching for the threat.

As Bob drove Susie home, she hit him with another surprise. "Bob, there is something else that I have been holding back." Bob wondered what it was this time. With those fighting skills, who knew what she could be. "Bob, I actually am a Mormon. My parents are both converts and very devoted. And I'm not really rebellious; I am very close to my parents. I didn't tell you right off because I wanted to see how you would act if you thought that I wasn't a latter-day saint. You did great." If Bob had felt pressure to become a better member of the church before, he really felt it now. He would talk to his bishop about preparing to be ordained an elder.

Chapter 24 – Brain Overload

George needed time alone to analyze the new memories, which were much sharper than those from Arnold Swanson. Swanson's memories had gone hours unrefrigerated and then were frozen. From the new memories that flooded into awareness, George learned that the infamous Mr. C. was a double agent, a trained KGB operative. He had been a world-renowned artist and had pretended to defect to the United States during an art exhibition in Los Angeles. His mission was to destabilize America by encouraging, training, funding and aiding in other ways subversive movements of all kinds, even purely criminal groups. His organization operated on the "my enemy's enemy is my friend" premise. Mr. C's full name was Pavel Chernoff. George had thought that Cleave's life was surprising and interesting, but in some ways, Pavel's was even more so. Cleave on the surface had been a loveable grandfather and Boy Scout but secretly a highly trained killer. Pavel, to his close associates, was a deadly KGB agent but inwardly did not have the heart of a killer. Pavel had grown up with a great desire to obey and please those in authority. He had been a very obedient son. His father, who was also a member of the KGB, had encouraged him to follow in his footsteps. His mother had persuaded him to study art. Even when he married, it had been to a woman that his mother had suggested that he date. He had learned to love his wife and had been a devoted husband until her untimely death from a very aggressive form of pancreatic cancer. After her death, his KGB bosses convinced him that a feigned defection to the United States would be a good way to get over his wife's death and make a fresh start.

It occurred to George that had Pavel been raised in Bountiful by his parents he would have been a model latter-day saint and citizen. Pavel's life forced George to ponder on how much we are influenced by our upbringing and those around us. How little right we have to judge those from a different background than our own.

Pavel was extremely intelligent and learned both intellectual matters and physical skills very quickly, even when he had little interest in the subject. He became a world-renowned artist even though he started with little personal interest in art.

George realized now why Pavel looked so familiar to him. Pavel looked remarkably like George. George pulled off to the side of the road and looked at Pavel's wallet. It contained a picture taken with his family when he was about George's age. They could have passed for brothers. Their builds, coloring and complexion were nearly identical. Pavel currently almost looked like an older version of George.

Pavel had a wonderful mind. Somehow, he had organized his thoughts and thinking in such a way that his mind was incredibly efficient, efficient at learning, remembering, analyzing. If George could consciously organize his mind the way that Pavel had subconsciously organized his, George could move to the next level of intellectual development.

Pavel's mind took in everything, everything that he saw, even in peripheral vision, everything that he heard, even in the background, everything that he smelled and tasted and even touched. He vividly remembered how a kiwi fruit felt in his hand the first time he picked one up in an American supermarket, a few weeks after his supposed defection. He remembered the smell of the alfalfa field that he passed on a drive through Idaho three weeks ago. He remembered how his first kiss felt, twenty-five years ago. He could still see the 15-year-old girl's face clearly in his mind. He could almost count her adorable freckles. He could still remember precisely every detail of his wife's funeral, including what his parents wore. It was not that Pavel had a mind that could not forget; he had jettisoned uninteresting memories. He enjoyed remembering details and had trained his mind to remember a prodigious amount of information.

George had taken Pavel's memories so that he could use them to destroy him. Pavel's mind was a treasure. George would no more destroy Pavel than bulldoze the Sistine Chapel. His goal would be to get Pavel out of the country.

Pavel's store of vivid memories was so voluminous that it overwhelmed George's memories from his own short life plus five other lives. The memories were like the tide rushing in, enveloping a small tidal pool. Because seemingly trivial matters were stored in such abundance, more significant memories had to be winnowed from the chaff of insignificant recollections. George stopped several times at rest stops and just took it all in. There seemed to be something that he should remember that was life-threatening to him, but he could not bring it to conscious awareness. Several times George checked his rearview mirror as if looking for someone in particular.

Pavel not only spoke English and Russian articulately, but he had also developed fluency in French, Italian and Greek. Although he cared little about fighting, spying and military matters, he had absorbed a phenomenal amount of information and skills during his years of KGB training. He was always top in his class.

All too soon, George was back in Idaho at the motel where they had agreed to meet. He had not figured out what to tell Tony and Luanna. He would just have to wing it, but he was getting good at that, or rather had absorbed that skill through acquisitions. George went to the office where Tony had left a note telling him the room number. George went to the room and knocked.

"Yes?" inquired Tony through the door.

"It's Buck." Tony opened the door. Luanna was with him. She ran to George, threw her arms around him and hugged him tightly. George let Luanna finish her hug and slid his hands down her arms as they parted until he was holding her hands. He looked at Luanna as if for the first time, seeing her through new eyes. Pavel found her facial features very interesting. He would have loved to paint her.

Tony was annoyed by all of this hugging and hand-holding. "So what did you learn?" he demanded.

"Tony, Luanna, can you keep a secret, even if your life is on the line?"

"I would never betray you," responded Luanna passionately.

"I can keep a secret," grunted Tony, upset by Luanna's total devotion to George.

"Did you guys ever watch Star Trek?"

"Sure," replied Luanna as Tony nodded.

"Do you remember the Vulcan mind meld that Spock does?"

"Of course," replied Tony.

"Kind of," responded Luanna.

"I can do something like that. I won't tell you how or any details, but that is what I did to Mr. C., otherwise known as Pavel Chernoff. For me, the process is more complicated and dangerous than it is for Spock. Pavel is now part of me. His brilliant mind is now overwhelming my mind. We will not conspire to destroy Pavel. He is a good man. Pavel has never hated America or wanted to destroy her. He is just doggedly following orders. But don't underestimate Pavel; he is a brilliant and highly trained KGB operative. He can be very dangerous. However, his boss, K.T., short for Katarina Taras, is the real problem. She is a former ballet dancer who, like Pavel, is a KGB secret agent masquerading as a defector. Unlike Pavel, she hates us and is passionate about destroying America. She takes orders directly from Moscow."

The three headed back to the safe house so that they could check the voice recordings from their phone tap. There were two hours of phone conversation, most of it of no value. George's attack on Pavel was not mentioned. George suspected that Pavel had asked his bodyguards to keep it a secret until he had figured out what had happened and why.

They had a great training session. Both Tony and Luanna commented that George fought differently than before. In addition to a new repertoire of attacks and defenses, there was more grace and fluidness to his motion. George consumed less energy and did not tire as rapidly. He was more efficient. George sensed that Tony and Luanna were envious of his newly acquired skill and knowledge. He was not about to start injecting them with cranial fluid, but he did think of a way to teach them some useful things that he had learned from Pavel. "Let's go for a drive," George invited.

"Can we get out and walk?" asked Luanna. "I have cabin fever."

"Sure." They piled into the GTX and headed towards town. "Drive slowly and be observant," George instructed. After a few minutes, George asked, "Now, don't look back and describe the farmhouse and yard that we just passed." Tony and Luanna started listing things that they noticed, a yellow mailbox, a white house with a white shingled roof, a half-buried wagon wheel in the yard, etc. "That was actually quite good, but Pavel would have noticed, without even being asked to be observant, much more." George added to the list. There were two large windows on the front side of the house that were each divided into nine smaller windows by a wooden frame. The curtains were drawn on the north window but not the south window. There was a detached garage, whose door appeared to be broken. A green Chevy Impala was parked inside. The name on the mailbox was Raymond Jones. George went on and on. "Why do you think that Pavel sees and remembers so much more than you do?"

"Cause he's really smart?" offered Luanna.

"He is really smart, but that is not why. When he was only four years old, his father started this exercise with him as a game, just as we are doing now. He still plays the game, every day, wherever he goes. You are getting a later start in life, but you're both still young." They continued the exercise. They parked in town and walked the main drag. George quizzed them on window displays and people who passed them on the sidewalk. By the time they were heading home, Luanna and Tony were already showing significant signs of improvement. They dropped George off at the safe house and went back out on their own, continuing the exercise. George went to bed.

The next morning George was awakened by the energetic conversation of Tony and Luanna. They had found a way to resume the game indoors. They had filled a shoebox with two sets of dice and a dozen coins. They would shake the box vigorously with the lid on, then pull the lid off for a second or two, and then put the lid back on. They would try to recall not only the state of each die and coin but the location. George suspected that what kept them going was a combination of Luanna's thirst for knowledge and Tony's desire to be alone with Luanna. George showered and got dressed. Luanna had started fixing breakfast, with Tony teaching her some of his special cooking techniques.

George entered the kitchen. "That smells great," he commented.

"Thanks, Tony is teaching me how to cook. He says that if I learn well, I can work for his father. He is also teaching me Mandarin Chinese. I am one-quarter Chinese, you know." It seemed that Tony had just needed to see a little hand-holding to rekindle his interest in Luanna.

During breakfast, the trio brainstormed about how to get Pavel safely out of the country and away from his Russian handlers. They also conspired on how to take down Katarina. One of Pavel's many talents was the ability to mimic other people's voices, even those of women. George practiced several key voices that Pavel had mimicked. It just so happen that his vocal cords and mouthparts, combined with Pavel's talent, did an excellent job of mimicking the voice of Pavel's main Soviet handler, Major Federoff. With this discovery, they began to formulate a plan.

Chapter 25 – Cute As A Button

As Bob drove Susie home from the club meeting, he pondered on how to invite Susie to dinner again after church. Finally, he just launched into it. "Susie, my mother would like to have you come to dinner again after church. I have to warn you though; my dad will probably join us this time. As I mentioned when we first met, he is not a member of the church and well, he can be kinda crude and vulgar sometimes."

"Yeah, that would be a problem. Working at a truck stop among truckers all day I never hear profanity or vulgarity. I might just die of embarrassment."

"Okay, I get your point. Why does such a smart, talented girl as you work at café anyway?"

"You would be surprised how much money I make most days and I don't just mean from tips, although those are great. I tell you what; tomorrow's your day off. Come to the café and have breakfast but try to stretch it out. Don't act like you know me; just sit in a corner watching what goes on. Come about 10 and stay as long as you can."

The next morning Bob dressed casually and drove to the truck stop. He hadn't had breakfast yet so he was right hungry. The corner tables were all occupied so he took a seat with his back to an inner wall where he could easily see men come in through the front door. Susie was working the other side of the room so middle-aged Debbie waited on his table. Bob ordered a big breakfast and had the waitress bring food out one thing at a time so that he could eat slowly without the food getting cold. Nothing much happened the first hour other than men flirting with Susie shamelessly. It was a good thing that Bob was across the room or he might have thumped one of them. He worked hard to keep his cool. There was one little man that was there before Bob arrived and kept going out and coming back in. After about an hour he came back in and ran over to Susie and whispered something to her.

Susie sat down and Debbie brought her pie and milk as if she were on break. A man walked in that looked like he had a chip on his shoulder. The sleeves were cut off of his shirt and he kept his muscles tensed so that they looked bigger. A toothpick hung out the side of his mouth. When Bob didn't know someone's name, he liked to make up a name for them to help him remember things about them. He named the man Chip. Chip took a seat at the counter and asked for a cup of coffee while he looked at the menu. "You're a tough-looking one," commented Debbie. "We don't allow fighting, but we do see some arm wrestling. You any good at arm wrestling?"

"I can hold my own." Chip looked around with a contemptuous look on his face. "I would be willing to bet money that I could beat anyone seated here except for the big guy over against the wall."

Another man sitting at the counter said, "Fifty dollars says you can't out arm wrestle the waitress sitting there on break." Bob named this man Dealer. Chip looked over at Susie. Bob hadn't noticed it before, but somehow Susie had made herself look smaller and weaker. How did she do that?

"You're kidding, right?" said Chip.

"Dead serious," replied Dealer.

"No tricks?"

"No tricks, just good honest arm wrestling."

"You're on!" Susie ate the last of her pie and finished off the milk. Debbie cleared and washed the table. The man sat down across from her. As they clasp left hands lying across the table, the man was shocked to see and feel that Susie's hand was actually larger than his own. Not only that, but her forearms were thick. Bets were being made throughout the room. Hundreds of dollars were on the line. They grasp right hands in the air with their right elbows on the table.

Debbie gave the three-count. When she said three the man's right hand was slammed to the table.

"No fair," cried out Chip. "I wasn't ready."

"You said that you were ready and Debbie counted to three. What were you expecting?" asked Dealer.

"I don't know. I guess that it's my fault. I tell you what, let's do double or nothing, but this time we have to hold it for at least five seconds before anyone can win."

"I'll take that bet, but first let's see the other fifty," required Dealer. Chip pulled another fifty from his thick wallet and slammed it down on the table. There was a flurry of betting before the rematch began. "Are you ready?" asked Debbie.

"Yeah, proceed with the count," responded Chip.

"One, two, three." The stranger pushed against the woman's hand, but it didn't budge. The crowd was counting. When they got to five, he watched his hand slowly bend back until it was touching the table. How did she do that?

"No way," he said. There's something going on here. She's not really a woman is she?"

"Yeah, right guy. With a figure like that she's obviously a man," called out someone sarcastically. Susie stood, revealing the rest of her figure and standing several inches taller than her opponent.

Another patron called out, "Maybe men have hips like that where you come from, but here we called that a well-built woman."

"It's all fake!" called out the stranger. "I want to see some flesh." Bob had heard enough. There was a loud scraping noise as he scooted back his chair. The room went dead silent as Bob rose to his full six-feet four inches and 250 pounds. He walked over to Susie and took her in his arms. He kissed her passionately. She responded in kind. Bob turned to the man.

"Now, are you gonna try to tell me that I just kissed a man? There is no question that Susie is a woman, one hell of a woman." Cheers rang out. "The question is, are you really a man, or just some kind of weasel." The man looked around. He had no allies, not even among those who bet against Susie. He turned and stomped out of the café. Debbie placed a mug on Susie's table and men started filling it with money. When things had settled down Susie pocked the money and went back to work as a waitress. As Bob continued to eat and watch, he realized that there were two distinct groups in the café. There were locals who came to drink coffee and visit with each other and there were those who were passing through. The first group bet on Susie, the second against her. Retired men were not only paying for their coffee and meals but were actually making money by coming to the truck stop. Everyone benefited except for out-of-towners who bet against Susie. The owner loved having Susie there because more people came and stayed longer, spending more money. Susie was a gold mine for the truck stop and doing quite well for herself.

To Bob's surprise, the man who Susie defeated reentered the café. The room went silent. Chip quivered with anger. "No one cheats me like that and gets away with it!" The man pulled a gun from his pants pocket and raised it. Bob saw a blur of motion out of the corner of his eye and heard a clunk as the gun hit the floor. The man was clutching his right forearm with his left hand. The blade of a small knife protruded from his wrist. There was a camera flash as the owner took a photo of the man who had pulled the gun. Bob swung his eyes to Susie who was poised to throw a second knife. Her upper blouse was ripped open and he could see two small knife sheathes with their tops just peeking out from beneath the cups of her bra. The sheathes were tilted inward so that the knife handles would lean inward, allowing her to draw the left knife with her right hand and the right knife with her left hand.

Susie quickly closed the flaps of her blouse with her left hand. She moved to a wall and turned her back to the patrons, apparently re-sheathing the knife from her hand. She pulled a safety pin from a pocket and fastened her blouse closed. She turned back and squatted to pick up a button from the floor. She searched and found another but could not find the third.

The owner walked to the man and pulled the knife from his wrist and held it near his throat. "We can play this one of two ways. We can call the police and you go to jail. Every man here can and will bear witness to what happened. Or you leave the gun where it lays and get your sorry ass out of here and never show your face in town again. Your picture will go up on our wall of shame you can see there behind the counter. We will never forget you. Debbie removed your wallet while we were talking and is recording your driver's license information. We have also taken photos of your truck." While the owner was talking, Susie picked up the revolver with a fork and slipped it into a plastic bag. She wiped up the blood that had dripped onto the floor with a napkin and placed the napkin in a second bag. Debbie handed the gunman a napkin to use to put pressure on his wound and stuck the wallet back in his pocket. The man backed out of the door holding his arm. Someone followed him this time to make sure that he left without causing further trouble. The owner handed Susie her knife wrapped in a $50 bill. "Thanks for pulling our bacon out of the fire."

"Anytime, Boss."

"Take the rest of the day off, with full pay and here's a $20 for the tips you would have made." Susie resumed looking for the last button.

"Anybody seen my button?" she called out. An old man missing half of his teeth fished around in his coffee cup with a spoon and lifted out a white button. He raised the spoon high for all to see his trophy.

"Plopped right in my coffee," he announced to all with great pride on his face. "I wouldn't trade today's experience for a thousand bucks. No sirree. Susie Q, I gots to have this button as a souvenir. I'll give you ten bucks for it. You know, sometimes they say some girl is as cute as a button, but there's nothing cutter than you, Susie Q."

"You keep the button, Jack. No charge. You just keep watching my back." Susie bent over and kissed Jack on the cheek. "Bob, pay up and let's go."

"Oh no," said the owner. "It's on the house. You did us a real service today. It's nice to have a big guy like you around to keep the peace. You treat Susie good; you hear."

"Yes, Sir, nothing's too good for Susie."

"You got that right, boy." Susie gathered up her stuff, including the evidence that she had gathered and the happy couple exited the café.

"How did you make yourself look so small and weak before the contest?" asked Bob.

"The most important part is to be sitting down with my legs hidden. Most of my height is in my legs. Sitting with my shoulders rotated forward and slouching, I look like a tall girl but not six-one. My face is slender, so people expect a slender body to go with the face. When I need work done on my car I make myself look big and strong like I did when I walked into your shop. Men often take advantage of women when cars are concerned, thinking that women are weak and ignorant of how cars work. I like to project strength and understanding. I get a better deal and more respectful treatment that way. You probably picture me in your mind as bigger than I really am because of that first encounter."

"Okay, but how did you so easily defeat that jerk?"

"There are two things that you need to know about arm wrestling. First, technique is more important than strength. I know that is not at all intuitive, but trust me, it's true. The arm wrestling champs are seldom the muscle-bound looking guys. Secondly, the most important muscles are in the forearms and on the chest. You'll notice that I have big forearms. I have very large pectoral muscles, but thanks to these wonderful decorations that God has given me, they remain disguised."

"Will you teach me your technique? With my size and strength, it would be embarrassing to be beat by a much smaller opponent."

"Well, we wouldn't want you to be embarrassed, would we?" responded Susie. "I will teach you, but there are more important things that I want to teach you. I want you to serve a mission and I want to teach you Russian before you go. I know that there are not any missions in Russia because of the Iron Curtain and all, but there are Russian people around the world. I would love it if you could teach my people. My mother was born and raised in Russia. My American father spoke some Russian when he met my mother, but she has taught him to speak it fluently. At home, every other day we speak Russian instead of English. My mother is a wonderful, loving person, but she is very demanding. I have noticed that you have an excellent recall of details. I believe that you will find learning languages much easier than the average person."

Bob was in a state of shock. Susie wanted him to serve a mission. He could tell that it was not an idle wish but more of a requirement. Bob had never liked anyone pushing him around; he got enough of that from his father. However, he had told himself that he would do whatever it took to win Susie. She was already thinking of their relationship as long term. He thought about how he had wanted to relive his childhood so that he could be nicer to people. Maybe a mission would be a way to partly make up for his past bad behavior. It would also get him away from his dad and the shop for two years. Maybe a mission would be just what he needed. If he did serve a mission, he did not want to be an ineffective missionary. He would have to do a lot more studying of the scriptures and pay more attention at church. If he did speak Russian fluently, that might get him to some exotic country. He would go along with this mission/ Russian thing for now.

"By the way, Susie, what are you going to do with the gun and the blood sample?" asked Bob.

"I have a friend in the FBI. He pays me for evidence. I'm sort of like a paid informant. He will take fingerprints off of the gun and analyze the bore. It may help solve a crime. Sometimes I get a big reward. My friend says that someday they will be able to uniquely identify people from their blood or other tissue samples. Down the road, the blood sample may be more valuable than the weapon as evidence."

Susie was fascinated by the Bountiful Tabernacle where Bob's congregation, the Bountiful Third Ward, met. It featured pioneer craftsmanship and a balcony with two beautiful staircases leading up to it. Susie insisted on sitting in the Balcony. She was impressed that Bob paid rapt attention to the speakers during Sunday school and sacrament meeting. He even sang the hymns with vigor. During the few weeks that they had been dating, he had become leaner and more fit. He was a handsome man. Physically, he was perfect for her. She was a couple of years older than he was, but that didn't bother her. She thought about the advice her mother had given her years ago.

"Susie, you can find and marry a good man who is mostly what you want him to be. Chances are that you will be happy, but he will probably never be everything that you want him to be. On the other hand, you can find a man with the potential to be all that you want in a husband and is crazy for you. If you find that you can shape him and mold him into what you want, you can have, over time, exactly what you want in a man. I have done that with your father. It would have been easier if I could have met him when he was much younger and more flexible, but I managed it. However, do not marry a man that does everything that you ask him to; you want a man with backbone."

Susie thought about all of the changes that Bob had made already to please her. He had become active in church; he had started taking better care of his body; he had started being nice to everyone, something that she doubted that he had been doing before. When she asked him to just observe at the café he did so until he felt that she needed him and then he stepped in. She was glad that he had not followed orders. She sensed that he was much smarter than most people gave him credit. He had great bloodlines on his mother's side. He had great potential. It was exhilarating watching Bob grow and develop.

Chapter 26 – Turning the Tables

The first part of his plan required George to impersonate Pavel. George began a transformation to take on Pavel's age and grooming. George shaved so that his sideburns were shorter and his goatee resembled the one that Pavel wore. With Tony's help, he added slight graying highlights to his hair, eyebrows and beard. Using some special makeup pencils, Tony drew faint lines into the natural creases in George's face that added decades to his appearance. With Cleave's equipment and some extra that they had recently purchased, Tony photographed George and created a Pavel driver's license. They had the driver's license that George had stolen in the elevator, but George feared that a close examination of the photograph would reveal the ruse. Luanna trimmed George's hair and touched up the grey highlights again. George donned a long-sleeve white shirt, conservative tie and a dark suit.

George drove the station wagon to the bank where the organization did business. He walked to the desk of the woman in charge of safety deposit boxes. Mimicking Paval's voice, George addressed Miss Stevens, whom he recognized from Paval's memories of earlier visits. "Miss Stevens, you're looking lovely this morning." Pavel always flirted with pretty bank personnel so George felt obligated to maintain the habit.

"Why, thank you Mr. Chernoff. You somehow look younger today. Have you lost weight or gotten a new hair cut?"

The flirting thing was complicating his impersonation, but George played along. He actually was thinner than Pavel. "As a matter of fact, I am 10 pounds lighter than last time you saw me and I did recently get a trim. Thank you for noticing." George held out the key to Pavel's safety deposit box. The key had been in the stolen wallet. He also pulled out his wallet and presented the fake driver's license. Next came the scary part. George had to sign a form. He had been practicing Pavel's signature. When he started to write Pavel Chernoff, his hand automatically signed it just like Pavel would have. At least it looked that way to George, but he was no handwriting expert. Miss Stevens compared his signature to one on file and was satisfied.

She escorted George to the vault that contained the safety deposit boxes and unlocked the steel cage door. She inserted the bank key into his box and he inserted his key. Miss Stevens pulled out the box and placed it on a counter. "I'll give you some privacy while you look at your box." She then left the vault. George removed everything from the unit and stored the loot in a briefcase that he had brought.

At the safe house, the conspirators examined the take. There was cash, fake IDs and passports that had Pavel's photograph on them. There were also fake IDs and passports for Katarina. Luanna put on makeup and hair coloring and age-appropriate attire to make her look Katarina's age. With Katarina only being thirty-two it was much easier for Luanna to look the right age than it had been for George. Luanna wore her long black hair up in a bun. Tony photographed Luanna and created a Katarina driver's license but with the photo of Luanna. While Tony developed the photos and finished the driver's license, George helped Luanna change her appearance to differ in subtle ways from the photo just taken. They went to a different bank branch where Pavel and Katarina's faces were not known. Luanna, playing the part of Katarina, set up a new account in Katarina's name and transferred $200,000 into it. The account was set up with a credit card and checking account. A few days later, they went shopping and bought new clothes on the credit card. They looked at cars and bought a new, red Jaguar sports car. They also purchased a new Lincoln Continental. They drove the Jaguar to Katarina's mountain cabin and left it parked in the back.

They returned to the safe house and staged Pavel's death, while George still looked like him. They dug a deep hole and George climbed down into it. He had what looked like a bullet hole in his forehead with real blood oozing from a superficial wound shaped like a bullet wound. George's hands were tied behind his back. Tony took several photos, including some with dirt covering most of George. George held his breath during this part. As a Navy Seal, Cleave had learned to hold his breath for long periods. George had practiced to see how long his body could go without breathing and was up to over three minutes. Tony developed the photos and mailed a copy to Major Federoff. Luanna and George returned to their youthful appearance after bandaging his wound. George removed any remaining facial hair.

George called the restaurant where he knew that Pavel would be having dinner with a woman that he had been dating. He had Pavel paged. When Pavel picked up the phone, George spoke in the voice of Major Federoff in Russian. "My friend, I have some grave news. It seems that someone has been skimming money from the operational bank account. K.T. has implicated you. I know you, my friend. You do not care about money, you never have. I believe that K.T. is the guilty party, but she has done too good a job of framing you. By the way, that little incident in the elevator was my doing. We were making sure that you possessed no incriminating evidence. Your things will all be returned shortly. Here is what I want you to do." George gave instructions.

The next day George, Tony and Luanna drove to the Little America Hotel in southern Wyoming. Tony acted as the lookout, watching for Pavel. This hotel had been chosen because it had a row of four old-fashioned, fully enclosed, phone booths. At precisely 2:15 PM, Pavel entered the first available phone booth in the row of booths. Luanna was elegantly dressed in a mid-calf length black dress, black high heel shoes, black evening gloves and a black, wide-brim diva hat that obscured her face. She gracefully walked by Pavel's booth and deposited a shopping bag in the adjacent booth. She continued walking and left the hotel. Tony watched to make sure that Pavel picked up the bag.

As instructed, Pavel took the bag, which contained the wallets, weapons and watches taken from Pavel and his bodyguard, $50,000 in cash, most of his fake IDs and passports and a key to the Lincoln Continental. He delivered the bodyguard's things to him where he and the other guard waited at the bar. Pavel said that he needed to make a phone call before they left. He walked out the side door and got in the Lincoln. He drove to the Salt Lake International Airport where he began a circuitous journey to Greece. He had been instructed to wait as long as needed for Major Federoff to contact him with further instructions. Until then he was to maintain a low profile.

Tony and George joined Luanna in the GTX and drove to the airport to pick up the Lincoln. "Hopefully, my friends, I will be safe now," George suggested. "I expect that Katarina will soon find herself in hiding, dead or a prisoner back in the Soviet Union. Either way, she will not be coming after me. I hope that you are not disappointed that we did not have occasion to use our highly honed fighting skills. At least, Luanna, if you ever come across your stepfather again, you will know how to put him in his place. I give you my deepest thanks for your help and your company. I was going nuts with loneliness before we joined up. What are your plans now?"

"Tony has offered me a job back at the restaurant. He thinks that he can hang onto his money now and not draw attention to himself. We will be heading back to El Paso."

"Remember that you need to ditch the Lincoln and thoroughly wipe it to remove all prints. It will lead the Russians right to you if you hang onto it. Tony, are you okay with how things are turning out? You spent a lot of money. Do I owe you anything?"

"No, I'm good."

"How about you, Luanna? Are we square?"

"Not yet. You owe me a date. We have been roughing it; now it's time for you to show me a good time."

"It would be my pleasure to go out with you."

Chapter 27 – Making the Old Man Laugh

After church, Bob took Susie home for dinner. He led Susie into the den to meet his father who was sitting in the recliner watching TV. "Dad, I would like you to meet Susie Flanders. Susie this is my father, Roger."

"Hello, Susie, Bob speaks very highly of you."

"Thank you. Bob has told me a lot about you." Mr. Wall was a little surprised at Susie's response. It was not exactly rude, but it reeked of honesty. She did not say that Bob spoke highly of him, just that he had a lot to say about his old man. Mr. Wall prided himself on speaking his mind so it was hard for him to object to this directness. It might be interesting to get to know this girl. He had misjudged her; she was no giggling bimbo. Bob led Susie past the dining room, into the kitchen where they found his mother.

"What can I do to help?" offered Susie.

"Everything is ready. You and Bob can carry out the food to the table. I'll get Bob's father." Bob noticed that his mother had prepared some of his father's favorite dishes. He thought to himself, "Good idea, Mom; soften up Dad." When everyone was seated, Mr. Wall asked Bob to give thanks. After a short prayer, they all began dishing up.

"So, Susie, what motivated you to move to our neck of the woods?" asked Mr. Wall.

"I work for the FBI as an undercover agent. I'm investigating a ring of tire thieves. Have you bought any shady tires lately?" Actually, he had bought some tires a few months ago in a deal that seemed too good to be true, thought Mr. Wall. Suddenly Susie burst out laughing. "You should have seen the look on your face." Mr. Wall flushed with embarrassment.

"I should have warned you, Dad. Susie loves to kid. You won't believe what she told me."

"Oh, what was that, Son?" Mr. Wall had made an effort not to call his son meathead.

"I told him that I was really a man," interjected Susie in a deep, masculine voice. Mr. Wall smiled.

"So did he believe you?"

"I think that he did until I told him that I was kidding and gave evidence to the contrary." Mr. Wall stared for a long time at Susie and then burst into ruckus laughter.

"Don't get any vulgar ideas, Dad. She just gave me a quick peek at her cleavage." This only fueled the laughter and soon everyone was laughing.

"So why did you really move to Utah?" asked Mr. Wall.

"I grew up in Minnesota. There aren't many Mormons there. I wanted to experience living among Latter-Day Saints."

"So, you came to get a husband," thought Mr. Wall. She probably thinks that Bob will inherit the shop and support her in style.

"Did you graduate from high school?" asked a suspicious Mr. Wall.

"Roger!" chastised Mrs. Wall.

"I quit going to high school when I was 16."

"Just as I thought," contemplated Mr. Wall. "Why was that?" he asked.

"I graduated. They make you stop coming after you graduate, except maybe to come speak at graduation, but hey, I've already done that as valedictorian. I have been accepted into the master's program at the University of Utah. I have a B.S. in International Law with a minor in German." Mr. Wall sat dumfounded. What would this pretty, intelligent young woman want with Meathead?

"So, you speak German?" asked Mrs. Wall.

"Not as fluently as I would like, but it is coming along."

"She speaks Russian like a native," offered Bob.

"Really, how did you learn Russian?" asked Bob's mother.

"We speak it at home every other day. My mother was a KGB spy." Her audience looked shocked. "Oh, I'm only being serious," she added. Bob thought to himself that if her mother had been trained as a spy that explained how Susie learned to fight and throw knives. While other girls were learning how to bake brownies, Susie was being taught how to beat up and kill. "I started teaching Bob Russian a couple of days ago. He has a gift for learning it, I think."

The two launched into a conversation in Russian. It gave the impression that Bob knew much more than he really did. They had actually memorized a script. Bob was very good at remembering text and had picked up the pronunciation quickly. Susie had spent over 16 hours teaching Bob what he now knew. Her intent was to shock and awe Bob's father, to forever change how he perceived his son who was certainly no meathead. The ruse seemed to work. Mr. Wall sat dumbfounded.

Later that night, Susie was surprised to get a call from Margaret Medefin. "Susie, I want to visit my grandmother who lives in northern Idaho. My parents don't want me driving that far alone. Any chance that I can talk you into coming with me?"

"Sure, when do you want to go?"

"My schedule is pretty open. When do you have a day off work?"

"I have Tuesdays off. Do you want to go the day after tomorrow?"

"That would be great. Could I pick you up at eight?"

"The time is fine, but let me drive. That way I can drop you off and explore northern Idaho while you visit family."

"Okay, but at least let me buy gas." Margaret wanted to get alone with Susie so she could tell her that she understood why she was here and appreciated her presence. Two sets of eyes watching George's back were better than one set and she was confident that George would be back again soon.

Susie was delighted by Margaret's request. She saw the activity as a wonderful way to have Margaret as a captive audience and be able to pump her for information.

Tuesday morning Margaret watched from the front room window as Susie pulled up in her red Corvette. Margaret called goodbye to her mother and ran out the door carrying a basket of food and drinks, her mother's idea. The Corvette lacked a backseat, so Margaret placed the basket on the floor at her feet. At least the Corvette had generous legroom with the seat fully retracted.

At first, the girls just did small talk; then Margaret got serious. "Susie, I think that I understand why you are here and I am happy for it."

"What do you mean, Margaret?"

"I mean that the daughter of a former Russian spy and a current American spy is not in Davis County by accident. You are here to find out why George has been kidnapped twice and why there is a connection to the Soviet Union. By the way, I don't know what you have told Bob. I did not learn this from him." Susie certainly had not expected Margaret to see through her cover. She didn't seem like the streetwise type. At this juncture, there was no point in denying her purpose.

"Okay, you're right. I'm here to investigate and protect. I don't know how you and George got yourselves involved or how you two have managed to stay alive. The NSA feels that you and George have strategic importance, sort of national assets. The FBI has been trying to pin something on Rico and Stuart for a decade and you two apparently took care of them. While you are underage, the agency will just watch, but when you are adults, the CIA will try to hire you."

"I can't speak for George, but I might be interested in working for the CIA or NSA. We have just been trying to save lives, especially our own. I will tell you whatever you want to know, as long as it doesn't incriminate or endanger us. If I tell you that I can't tell you something, leave it at that."

"Deal. How did this all start?"

"George learned about a plot to blow up the Pineview Dam. He told the FBI about it."

"How did he learn this information?"

"Can't tell you." The conversation went on that way with Margaret volunteering information that she considered safe while withholding vital secrets.

After dropping off Margaret, Susie visited several truck stops to listen and ask a few questions. She heard a few rumors about a big girl in Utah that was hustling truck drivers but nothing about George or Margaret. Maybe she was going to have to keep a lower profile.

Chapter 28 – First Date

At the airport, George and his friends drove around long term parking until they found the Lincoln. Tony dropped off Luanna and George. George donned a pair of light cotton gloves. Luanna asked him to drive. He soon found out why. George opened the passenger door for Luanna and she got in, still dressed in her elegant dress, which accentuated her figure. By the time he had walked around and opened his door, Luanna was practically sitting in the driver's seat. George slid in and nudged her over a little.

"Here are the date rules, George M. Horton. They are not negotiable. We are not pretending to be shacking up or pretending to be married. We are not going to be sleeping under the same roof, so loosen up and at least treat me with as much physical affection as you would your redheaded girlfriend. Don't try to deny it. I found two red hairs on your shirt after your little trip. She isn't the one who has been putting her life on the line for the last several weeks, I have. It's time to pay up."

"Yes, dear," replied George, realizing that more of his secrets had been discovered.

"Now kiss me proper." George was conflicted. It wasn't that he didn't find Luanna attractive or want to kiss her, but he did not want to heat up a relationship that he could not see going anywhere, especially now that things with Margaret were on the mend. Finally, he just let Pavel take over. He knew how to kiss a woman properly and his memories had none of George's misgivings. When George found his body starting to get carried away, he throttled back Pavel and ended what had turned out to be a much longer and more passionate kiss than what he had intended.

"How was that?" asked George.

"That was ... surprisingly wonderful," responded Luanna in a bewildered and subdued voice.

Luanna tugged on George's shirt. "You look underdressed for tonight. I want to keep wearing this outfit so you need to dress up. Tony gave me some spending money just for the occasion." George drove to the ZCMI department store in Salt Lake City. On the way, Luanna tickled and caressed his back and shoulders. After George tried on several suits, Luanna settled on a high-end dark blue one with subtle, narrow pinstripes. They bought a tie, shirt, belt and shoes to go with the suit.

Then they were off to dinner. "I want to go someplace expensive," demanded Luanna. George drove to the La Caille Restaurant. He had never been there but had heard about it. Fortunately, being a weekday and relatively early in the evening, they were able to get a table after only a short wait. George enjoyed seeing the excitement and joy on Luanna's face. She was thrilled to be in such an upscale establishment. George ordered lobster and Luanna ordered a filet mignon steak. With Luanna's talent of being able to mimic what others do, she followed George's lead in table etiquette, thus avoiding any embarrassment or disappointment.

"George, tell me about what you were like before all of your Spock stuff."

"Well, I was just a dorky fifteen-year-old kid. I wasn't into sports. I wasn't a particularly good student at school, but I was always learning stuff on my own. I even have a small laboratory where I did experiments. I have a much older sister who is on a church mission to France. I have wonderful parents. They are good, honest, loving people. My parents are super athletic and hard working. I wasn't very popular, but I really didn't notice or care. I never had a girlfriend; it wasn't that I didn't like girls; I just didn't like the ones that liked me. How about you?"

"My life was wonderful until my dad got cancer. I was much closer to my dad than my mom. I suppose that in some ways you remind me of him. He was very smart and well educated. Like you, my dad didn't get angry or raise his voice. My mother did plenty of that. He never spanked me that I can remember. He always told me how smart and pretty I was. My mother didn't handle his death very well. I became the mother and she the child in some ways. That was two years ago. Then a year ago she remarried." It was obvious that Luanna was uncomfortable with that subject so she changed it.

"So what's it like having all of the memories?"

"The skills and intellectual knowledge are great, but to know every personal detail about strangers can be challenging. I even know their dominant thoughts. Sometimes it is like they are living in my head, sharing my body with me. Do you remember how I treated that biker when we first met?"

"Yeah, you were really rude and abrasive. I thought that you were a tough-guy jerk."

"I have the memories of two evil men in me. I let the abrasive one take over just to get that biker to show his true colors. I was never a confrontational kind of person. When I need to be confrontational, I just let someone that is good at it do it."

"How convenient, you can act like a jerk and let someone else take the blame," she said with a chuckle and a sly smile.

"I still take responsibility. The memories only take over when I let them."

After dinner, the couple went dancing at a dance hall in Salt Lake City that did not serve alcoholic beverages. Years earlier, Luanna's dad had given her some dance lessons. With those lessons and her ability to follow a lead, she did quite well on the dance floor. Sometimes they just slow danced, holding each other close and gently moving their feet. George had to admit to himself that he enjoyed that part immensely. They danced until the hall closed at one.

As they walked to the car, a seedy-looking man emerged from the shadows to block their path. He held a long knife in his right hand. "Gimme yur wallet!" he commanded.

Luanna leaned to George and whispered into his ear, "Please, let me handle this. I have been dreaming of a moment like this for weeks." George silently nodded. Luanna hiked up her dress so that it would not inhibit her freedom of movement. The mugger did not know what to think about this but enjoyed the extra display of leg. In a flash, Luanna's right leg shot up from the ground. Her foot, still wearing a lovely high-heel shoe, struck the middle of the man's forearm from below. The inertia of the heavy knife was enough to keep the hand from accelerating fast enough to prevent breakage of the forearm. One of the two delicate bones snapped. The knife clattered to the sidewalk. In agony, the man cradled his right hand in his left hand. Luanna picked up the knife as a souvenir to show Tony. She turned to George, "I didn't think that it would break his arm. I was just trying to disarm him."

"Let's get out of here," George suggested. "I don't want to meet up with more trouble." They hurried to the car. Luanna was exuberant about how easily she had disarmed and incapacitated the man. She settled down after they had driven for a few minutes. She turned to George.

"I think that I can sleep now without having you nearby. I'm not afraid anymore. First, you saved my life and then you saved me from living in fear. You know that I love you, George. I always will. This is not some childhood crush, some momentary infatuation; I really love you. You are everything that I ever wanted in a man. You are virtuous, kind, brave, smart and wise. You can protect me and support me. You like my intelligence, rather than being intimidated by it. You are willing to patiently teach me. It doesn't hurt that you are tall and sort of cute but not too cute. I don't trust men with striking good looks." Luanna put her head on George's shoulder and held his upper right arm. Even with all of the memories, George could not think of an appropriate response, so they drove in silence.

In fifteen minutes, they were in Bountiful. George pulled into the Viewmont High parking lot and stopped. Since Luanna had called him by his real name, he thought that he should reciprocate. "Thank you, Vicky Lee, for a wonderful evening. It's time for me to go home and for you to join Tony."

"Not so fast, George; it's my turn to kiss you." Vicky encircled his torso with her strong, loving arms. She pulled their bodies tightly against each other and gently pressed her lips against his. The kiss was affectionate, not aggressive or demanding. She pulled her lips just far enough from his to be able to speak.

"Even though there is another girl in your life and maybe you even love her, can't you at least accept the possibility that I might be the girl for you, that you could fall in love with me? Don't answer; just think about it. Consider that I might make changes that make me exactly what you want someday in a wife. I know that you enjoyed our kiss. The rest can easily fall into place. Think about it." George had to admit to himself that he was thinking about it and if he did not get out of that car, he might not have the will to go back to his normal life. Vicky released him from her embrace. George could tell that she wanted him to not feel trapped but invited into her life. He studied her face, memorizing every feature. In the soft lights of the parking lot, her face was adorable to him. Her high cheekbones and large, almond-shaped dark eyes gave her an exotic, alluring look. George opened the door and stepped out into the night. He grabbed his duffle bag from the backseat and gave one last wave goodbye. Vicky slowly drove away. Would he ever see her again?

As he walked the dozen blocks to his house, the intense loneliness that George had felt before finding Vicky returned. He wondered if he would feel this emptiness until they were reunited. It was kind of funny. Not long ago, George was turned off by any girl that liked him. Now a girl liking him made her much more attractive. George was not sure if that was the natural course of maturing or the effect of the memories.

Vicky had just told the boy of her dreams that she loved him. He did not flinch or pull away, but he had said nothing, not one word of encouragement! Somehow, that made her love him even more. Vicky knew in her heart that George was attracted to her. She also knew that he had a girlfriend, probably some meek, petite little thing. Of course, as a gentleman, George was trying to be as faithful to her as possible while being kind to Vicky. He had never initiated a kiss with her, except when she ordered him to, and that can hardly count as initiative on his part, but he did kiss her back. She was not going to accept defeat. Vicky drove east to Main Street and headed south. She tried to memorize as much of the town as she could. She noticed that there was an office for the Davis County Clipper, a local newspaper. She memorized the address. She was going to find out as much about George and his town as she could. George had said that he was a very public figure. Vicky was going to find out just how public.

Before George, every boy had been intimidated by Vicky's high intelligence. Until George, this had made romance nearly impossible, not that she was looking for love with all that was going on at home, but Vicky was envious of her friends who had romance in their lives. She loved how George looked at her, not with ogling eyes but with respect, appreciation and genuine affection. He found her attractive, but he was so discreet about it. Vicky could go her whole life and never meet another George. That would not be necessary. She was going to make him hers. She would become everything that he ever wanted in a girl. She would study his religion, and if it was not repugnant, embrace it. She would educate herself and give herself as much in common with George as possible. She would learn to bake bread better than his mother's, bottle fresh fruit or whatever other homemaking skills that George found valuable. Vicky would make herself irresistible to George.

Chapter 29 – Run for Your Life

When George was a block from his house, he interrupted his ponderings to scan the street for hidden dangers. There was a car parked in the street about half a block from his house. He did not recognize it as belonging to any neighbors. He stopped to consider how to approach it. Suddenly the flash of a match igniting briefly illuminated the interior, revealing the presence of a heavyset man sitting in the driver's seat. The car was facing away from George so he could not see the man's face. Pavel's memory that George had been trying to bring forth exploded into his awareness. Katarina had asked Pavel to recommend an assassin right after the news story broke about Rico and Stuart's slaying. She had not said why, but now it was obvious. The man in the car was Jake Lancaster, a thorough and ruthless killer. George turned as if to enter the home adjacent to him. He heard the car engine start. Knowing that he had been recognized, he dropped the duffle bag and dashed between the houses and onto 200 West. George could hear tires squealing. He reversed course. By the time the car had turned onto 200 West, George was back to 100 West.

Pavel had only seen Jake once and that had been over five years ago. He had hired Jake by mail to perform an assassination. Pavel had clandestinely watched Jake from afar by staking out the target. He liked to know whom he was doing business with while leaving the hireling knowing as little as possible about himself. Knowledge was power and offered a degree of protection. Back then, Jake Lancaster was lean and relatively fit. Even though George had only gotten a glimpse of Jake's face, he discerned that Jake had put on weight and looked much less healthy than five years ago. George hoped that Jake was not up to the job for which he had been hired.

The streets of the Bountiful core section of town were straight and regular, lacking twists or alleyways. At this time of night, virtually everything was closed. There were no large buildings in which to hide. George had the advantage of agility and off-road mobility. In addition, he knew the city much better than his assailant did. The assassin, possessing a car, had the advantage of speed and endurance. George needed a plan. He was in good shape and could stay ahead of the car for a while, but eventually he would fatigue. He needed to go where the car could not follow but not to escape; George needed to finish this. Otherwise, he endangered all of his love ones.

The faces of all whom George loved came into his mind as he ran, now passing between homes and businesses onto Main Street. One of those faces was his maternal grandfather. Before working for Uncle Martin, George had spent weeks in Idaho on his grandparents' farm every summer. He had also worked on Barton's farm, just east of 400 East in Bountiful. In addition to being east of his position, the farm was a dozen blocks north. With the sound of screeching tires pursuing him, and Jake catching a glimpse of George now and then, he headed northeast. George's pursuer apparently noticed the general direction that George was now heading and began to anticipate his movements. A couple of times he fired shots at George using a silencer equipped handgun. One slug came so close to George's face that he could feel the rush of air!

Being chased by an automobile reminded George of when his family would play tag at the park. His older sister and parents were so fast. They could easily catch George and had to pretend to be running their fastest while running slowly. George realized that his comparison of himself with his family members was why he had always thought of himself as a slow runner. Now he was taller than his sister and mother and could look his father straight in the eyes. He should be as fast or faster than they were. Suddenly, it was as if a heavy weight that George had been carrying his whole life was lifted from him. He shot forward, running faster than he had ever run before. George thought of one of Cleave's favorite sayings, "As a man thinketh in his heart, so is he." George began taking a less direct route and often eluded Jake for blocks.

When he finally reached the farm, he found that the plot nearest him had been planted in a spring crop that had just been plowed under. George ran into the field to distance himself from the road. Jake was not only a smoker but also middle-aged and apparently overweight. George wanted to make him run.

Jake parked at the field's edge and got out of the car. He raised his silencer-equipped pistol to shoot at George. George doubted that in the dark and with a silencer, Jake could hit him at that range, but he dove to the ground anyway, soiling his new suit. After a couple of shots at that range, Jake started into the field after George. George leaped up and continued his run in a northeast direction and then turned due north. He easily increased his lead, even though Jake was able to run a more direct path. George lost sight of him in the darkness as his lead grew. George was sure that his young eyes could see better in the dark than those of his much older assailant. If George could not see Jake, Jake certainly could not see him. George turned due west, heading straight for the barn.

There was an old John Deere tractor parked behind the barn that was very similar to the one that George had driven on his grandparents' farm. Fortune had really smiled on George. The tractor was currently equipped with a front-end loader. George started the tractor and raised the loader scoop to a position a few feet off the ground so that he could use it as a shield. He headed southeast on an intercept course with his assailant. Standing on the running boards, George could just see over the scoop to navigate. Jake came into view. As he turned to shoot at George, George ducked below the level of the scoop. The bullet hit inside the top lip of the scoop and ricocheted back towards Jake. The redirected slug did not come close to Jake, but it made him more cautious. He lost his nerve and turned south. George maneuvered to cut off Jake's retreat. Jake was breathing heavily by now.

Suddenly the barn lights flashed on! "Old Man" Barton appeared, wearing a bathrobe and carrying a shotgun with a flashlight mounted to it. George put the tractor in neutral and let it coast to a stop. He slipped to the ground and hid behind the far rear wheel, squatting so that he could see Jake by looking under the scoop. Barton yelled, "Stop or I'll shoot." Jake, highly visible with Barton's flashlight shining on him, stopped and turned his pistol on Barton. Barton fired. At that range, the shotgun had a very wide spread. Several of the lead pellets embedded themselves in Jake's flesh, not doing major damage but causing serious pain. Jake fired, missing Barton.

Jake found himself wishing that he had brought the rifle and not the pistol, which equipped, as it was, with a silencer, was difficult to aim and inaccurate, especially at long range. Business had been slow the last few years and Jake had spent far too much time smoking, watching TV and snacking on junk food. He had been thinking of retiring after this job, but now it looked like he would be lucky to live through it, let alone earn a paycheck. He should have thought about how most farmers owned firearms and knew how to use them.

Barton, on the other hand, had his favorite weapon and had a reputation of being tougher than nails and not afraid to stand up to anyone. He fired at Jake again and ran towards him. Jake fired and missed again. Barton fired and this time enough pellets hit Jake to jolt his body. Barton kept running and firing. Jake shot once more but harmlessly into the dirt just before dropping the gun. Barton continued shooting until his shells ran out. From George's vantage point, it appeared that additional shots would be redundant.

Using the tractor as a shield, George ran in a line that kept the tractor between Mr. Barton and himself. George scrambled over the east fence and onto the road. With more sure footing, he sprinted south, heading home. George thought about hiding out for a few days but was afraid that his parents would think that he was dead. As George ran, he pulled off the cotton gloves that he had donned before entering the Lincoln. No prints would link him to the tractor in the field or to the Continental. He slowed to a brisk walk. After walking a few blocks, he took off his jacket and shook it to remove as much dirt as possible. George used his handkerchief to brush off additional dirt. He also brushed off his pants. Fortunately, the scrambling in the dirt had not torn the fabric of his new suit. George walked slowly the rest of the way home so that his perspiration could dry and his heart rate slow to normal. Police sirens and ambulance sirens interrupted the silence of the night.

Chapter 30 – Home at Last

On the way home, George recovered his hastily discarded duffle bag. He arrived at his house and knocked on the front door. The sirens had already awakened both his parents. His father opened the front door and, without speaking, grabbed George's left arm and pulled him into the living room. He stuck his head out and looked both ways and then closed and bolted the door. He threw his arms around George and nearly crushed him with his powerful arms. Then he suddenly released George. "I'm sorry, Son, have you been wounded? I forgot to look or ask."

"Not a scratch on me. I'm fine."

"What's the bandage for?" he asked, looking at George's forehead.

"Just a self-inflicted superficial wound I employed as part of a plan." Mr. Horton peeked through the curtains searching the street.

"The snoop is gone. He has been watching our house for days. I called the police several times, but he always left before they came to investigate."

"He's not coming back, Dad."

"You killed him?"

"No, Dad, watch the mornings news; it will explain everything that you need to know." George's mother rushed into the room and threw herself at him. He had only seen his mother weep openly a few times in his life and this was one of them. George's dress shirt that had been damp from perspiration now received additional moisture. His mother hugged him for a long time. She looked older than George had remembered. Her normally well-groomed hair stuck out in random wisps. George felt a pang of guilt, realizing what pains he had caused her.

"I know that you are trying to protect your mother and me with your silence, Son. But is there anything that you can tell us about what you have been up to?"

"Dad, tell me what you already know and I will try to fill you in as much as possible."

"Well, Margaret slipped me a note from you and I followed the instructions. When your car and the bodies were found, we had a good idea of what had happened."

"Yea, I hung around Utah for a while so that I could hear the local news."

"Margaret is very shaken. She has been over here watching the news with us often. We assumed that she had been your rescuer. We didn't know your plan but figured that you were putting distance between you and the rest of us for our protection. We thought that you might even be in Mexico. A man showed up a few days after your disappearance. He never spoke to us, but he kept hanging around, watching the house at all hours of the night and day. That's who I was looking for outside."

"Mom, Dad, I have had to travel in disguise. I felt compelled to do some things for our protection, but I have remembered your teachings and tried to follow them. I made a few friends along the way who, incredibly, risked their own lives to help save ours. I have picked up some new skills. Hopefully, I am a little wiser.

"I was in no physical danger until I got home and encountered your snoop. That is what the sirens are all about. I am so sorry for all of the worry and heartache that I caused you. You are the best parents in the world." By now, George was weeping and he put his arms around both his parents. They wept and talked until dawn. Mom fixed breakfast while they all listened to the morning news on TV. The shooting in Barton's field became the lead story in the local news. They had a great breakfast together. It was so good to be home with his parents. They started joking about "Old Man" Barton's reputation and how this would add to it.

"The local kids are already terrified of him," commented George's mother. "Imagine how afraid of him they will be now. No one will dare swipe a melon from his fields." They all laughed hysterically. It was great to relieve the built-up tension. George's father called the city police and the FBI to report that George had returned. A couple of local officers came by to question him. George told them that his disappearance related to his previous abduction and that he could only talk to the FBI about the details.

George called Margaret to let her know that he was safely home and to arrange a time to debrief her as much as possible. He did not want her to get upset again about secrets that he was keeping from her. That night they shared a picnic dinner in Mueller Park, a Bountiful canyon recreational area. After the meal, they walked, talked and kissed. "Are you going to be okay with only half the truth?" George asked Margaret.

"I hope so," replied Margaret. "Especially since it nearly cost me my sanity last time when I insisted on knowing everything. I'm just really happy and relieved that you are safely home. I don't even care if a beautiful girl with long black hair and big brown eyes helped you out along the way." It was too dark to see it now, but earlier Margaret has spotted a long black hair stuck to the back of George's shirt. It was not causally lying there. It was stuck on as if the hair and shirt had come out of the washer together. Margaret shuttered to think what that implied. She had let her mind run rampant after George's first abduction; she was not going to do that again. She just needed to trust George.

The next day, George set about destroying all notes and other evidence of his experiments. It would be tragic if his discovery fell into the hands of the Russians or even just criminals. What he had learned over years of research was burned into his own mind and that of Margaret. They didn't need any notes. With help from his mother, he even repainted the room, partly to cover up any lingering smells from his animal experiments.

George had only been home two days when Bishop Williams called to ask if he would sing the national anthem at the ward Independence Day breakfast and devotional. Brother Bradford, who originally had been asked to sing, had been called out of town for a family emergency. George had only attended a couple of these meetings in the past. They were held at seven in the morning and that just seemed too early to him to have to be somewhere on a holiday.

The next morning George dressed in his scout uniform for the devotional. To his surprise, he could hardly fit into the shirt. He arrived early for the ceremony and helped set up chairs. The event was held on the front lawn and was in conjunction with the other ward that met in the Bountiful Tabernacle. To his surprise, Bob Wall showed up with a very cute stranger. He hardly recognized Bob. He was leaner and more muscular. He looked very fit. When Bob saw George he smiled and walked his way, holding hands with the pretty, tall blond. Bob had never smiled at George unless it was a malevolent grin. How had so much changed in such a short period of time? Bob warmly extended his hand to George. He shook George's hand vigorously and greeted him. "George, I would like to introduce you to my girlfriend, Susie Flanders. Susie, this is George Horton, the star of our football team and an all-around great guy." Somehow, the unexpected compliments sounded genuine. Apparently, Bob had made as great of a change on the inside, maybe greater, than he had on the outside.

"It's great to meet you, Susie. Are you new to Bountiful?"

"Yes, I moved to the area this summer from Minnesota. I love your climate so far and Bob has begun showing me your beautiful state. I hear that you have been out of town for weeks. Where have your travels taken you?"

"Welcome to Utah, Susie. I would love to be able to share my adventures, but I can't at this time. I need to check on preparations for the program." George hurried off and tried to look busy. Soon it was time to begin and George found a seat on the front row. The program began with the scouts formally presenting the colors. Once the flag was in place, one of the scouts led them in the Pledge of Allegiance. Then it was George's turn.

As he sang the national anthem, something triggered in him. He felt a burning sense of appreciation for his homeland and a desire to serve his country. Both the memories of Cleave and those of Pavel contributed to this patriotic reaction. George wanted to follow in Cleave's footsteps and serve his country in every way that he could. He wanted to defend her from ruthless enemies who were trying to bring her down. George had sensed during his singing that his voice seemed to have much greater artistic appeal than when he sang in the play.

Bob felt mixed feelings as George sang. As his life had been changing over the last few weeks since he had met Susie, he had not only felt closer to God but also to his country. George's singing inspired him, but he also felt a twang of envy. Did George have to be so good at everything? Couldn't he stop at being a great athlete? Did he also have to be brilliant and talented? He was good in the school play, but now he sounded like he could sell records of his singing. Some of the women, including Susie, were nearly swooning over him. Well, envy was just another weakness he would have to learn to overcome. Besides, Susie was his girl, and if he were not mistaken, he saw a little envy in George's eyes.

After a week back at home, things settled down to near normal. One difference, however, was that George's workload was reduced. Margaret had volunteered to fill in for George at the mortuary while he was gone. She had explained to Uncle Martin that George had shared with her the details of his duties so well that she could do them herself. She had to demonstrate her skills to Uncle Martin to convince him. After George returned, they split duties, with George preparing the men and Margaret preparing the women.

George got a call from Francesca. They met at a park and had a long talk. George shared with her some information but none that would implicate Margaret in the deaths of Rico and Stuart. He told her about an unidentified mole within the FBI. She said that she would look into the status of Katarina. They met again a week later. Katarina had been killed by a hit and run driver a few days after George's return home. The agency mole had not been pinpointed, but the search was on. It appeared that the plan to make the country safe for George had succeeded.

In private, George wept for Katarina. He had not killed her with his own hands, but he had certainly caused her death, as surely as if he had sat in the driver's seat of the automobile that took her life. She had not been a wicked woman, just a soldier doing her job and doing it well. Her death was necessary, but that did not mean that George had to be pleased about it.

George's mind and attitudes continued to evolve as Pavel's memories and thought patterns became more and more part of his life. His experiments with planarians had changed his life far more than he could have imagined. George started out on a quest to improve his memory. Early on, he stole the memories of others, but now he could memorize what he wanted to remember with ease. George got what he sought, but his goals had changed. He had not set out to be the lead in a play or the star quarterback. He just wanted to be able to remember the scientific principles and facts that he was studying. In the course of events, George had lost his passion for science. Instead of dreaming of being a Nobel prize-winning scientist someday, he wanted to be some kind of super-spy for his beloved country. With the knowledge and talents that he had gained, he felt like he could do almost anything, except feel at ease. Even though Katarina was dead, along with the assassin that she hired, George did not feel completely safe. There were too many loose ends.

The End

Dedication

This novel is dedicated to two of my daughters, Stephanie and Amanda. Stephanie inspired me to tell the story verbally to her when she was 10 and years later encouraged me to write it down, which began my hobby of writing novels. Amanda spent many hours reviewing the manuscript, vigorously encouraging me to make needed changes. She also took the photograph for the cover image.

About the Author

Lloyd G. Miller is a successful engineer (US patents #6,491,773 and #8,042,594) who started writing as a hobby over two decades ago. After writing several novels and spending years refining them, he decided to try publishing. After experiencing creative differences with a publisher who had contracted to publish one of his novels, he decided to publish eBooks through Smashwords. He lives in Utah where most of the story takes place.

Other Novels by Lloyd G. Miller

The author has also written The Computer Who Loved Me, a sci-fi novel published as an eBook and Reckless Beauty, a sequel to Reckless Brilliance.

Also by Lloyd G Miller

Powerful Minds
Reckless Brilliance
Reckless Beauty

Standalone
The Computer Who Loved Me

About the Author

Lloyd G. Miller is a successful engineer (US patents #6,491,773 and #8,042,594) who started writing as a hobby over two decades ago. After writing several novels and spending years refining them, he decided to try publishing. After experiencing creative differences with a publisher who had contracted to publish one of his novels, he decided to publish eBooks through Smashwords. He lives in Utah where most of the story takes place.